This is a work of fiction. The authors have invented the characters. Any resemblance to actual persons, living or dead, is purely coincidental.

If you have purchased this book with a 'dull' or missing cover-- You have possibly purchased an unauthorized or stolen book. Please immediately contact the publisher advising where, when and how you purchased this book.

Compilation and Introduction copyright © 2009 by
Triple Crown Publications
PO Box 6888
Columbus, Ohio 43205
www.TripleCrownPublications.com

Library of Congress Control Number: 2009927420
ISBN 13: 978-0-9820996-4-3


*Editor-n-Chief: Vickie M. Stringer*
*Cover design: Valerie Thompson, Leap Graphics*
*Photographer: Treagen Kier Colston*
*Make-Up: Candace*
*Model: Erika*

Printed in the United States of America

FIRST TRADE PAPERBACK EDITION PRINTING JUNE 2009

10 9 8 7 6 5 4 3 2 1

Printed in the United States of America

# Innocent

# *Dedication*

In memory of my mother Evette L. Sullivan
August 7, 1947- June 9, 2006.

There is not a woman alive that can take your place.
There has not been a day that passes that I don't think of
you and miss you dearly! You will forever live in my mind,
in my heart and imbibed in my soul.

I cherish the rare times you visit me in my dreams as I languish
immersed in the hideous concrete and steel cage.

I love you mama!

# Chapter One

## INNOCENT

As I drove, the green pastoral scenery and sublime blue sky beckoned me with the promise of a new day and better tomorrows. I drove with the wind in my face and my elbow out the window. I whistled a soft, melodic tune, recalling my grandmother's verbal incantation. She was an old, black woman with a staunch love and dedication for her grandson. In my mind, I could still envision her beautiful mahogany face, a reflection of strong black women that had come before her.

My grandmother, whom I often called "Gramma", raised me and my twin brother TC after our mother was murdered by an ex-lover. She barely made it to her 18th birthday. My brother and I witnessed the murder. Even though we were three years old, I can still hear her sorrowful pleas and plaintive cries. "James, please don't hit me no mo'. Not in front of my babies."

Her cries fell upon deaf ears as the man used his fists to shatter every bone in her pretty face. Then he strangled her.

By the time the cops finally arrived, the man stood weary and befuddled, saturated in her blood. He appeared to be on the verge of some type of psychotic delirium. He began to cry in a crescendo of sobs that rocked his body. And his feet shuffled in place, as if he were marching to a beat that only he could hear. We were only three years old when it happened. My brother says he can't remember a thing—but I can't forget.

Everybody called Gramma, "Big Mama". We moved into her big, rat-infested house. In the winter it was brutally cold and the summers were excruciatingly hot. There were days the electricity and the gas got turned off, but my grandmother always managed to make do.

Big Mama was the neighborhood candy lady and she sold boot-leg liquor after hours. She even ran a gambling house on the weekends. Because of her financial endeavors my brother and I lived better than most of the neighborhood kids.

By the time we reached sixteen, our once beanpole bodies had transformed into strong, hard-bodies and we drove the chicks crazy. I had become a gifted athlete and was looking at several scholarships from prestigious universities across the nation. I ended up accepting a scholarship from Georgia State University, but my twin brother took a different route. He fell victim to the call of the streets. It may have had to do with the fact that Big Mama's half-brother, David, was in a gang called the Black Gangsters. He was an OG, a shot-caller. My brother admired the hell out of David and the two were inseparable. As soon as TC was old enough to hold a gun, David initiated him into the gang. TC already had a natural inclination for violence, and he quickly excelled within the ranks of the Black Gangsters with David as his mentor.

Two months before I made my decision about which college I would attend, David was murdered as he sat on the front porch drinking beer. TC had run out of the house to discover David's idle body lying in a puddle of blood. It should have sent a message to my brother that it was time to get out of the gang, but instead, it made TC even more cold and heartless. He and the other Black Gangsters avenged David's death by killing rival gang members. TC was officially made a shot-caller for the south side of Chicago, replacing David.

The day I left for college everybody gathered at Big Mama's to say goodbye. It was a festive occasion for family and old friends.

"This is for you, bro." TC coolly tossed me a bag of dro and the keys to his midnight blue, tricked-out '73 Chevy Impala with 24-inch rims. The car had a booming sound system and 15-inch speakers that made the trunk rattle like there was a gorilla trapped inside.

"Thanks, bro." I grinned and gave TC aone-arm hug. I saw something palpable in his somber brown eyes, something that mirrored my own. Besides the brief stints TC did in Juvenile Hall, we had never been away from each other for a long period of time. Today was different.

I threw my bags in the back and told everyone goodbye. I was ready to leave when I saw Tamara Jenkins, my first love, leaning against my car. Tamara had helped me discover my manhood. She had stolen my virginity. She had a body with crazy curves, and I used to have fun exploring every inch of her.

I was older than Tamara by almost two years, but she was much more mature than I was. I think that was where the problem started, or should I say ended. We experienced love, hate, and pain far too young. Even though she let me do what I wanted to do with her, I started messing with other shawties on the side and somehow Tamara got lost in the shuffle. It didn't matter though, because she always came when I wanted her. Big Mama didn't like Tamara from the beginning, but she held her words. She knew I was growing up, and she said it was just a phase. That was until she caught us in bed together one Sunday morning. I thought Big Mama was at church calling the Lord's name at the same time I was delivering my sermon to Tamara. She was calling for God herself. I had her bent over my bed, pounding the shit out of her. From that point on, Big Mama referred to Tamara as 'that fast ass heffa' and forbade me from bringing her to the house.

Tamara leaned against my car with her arms folded over her ample breasts. I couldn't help but admire her sensuous curves. I noticed her pursed lips, and I could sense an attitude.

I turned and looked at my front porch. Big Mama was standing there with a disgruntled look on her face. I turned to Tamara and spoke. "I'm glad you came by." I leaned forward to kiss her.

Tamara twisted her lips to the side and gave me her infamous hand to my face gesture.

"Why you got to embarrass me in front of my homies and family?" I asked harshly. I could feel my face turning red.

"Nigga, I'm pregnant!" She spat with a hurtful scowl written on her face. "And yo ass burnt me. I know it was you, because you da only one I been wit."

I fought the urge to look over my shoulder to see if Big Mama had heard her. Instantly, my mind flashed back to the morning

I went to take a leak and an excruciating pain shot through my dick, almost buckling me to my knees. That shit hurt like a muthafucka!

I went to the free clinic on 51st Street. It was a virtual class reunion up in that bitch. Kanisha Williams was sitting there with her mother. She couldn't look me in my eyes. She had been one of the many chicks I had been having sex with and the most likely candidate to have burnt me.

Tamara's words made me feel nauseous, like I had been drinking for days.

I wanted to run away, hoping that all this shit would disappear. Thinking of nothing else, I reversed the situation and lied. "Burnt you? Girl please, you betta get outta my face. If you burnin', it's probably from that other nigga you fuckin' wit."

"What other nigga?" Tamara asked with an attitude.

"That nigga you pregnant by."

Tamara jerked her neck back like she had been slapped. She shuffled her feet. "I ain't been with nobody and yo ass know it, bitch!" she yelled with her face balled up.

I knew she wanted to slap the shit outta me.

Tamara shuffled her feet again, but this time I heard something. I looked down and noticed a beer bottle by her leg. I wondered whether it had already been there or if she brought it with her. Cautiously, I glanced over my shoulder and saw Big Mama on the porch watching us closely. I desperately needed to get away. I couldn't be nobody's baby's daddy. I needed to go to college and get an education so I could help myself and my family. That meant getting out of the ghetto.

Wringing her hands together, Tamara nibbled on her bottom lip and choked back tears. "I, I know I'm only fifteen; and I know you didn't do this to me on purpose. Innocent, I can forgive you. I love you. Please don't leave—" She broke down into tears.

I pretended that I was looking up at the blue sky. I wanted to reach out and hug her, hold her in my arms and assure her that everything was going to be okay.

Tamara grabbed my shirt and pulled me close against her body. Her breasts pressed against my chest. "Don't leave me. I can get a job as a waitress. You can go to school at night. I'll do anything, just don't leave me, please." Tamara gently placed my hand on her flat stomach.

I was temporarily captivated. But then something in my head

went off. This girl represented everything I was running from. This was everything I wasn't trying to become. Tamara was the obstacle: welfare, young fatherhood, teenage pregnancy, too many people and not enough jobs in the ghetto. I shut my eyes tight and told my confused young mind to deny the existence of my seed growing in her womb.

"That ain't my baby!" I said coldly. I jerked my hand away from her stomach and pushed her off of me.

She resisted and grabbed for my arm.

"I'm out of here." I reached for the car door, opening it. After getting in, I cranked up the engine and put the car in drive. I drove off.

Tamara picked up the beer bottle from off the ground. She hurled it at the car, hitting the bumper.

# *Chapter Two*

Nine hours into the journey to Atlanta, Tamara's sad face was still on my mind and weighing heavily on my conscience. I smoked a blunt, a habit I picked up in the last year or so, and now I had developed a bad case of the munchies. I made a pit stop at a Dairy Queen in a little ass town.

As I left the Dairy Queen a big white dude pulled up next to me. I shoveled some of the Oreo Blizzard into my mouth. He rushed out of his car and bumped into me, almost knocking the blue cup and brown paper bag out of my hand. I started to check him, but instead I got back in my whip and dipped.

Once again I was back on the road. I put the Blizzard cup between my legs and threw the bag in the back of the car. It landed in the back window. The sunshine and the smell of cow manure were exciting to a young city boy like me. I zoomed across vast flatlands with my system booming and basketball on my mind. I reached for the partially burned blunt in the ashtray and noticed a sign that told me that there was ninety miles to Atlanta. I bobbed my head, sparked the blunt and inhaled deeply. This was the shit. I looked up and a patrol car was sitting idle in the median. It seemed to be waiting like a giant snake in the tall grass, and I was its prey.

My heart beat wildly and I nearly choked on the smoke.
I snatched the blunt out of my mouth, nearly busting my lip. The
radar gun was pointed right at my car. I wasn't speeding but I was
still scared.

"Fuck!" I scoffed when I looked into my rearview
mirror.

The long, black car crawled onto the shoulder of the road
like a serpent. I eased the bag of dro out of my pocket, placed it
under the ashtray and tossed the blunt out the window. Normally,
I'm not a religious dude, but this time I began to pray my ass off.

"Lord, please don't let these crackas pull me over." I turned
the music down. The sound of the Dairy Queen bag in the back
window, rattling in the wind, was annoying. I looked again into
my rearview mirror, but couldn't see the police car because of all
the traffic.

"Don't panic, don't panic!" I told myself as I gripped the
steering wheel so tight my knuckles paled. I quickly did a visual
sweep of the car; candy wrappers, soda cans, and clothes were
strewn everywhere. In the backseat were two large basketball
trophies.

Again, I looked in the mirror and still didn't see the cop car.
They were gone. I had just panicked. I sighed in relief as I turned
the music back up and pressed on the gas.

The next sign told me that I was eighty-five miles from Atlanta.
For some reason, I began to think about the father I'd never had.
Big Mama had told us that our father was in prison. He had never
wrote, never called, never cared. "How could a human being be
so cruel?" I asked myself. Then my mind flashed back to Tamara.
*That ain't my baby,* I remembered myself telling her. Damn, was
I repeating the same cycle?

While daydreaming, I noticed the camper behind me veer
to the left. There it was. The police car was approaching at dare
devil speed. It rode my ass for miles. My paranoia was so bad
that I almost wished that they would pull me over and get it over
with.

"Shit, I don't have the car's registration and insurance," I said
to myself over the loud music. I was going to get that handled as
soon as I had made it to Atlanta.

I just fought to keep my composure as other motorists sped by
giving me dirty looks like I had done something wrong.

Finally after miles of the maddening charade, the cop's lights flashed and their siren screamed, "CHIRP! CHIRP!" It was the sound of the beast.

I felt a pang in my stomach as I pulled over to the side of the road. I squirted a little bit of the cherry-scented air freshener that TC always kept in the console because, according to him, it killed the weed smell.

In the mirror I watched the cop step out of his car. He was a huge man. He wore mirrored sunglasses and one of them ten gallon hats. He was more than pink and irritated; he was red and angry. His name tag read Stanley Burns. The other cop, his partner, was short and chubby. His partially unbuttoned shirt was wet with large sweat stains under the arm pits. With one hand he mopped at a tuft of unruly hair on his forehead as he approached my car from the opposite side of his partner. He placed his hand on his gun and he frowned at me.

"Boy, lemme see yo license, registration and insurance card," Officer Burns demanded with a heavy southern drawl that made my flesh crawl.

It took a minute for me to figure out what he'd said. I tried to fake a polite smile as I reached into my pocket. The other cop had taken an interest in something on my backseat. I passed Officer Burns my license. I prayed like hell that he would forget about the registration and insurance cards. I looked up at him. The glaring sun burned my eyes.

He shoved his sunglasses up onto his forehead. "IC Miller?" The cop exclaimed. "what de daggon kinda damn name is dat?" The cop asked.

"That's my name, sir." I didn't want to tell him the "I" stood for Innocent.

"Lemme see yo registration and insurance," he commanded, narrowing his eyes at me.

"My birthday is tomorrow, June 6th. I'll be eighteen. I'm on my way to college to play point guard for Georgia State." My mouth was a flood gate. I hoped my talking would take his mind off of what he was asking for. I didn't want to go to jail.

"Registration!" He barked with his hand on the car door like he meant business.

"Huh?" I returned his frown. I then reached for the glove compartment in search of something I knew wasn't there.

I noticed the other cop at the passenger door. The bag of weed that I thought I had stashed under the ashtray was in plain view.

My stomach did cartwheels.

"Yes, IC Miller." I heard my name being called in over the radio. Officer Burns was running a check on my license plates.

I acted flustered and frustrated which wasn't really hard to do with that bag of weed staring me in the face. "Dammnit! I know it's in here somewhere," I said, stalling for time.

"Boy, step outside the car," the officer commanded as he flung the door open. "Out!"

I saw nothing but pure hate in that white man's blue eyes. He deposited my license in his shirt pocket when I stepped outside the car. The hot sun beamed down on my face, and my white T-shirt was pasted to my skin. "What did I do?"

"You was speeding, boy."

"No I wasn't," I retorted.

His face turned beet red. "Boy, you talk only when I ask you to. You was speedin'!"

I noticed his partner had honed in on something in the car. I hoped it wasn't the weed. I was already in major trouble without the registration, but if they found the weed I could kiss my scholarship to college goodbye.

The cop opened the car door on the passenger side. They never asked if they could search the car.

Their radios crackled to life. "ALL UNITS! ALL UNITS! Be on the lookout for a late model Ford or Chevy Sedan, possibly dark blue. The Dairy Queen on 4th and Main has just been robbed at gun point. One homicide victim discovered inside. I repeat, ALL UNITS!"

The cop on the passenger side of my car slammed the door shut and exhorted, "Let's go! Elmo's niece works there."

Officer Burns reached into his shirt pocket and handed my license back to me. "Don't eva let me see you driving this piece of shit again. Ya hear me boy?"

"Yes, sir," escaped my lips.

As they turned to walk away from me I wanted to applaud their departure; but instead, I sighed with relief and turned to get back into my car. Before I was totally off the hook, though, Officer Burns abruptly turned around. He was looking at something in the back window of my car. He walked back toward my car. He pushed his hat back, scratched his forehead, and then walked toward me.

"Boy, where you comin' from?" He once again looked

suspiciously at the back window of my car and then at me.

"Chicago. I, I'm on my way to college to play ball for—"

"Where'd dat Dairy Queen bag come from back derre in yo window?"

"I, mmm, I stopped for some ice cream," I stuttered regretting the words as soon as they came out of my mouth.

He approached me in a blink of an eye. "Boy, put your hands up against da car, turn around, and spread yo legs!"

"For what?" I asked not wanting to believe what I was hearing. If I was going to be arrested, I wanted to know why. "What did I do?" I yelled, standing my ground.

The other cop rushed back around the car with his hand on his gun. His cheeks were flushed rouge with exasperation.

I raised both my hands, palms up and asked again, "Officer, what did I do?"

Officer Burns shoved me against the car then reached for the radio attached to his shirt. "I need assistance! Need assistance! I'm on Highway 75 with a possible suspect in the Dairy Queen robbery. I have him apprehended."

"What did I do?" I asked again, terrified.

Burns yanked my arms behind my back and his partner joined the scuffle.

Even though they were both large, strong men it felt like I was being attacked by two old ladies. Trying to secure my arms behind my back, the officers were wrestling and stumbling over each other.

"Need assistance! Need back up!" I heard Burns yell into his radio as he gave his location again.

Suddenly my arms were pulled behind my back and yanked high with so much force that I felt excruciating pain ricochet through my body. "Ouch!" I shrieked in pain. Dust and debris scattered around us like a small tornado. I managed to stay on my feet with two angry white cops on my back. "Man, what did, I—" I tried to ask again.

Both officers were grunting trying hard to slam me down to the pavement or to break my arms.

"Ahhhh!" Both my shoulders were about to be dislocated from the joint. The pain was more than I had ever experienced in my entire life. I had no choice but to spin around, freeing my arms. I hauled both cops off of me.

The short chubby one fell to the ground in a heap. Officer

Burns staggered backward but managed to regain his balance. I saw something more than hate in the dark pools of his blue eyes. He reached for his gun.

I threw up my hands. "Nooo!"

Burns staggered and aimed at my chest. He pulled the trigger.

A single shot rang out.

With his lips pressed tight, his mouth creating a thin pink line in a lupine sneer, Officer Burns took a step toward me as if he was about to shoot again.

I saw his rage, felt his hatred. My body stumbled back and I felt a burning sensation inside of my chest. My eyes scrolled down and what I saw frightened me. There was a gaping hole in my chest that spewed crimson blood. It stained my white tee. "Oh God!" I shouted. My eyes bulged as I clasped my chest. The heel of my hand felt nothing but broken bone. Clouds sailed above me while beneath me rivulets of blood quickly saturated the earth.

Both cops stood over me. They exchanged knowing glances.

"Steve, he went for my gun. I had to shoot 'em. Ya hear me?" Burns said to his partner.

The chubby man nodded his head, still hunched over trying to catch his breath. They both looked down at me as I blinked away tears. In the distance, I heard sirens.

"You one lucky nigger," Burns said to me.

I closed my eyes in an attempt to escape the pain that was invading my body. Choking back tears, words lodged in my throat. "Officer, sir, what I do?" I croaked dryly.

"Shut the fuck up!" Burns ordered, kicking my legs apart. He patted me down.

The roar of police sirens came to a screeching stop. There was chaos everywhere. A cop was bawling hysterically while several other officers were trying to hold him back.

"Elmo, no!" I heard one of the officers yell. "Stop him!"

I heard a growl above me, "This black son of a bitch raped and murdered my niece in that robbery!"

"Hold him!" an officer ordered.

But before I knew it, the heel of a boot came crashing down on the side of my forehead.

The world flickered around me like a strobe, and all the pain disappeared into that deep abyss of my mind.

# *Chapter Three*

## TAMARA JENKINS
## FIFTEEN MONTHS LATER

"Henny and Coke please," I spoke to the waitress who took my order. As she walked away, I looked around the lounge of the plush Four Seasons hotel, admiring its splendid beauty. I needed something to pass time before I went back to my room to wait on the phone call that could change my life.

A week and a half ago, while riding the L-train to work, I had spotted a discarded newspaper on the seat next to me. I had always liked to read the horoscope section, so I scanned through the pages until I found Pisces, my zodiac sign.

*"You are in for a big career change. More money in the immediate future."*

On the next page, I saw one of them big-ass advertisements. It was the kind that takes up the entire page. There was a picture of a black woman who was dressed very nice, sophisticated even. She had one of them shit-eating grins on her face like she was living large and enjoying life to the fullest. The caption above her head read:

THE ATLANTA JOB FAIR EXPO

*Are you tired of your dead-end job with no room for advancement and no plans for the future? Recruiters from top companies want to talk to you! Entry level to Executive positions available. There is a job for you!*

"This must really be big since they're advertising here," I muttered to myself, eying the list of employers and the dates of the fair. I began plotting as the train drove me closer to the job I had been forced to take. My caseworker was threatening to kick my ass off Welfare, Section 8, and the WIC program. Ain't that some shit? The WIC program! How was they gonna kick me off something that's free because I didn't feel like working? Damn!

So every day I dragged my ass to an office located downtown in the Water Towers building. It was a real nice joint with an inside shopping mall and lots of expensive stores and restaurants. When I started working I thought I was going to be a clerk. I thought I would be typing and answering phones. Come to find out, my job title, *clerk*, required me to do everything but type and answer the phones.

They had me toting big-ass trash bags, mopping floors, and cleaning toilets. They used me for a janitor, a maid, a flunky, and a gopher. Somebody should have reported these damn people to the Illegal Slave Trade Commission because at $6.50 an hour, them white folks tried to work my ass like a Hebrew slave.

One time, the white chick who hired me caught me sitting down with my shoes off sneaking a break.

"Excuse me," she said rudely. "What are you doing?" She turned up her nose, focused her fake green eyes on the clock above my head and said, "it is not break time yet."

I looked up at her, rubbing my sore feet, and gave her a look like, *Bitch, does it look like I give a fuck?*

She waddled her fat ass off and left me alone.

A couple of days later, her purse came up missing. She never said anything to me about taking an unauthorized break after that either. I bet that bitch wouldn't leave her shit in the break room no more while I was cleaning—with her broke ass.

When I got home from work, my clothes were always dirty, y back hurt and my feet were swollen and sore. My son was always crying and my mother was always complaining about money for Pampers. I was so tired, I could have fallen asleep anywhere. Oftentimes that's what I had done. I'd even fallen asleep on the toilet. But I needed all the overtime these honkies would give me. You see, at the mall I had seen this fly-ass, one-piece Baby Phat jumpsuit that I wanted to buy and wear to the club. Actually, it was either buy or boost—whichever came first. That's a hood chick for ya.

One day, I had arrived at work early and had snuck on the computer to go online to look at some porn sites. For some reason that morning, though, I remembered the job fair. I Googled my name, and to my surprise ten different chicks with the same name as mine, Tamara Jenkins, came up. That shit had me mad buggin' because some of them really had it going on. My mind flashed back to the newspaper ad I had read on the train. I remembered what my horoscope had said: *You are in for a big career change.* So what I did was create a resume by using some of the information from the chicks with the same name as mine. Tamara Jenkins, teenaged mother and high school dropout, now had a future. Now, I know what you're thinking, but don't try to knock my hustle by trying to judge me—especially if you never walked in my shoes. Anyway, I was finally coming up because of a tiny white lie. Not bad for a chick that had been born and raised in the heart of the ghetto, Chicago's south side in the Cabrini Green Housing Projects.

In a week's time, I went from working a back-breaking job in Chicago, to cruising a job fair in Atlanta. As luck would have it, my resume produced three companies that were interested in me, but I managed to get a call from Barnes & Associates, a software company. I was just waiting for the lady who called me to confirm an interview time. Now that everything was working better than I had expected, I was suddenly scared to death. *What if they found out that I exaggerated a little on my application?* I thought. Could they throw my ass in jail for fraud?

Shit, what was a chick supposed to do? I was a seventeen-year-old teenaged mother and high school dropout. I did manage to earn my GED and was taking computer classes at a community college. Other than that, my life was going nowhere and fast. I was tired of being on Section 8, broke and poor. So, on a whim, I concocted a scheme to remedy the problem—to get me and my child out of the ghetto. Hell, I had made it this far—I would deal with whatever happened when it happened.

The waitress brought my drink and as I sipped on it, I noticed that I was surrounded by uppity black folks. These were the same people that would normally turn their snobby noses up at me, yet here I was attempting to be one of them. *Get in where you fit in,* was the motto in the hood. I just prayed it didn't backfire on my ass.

Although I was in Atlanta for the job fair, I was also motivated because my baby daddy, IC Miller was there, with his sperm-donating ass. The more I thought about him living the life of a college basketball player—free and with no responsibilities, while I was struggling, I became even more pissed off. The day I had learned that I was pregnant, I also found out that he had given me an STD. On the day he was leaving to go off to college, I confronted his ass about it and he tried to flip the script. Nigga pah-leez! That day I had made a solemn oath: if I ever saw his ass again I would make his life a living hell.

*So, this is how they livin',* I thought to myself, taking my mind off of IC as the waitress set down another drink. She smiled like she thought I was going to give her ugly broke ass a tip. Shit, I was broke, too. I looked at her when she walked away. Not only could I see the tracks of her hair weave but her braces made her lips protrude. I was glad my teeth were straight. I swear, if she smiled too hard she'd cut her lip.

For some reason, I was temperamental that day. Maybe it was the anxiety of not knowing, but hoping and praying that my life would change. Shit, I had a child at home with my mother who was a 'recovering' crack addict. No, she wasn't a former crack addict. She stopped smoking until she could recover some more money. Life is strange and people are even stranger. I guess when you're used to having nothing, the idea that you might get something means a whole lot. Not big things, just the ordinary things that people take for granted. Things like having food on the table, clean clothes to wear and a roof over your head. That's why I had to pull this shit off. I ain't never had nothing but bad luck and hard times.

I looked around the room at the black people with money and felt a little envious. Only another poor black person could understand what I was feeling. Even though I was out of my league, there was no turning back now. "God, if you can hear me, please help me," I prayed. I took a sip of my drink and nervously drummed my acrylic fingernails on the tabletop, trying to look unpretentious, unfazed—and pretty.

A mellow Jill Scott song played in the background. To the right of me was a large picture window that took my breath away when I first looked out of it. I never saw scenery that beautiful. My nerves were on edge waiting on the phone call and a million what-ifs ran through my mind.

I let my eyes roam the lounge, along with my imagination. There were some fine-ass brothas wearing really nice suit. Then, out of the blue, a dude stopped at my table. He was good looking and bald headed, with one of them thin goatee mustache jobs. His teeth were even nice and white.

He asked, "Is this seat taken?"

I noticed he looked at my breasts then his eyes darted downward.

For a fleeting moment I thought about fucking with him and calling him out on the shit he had just did. But instead, I politely nodded my head and replied, "Yes, it's taken." I flirted with my eyes.

He opened his mouth to speak, but thought better of it and walked away.

Lucky for his square ass 'cause I was jail bait. Once a brotha hit this tight poonany, he was sprung. Then I would tell him my real age. He would start trippin', but want to keep hittin' it. If it was good, I would let him and we would keep it our little secret on the low-low from his wife or girlfriend. Then I would start making my demands for money, lots of money. At five foot nine, 140 pounds with a strikingly bodacious body, a tiny waist, and a pretty face, dudes were always telling me that I looked like I was about 23 or 24 years old. Even though I carried a fake ID, I was never carded because I knew how to act. I looked around at more of the men in the lounge. They were handsome, they just weren't my type.

Just as I was gathering my things to go back to my room and wait for the call, in bounced this fine, slender brotha. He had long locs that hung on his shoulders and he looked to be about six feet four inches tall. He wore an oversized, blue Rocawear shirt with some baggy Red Monkey jeans. One wrist was iced out with two bracelets and on the other wrist he wore a Rolex watch. Around his neck was a platinum chain embellished with diamonds, showcasing the initials P.G. His eyes were low and slanted, a look I recognized all too well; he had been smoking some weed. A feeling that I couldn't explain surged through my young body. Just looking at him made my pussy moist. I noticed quite a few of the other people in the lounge checking him out, too. The older men looked annoyed as they gazed at his swagger, remembering their youth. However, the women stopped what they were doing and made him the center of their attention with flirtatious invitations as they walked by him. It was true that every woman wanted a thug, no matter what socioeconomic background they were from. As he walked, he swung his head slightly to remove a loc from his face. That shit was sexy as hell. I couldn't stop myself from staring. After he sat down at the bar, I watched him flirt with a few of the stuck up chicks, but he had yet to look my way.

Within moments, he casually turned to canvas the room. Then he saw me.

I tried to play it off, but he caught me staring. So I hit him with a subtle dick-tease. I crossed my legs, showing him a little thigh and he did a double-take that made me blush.

His high ass damn near fell of the bar stool he was sitting on. I had his attention, so I turned it up a notch. I took a sip of my Hennessy and Coke and circled the rim of my glass with my tongue. He sat straight up on his stool and looked past the waitress at me. She said something to him but he ignored her. He slid off the barstool and bounced my way. His eyes showed mischief and thug curiosity. His pants were sagging so low, I was surprised they didn't fall off of his narrow ass. He definitely was a testament to the new evolution of "Thugacracy."

Wearing a goofy-ass crooked smile, he pushed up on me. "What it do, shawty?"

I noticed his mouth full of gold and diamonds. He was tatted up and he reeked of weed. God, I hated that line; but from him, it sounded kinda gangsta.

"You tell me what it do, or better yet, what can it do?" I shot back, completely catching him off guard.

His diamond grill sparkled as he searched his mind for a witty reply, but he came up short.

"Do I know you from somewhere?" He stroked his face. "She said you were a dime-piece but damn!"

I sensuously puckered my lips in a way that suggested something sexual, although I had no plans to sex this man.

He shuffled his feet and groped himself as he looked at me with his sexy penetrating Ebonyze.

I seductively caressed my thigh again, giving him what I knew he wanted. I was going to have fun with this nigga. "No, I don't think we know each other but the question is, 'do you want to get to know me?' But first things first, who are you and who said I was a dime?"

He looked shocked at my admission.

"I'm Pharaoh Greene," he said with a cocky attitude, "you know, G," like I should have known.

His arrogance would have normally turned me off. I couldn't stand a nigga who thought everyone should know his ass, but I had to admit, he had my interest.

"Well, Pharaoh Greene, I'm not from Atlanta; I'm here on a business trip from Chicago."

I had no way of knowing that he was a major gangsta and a key figure in the prosperous drug trade in Atlanta. I had no way of knowing that he had made his first million dollars when he was nineteen, or that he had gone on to funnel money into the music industry and within a few years, had come up with a few one-hit wonders that he had produced himself. I had no way of knowing that G was a flat foot hustler that had his hands in everything legal and illegal going on in the city. That day I just wanted to flirt with him and maybe even smoke up his weed.

"I'm Tamara Jenkins, nice to meet you." I extended my hand. As he took it, I looked at the diamond Rolex on his wrist and thought, *Oomph, dude caked up.*

His hand was soft, but firm as our touch lingered. I saw his eyes grow cloudy as our conversation quickly turned awkward. Maybe he was stuck on stupid because smoking weed would get a nigga tongue tied. I got the feeling he was about to walk off, but just looking at him gave me the urge to smoke a blunt and chill with him. After all, I didn't know nobody and I had a big-ass hotel room all to myself, so I moved in for the kill. I gulped my drink, all the while trying to look sophisticated. I took a five dollar bill out of my purse and slapped it on the table. I quickly stood up, causing my firm breasts to intentionally brush up against him. It was fun teasing him; however, neither one of us was prepared for what would happen next.

"Ouch!" We both spat out in unison as we jumped back from one other. Static electricity shocked the hell out of us as my hard nipple pressed against his shirt. I caressed my breast and he rubbed his chest while we looked at each other and cracked up laughing. Our laughter was loud and vibrant. Anyone watching would have thought we were old friends.

"Damn, ma. We make sparks together," he joked as his eyes traveled down to my breasts like they were loaded 38s. He chuckled, "Damn, so you leavin' me?"

"Yeah, like I said, I'm here on business," I told him matter-of-factly, "so I can't let myself get sidetracked with pleasure, you know?"

He took a step closer. I found myself gazing up at him thinking again, *Damn, this nigga fine.*

"Well, it's my business to make sure your stay here in A-town is a pleasurable one." He licked them sexy lips like he was LL Cool J.

Damn! I wanted to slap his ass for being so sexy. Suddenly, that ugly-ass waitress showed up out of nowhere. She took a look at me and then at the five dollar bill on the table and rolled her eyes at me with an attitude. I'm the one who should have had an attitude. Six dollars for a Henny and Coke was ridiculous. She'd have to come up with that extra dollar because that was all she was getting out of me. I hadn't asked her to bring that second drink, so that was on her.

"You have an urgent phone call," she told G as she cut her eyes at me.

I was about to check her ass but then something popped in my head. Could she be this dude's chick?

"Tell'em I went to go handle some bidnizz," he told her. I blushed.

"But—" The waitress began, but abruptly changed her mind before turning away and stalking off.

"You ready to dip, shawty?"

"Dip? Where you think you're going?"

"At least let me walk you to your room. I don't bite, but I have been known to nibble." He smiled.

I couldn't help but laugh as I walked away, letting him enjoy my plump, round ass as it swayed from side to side.

And just as I knew he would, he followed.

*Got him!*

As we exited the lounge I saw the waitress on the phone. It looked like she was doing commentary of our every move to someone on the other end. Had I known then what I know now, I would have left dude alone.

# Chapter Four

All the way to my room Pharaoh had me cracking up. Being near him was intoxicating. I guess you can take a chick out the ghetto, but it's hard to take the ghetto out of a chick like me. He joked about Atlanta and told me stories about being raised in the Bankhead Court projects.

He had me in tears by the time we reached my room. I've always liked dudes that could make me laugh. However, once we walked inside the room the moment seemed to slow down. I saw a sparkle in his eyes as our laughter dissipated, giving way to something neither of us could deny. It seemed to give birth to sexual tension. I walked over to the love seat and Pharaoh followed.

"Have a seat."

He plopped down and I sat next to him, but not too close.

"So, tell me about yourself," he requested.

"I already did. It's your turn," I answered coyly.

"You smoke, ma?" He reached into his baggy pants pocket and pulled out an ounce of weed. He tossed it to me before I could answer.

I caught it and smelled it like a real weed connoisseur.

The only thing that could smell better was the inside of a new whip or a suitcase full of cash.

I watched as he dug into his pocket again. This time he pulled out a wad of bills and a box of wrinkled blunts.

I kicked off my shoes, impressed with his finesse. We smoked, chilled, just enjoyed each other's vibe. The weed was so good. I really wanted to keep some for myself.

"You like what you see?" I asked, noticing Pharaoh checking out my body.

"You look like a model." He leaned forward and kissed me.

I kissed him back. God, he was a good kisser. His lips were soft. His tongue lightly played tag with mine.

I pulled away from him and our sumptuous kiss. "I like chilling with you." I looked down and saw a big-ass print in his pants. I resisted the urge to grab a hold of his dick and play with it like a joy stick.

"Then why'd you stop, ma?"

Ignoring his question, I attempted to walk to the mini-bar to get some water.

Pharaoh gently took my hand and rested it on top of the protrusion in his pants. "You scared of this?"

My eyes fastened to the bulge under my hand and I felt my knees buckle.

"You must got a man or something." He let go of my hand; however it didn't move from its position.

"Nah, why? You got a chick?" I heard myself almost stutter, nervous energy running through my body.

"Nope, but I'm accepting applications for a classy lady just like you," he told me before taking a pull off his blunt. The haze of smoke hovered over his face and he pulled me close in an attempt to kiss me again.–

Weakly, I pushed myself away. "Stop," I told him timidly. But to him it must have sounded like "don't stop."

He squeezed my breasts like he was sampling a roll of Charmin tissue.

My arms tried to separate us, but my attempts were futile. He had his lips on my neck. His hand reached inside my blouse and pulled out one of my titties.

"Stop," I moaned.

Pharaoh's sultry lips walked down to my bare breast.

"Stop, damn!"

His hand moved up the inside of my thigh.

I tried to put the coochie-block on, but either I was too slow or he was way too fast. With one quick motion his hand pushed my thong to the side and he deftly eased three fingers inside of me. My pussy was gushing wet and my legs opened wide like a treasure chest.

"I'm hot as hell," I mumbled.

I fumbled with his zipper and he fumbled with my bra. My breasts spilled out, but I nearly had to wrestle to pull his dick out.

"Good Lord!" I said with nervous laughter. "Your shit is thick as my arm."

Pharaoh chuckled. "You like it, don't you?" His hand was on the nape of my neck, pushing my head downward. "Just put it in your mouth," he coaxed me.

Bending to my knees, I gently stroked his dick.

One of Pharaoh's legs began to tremble.

"Just relax," I encouraged him. I licked my lips and opened wide. I lowered my hot mouth on the head of his dick. Taking a little in at a time, I slowly bobbed my head up and down like a pro until I had created enough juices in my mouth for me to continue with ease.

Knowing that maybe this would mess up our momentum, I asked Pharaoh, "When you leave, can you leave me some of your weed?" I licked his dick like a lollipop. "Ummmmm," I moaned.

His body went rigid. "Shawty, you can have all of it!" He mumbled with his hand on my head, pushing it back down.

I continued, this time relentlessly bobbing my head up and down.

Moments later, his body started to erupt in convulsions and a series of fitful contractions. "I'ma...I'ma 'bout ta cum! Mmm, shit!" He groaned.

I wasn't lettin' this nigga cum in my mouth, so I bobbed and weaved with my head until he released his grip. I masterfully masturbated him with my hands until I pulled his milky fluid from his dick.

He shuttered and exploded.

"Day-um!" I exclaimed. The force was so strong that it jetted upward in a stream that nearly hit the ceiling. I glanced over at the clock on the table. I still hadn't received the phone call.

Pharaoh had a wild look in his eyes. He stood up, stroking himself strongly in front of me.

"What's wrong?" I asked.

"Nothing." He smiled. "You ready for some more?"

"Why don't you just wrap it and I'll let you beat it up," I purred. "Better yet, you can handle your bidnizz and eat it before you beat it," I challenged.

"Wrap it?" He asked, befuddled.

"A condom, nigga!"

"Oh." He looked disappointed.

Slowly I stood and leisurely slithered out of my clothes, one garment at a time, doing a dick-tease. I enjoyed watching him look at my body.

Finally he chimed, "Damn shawty, you got a bangin' ass body! Is all dat ass real?"

"You tell me what you think." I smiled and nodded my head. I padded across the room, giving him a nice dose of booty shake then struck a pose with my hands on my slim waist.

"Dammnit, man, you a bad bitch!"

"You did say I could have the rest of the weed, right?" I asked meekly with my forefinger on my cheek as I walked back toward him. "What's wrong, baby?"

I stuck my finger inside my wet pussy then pulled it out and attempted to trace his lips, but he pulled away. "What, you don't eat pussy?"

"Aye, shorty." He had a serious look on his face now.

*Niggas*, I said to myself. *Always want a chick to suck they dick, but they don't want to eat no pussy.* I moved away from Pharaoh, and all of a sudden the mood was destroyed. "That's cool," I said to him.

"So what's that supposed to mean? We ain't fucking now 'cause I won't eat you?"

I didn't say anything. I just walked away to get a condom out of my purse. Behind me, I heard a rustle. I looked back and Pharaoh was tearing off his clothes. He took off his jewelry and piled it next to the weed on the table. I grabbed the condom and dangled it from my fingers as I admired his beautiful muscular chest. Again, I looked at his dick. It took everything in my power not to jump on it raw but I had learned my lesson from doing that years ago.

"Are you serious?" Pharaoh asked, looking at the condom. "What the hell I'm s'pose to do wit dat?" He smirked. "Big boys need big toys." Laughing, he reached into his pants on the floor and pulled out a Magnum XL condom. "I don't know who you're used to being with baby, but I'm a man."

"Well, let me see what you can do, man." I jumped into bed. The more I looked at him the more he looked like a keeper.

I wondered if he really didn't have a lady like he had claimed, but at the time I didn't care. What she didn't know wouldn't hurt her.

He struggled to get the condom on. Finally, he climbed between my thighs. I felt his dick probing the dark, tight delta of my womanhood. The head of his dick was inside me. It felt so good. He placed one of my legs on his shoulder and lowered his body onto mine.

"Stop!" I yelled. I screamed so loud I scared myself.

*Innocent*

# Chapter Five

"Whaat!?" He raised his voice.

I could tell Pharaoh was pissed.

"I said 'stop'."

"Shawty, you trippin." Ignoring me, he pushed a little harder and continued to make his entrance into my pussy.

I squirmed away.

Pharaoh looked at me and appeared to be irritated. I began to caress his chest hoping that it would calm the beast inside him. I maneuvered my arm up a little higher just in case he slapped me for stopping him so late in the game.

I took another hit from the joint that lay burning in the ashtray beside the bed trying to relax so that we could try this again. "Uhhh, G, before you stick it in, you gotta get it right so I can cum."

"Whaat?!" He exclaimed pushing up on his elbows.

I could feel his dick easing in a little more. God, it felt good. "I don't cum easy, but when I do—"

"I can't tell you don't cum easy. You done soaked the fuckin' sheets and I ain't even hit it yet."

I kept my arm up, holding his stare as his body relaxed.

He lowered his head to tenderly suck on one of my brown

nipples. With a mouthful he said, "Damn girl, you're wifey material." Gradually he crawled down my body leaving a trail of hot saliva. His tongue stopped for a brief rest to lick my navel.

I urged him down to my neatly trimmed pussy. "Come on, right there."

He spread my legs and saw my tattoos: "Juicy" on one inner thigh and "Fruit" on the other. I could see that he was reading the words etched in my skin.

"Wha da fuck dat s'pose to mean?"

"You know, my fruit is juicy. Real juicy. Don't you want some?" I stroked my pussy and spread the lips apart just so he could see how wet I was.

Pharaoh looked at me and made a face. He replaced my fingers with his and spread the lips of my slippery wet vagina apart and blew on it lightly.

I lay on my back and moaned softly, "that's so good."

Pharaoh gave me a soft kiss and began to nibble on my clitoris like it was a morsel of fruit, while his tongue lapped at the most sensitive areas. He moaned loudly.

"Ohhh, shiiit," I sighed. The feeling was pure ecstasy. "Right there."

His tongue thrashed faster and faster before sliding back inside of me. He was slurping, sucking, licking, and thrashing his head back and forth. The sound echoed throughout the room.

As I tried my best to watch him, my toes spread uncontrollably and I closed my eyes. "Awww, shit, nigga! I'm about to cum."

He continued lapping, strong and long. All of a sudden the earth shook and my body quivered. I wanted to call out his name, but I just couldn't remember it at the time.

Like a good boy, Pharaoh began to lap up my juices. He inserted two fingers inside my pussy, stroking me like I was a kitten. He continued to fervidly suck and lick.

I felt another carnal climax about to erupt. I spread my legs wide allowing his tongue to gluttonously work its magic on me. Panting and moaning I held the top of his head with my hands. The feel of his locs on my fingertips heightened my sexual pleasure. Even his facial stubble felt ultra sensitive on the inside of my thighs. Suddenly, it was just too much to bear. This dude knew exactly what he was doing. Nobody had ever eaten my pussy like that before.

Pharaoh came up for air and cleared his throat. "So, what you think?"

My hair was matted to my face with perspiration. I smiled at him and finally spoke once my breathing became steady. "You fulfilled my wildest dreams." I caressed his forehead. I wanted to ask for an encore. "Boy, where did you learn how to eat pussy like that?" I asked, noticing my fingernail marks on his sticky, wet forehead.

"Shawty, lemme hit from de back." Pharaoh said, stroking his dick. He shoved me back down on the bed, climbed on top of me and went to work.

An hour later our bodies were covered with dewy sweat.

Pharaoh moaned some unintelligible words and finally his body went rigid. He jerked and convulsed and fell out on the bed. "Day-um! You got some good-ass pussy!" He panted. Even with a sex face, I couldn't help but admire his handsome features.

Basking in the glow of getting sexed real good, I looked at the clock. *Damn, still no phone call.*

Suddenly, there was an intrusive pounding on the hotel door. Pharaoh's eyes bucked wide. "Who da fuck is dat?" he whispered.

"I dunno," I said, less concerned about the level of my voice. I was in my room.

Dude looked at the door as the knocking continued.

"G, I know yo ass in derr!" Some chick outside the door screamed. He bolted from the bed like he had been shot with a stun gun.

"What the fuck is wrong with you? Is that your woman?"

Pharaoh shrugged his shoulders. "I don't know." He pulled on his jeans and shirt, searching under the bed for his shoes and jacket.

"I thought your ass said you ain't have no woman?" I reminded him. Now I had an attitude.

The pounding on the door continued. A woman screamed, "Pharaoh, I know your ass is in there!"

I stared at him with my arms folded in front of me. "Well, she called yo name so you know who it is. You need to go out there to check dat hoe before I do!" I huffed.

"Shhh," he hissed, placing his hand over my mouth.

"Nigga pah-leez," I huffed back, pushing him away from me. "You need to handle yo business. This shit ain't cool."

"Nigga, I know yo ass in derr with some stank bitch!" The

voice entered the room from the other side of the door.

"No she didn't just call me a '*stank bitch*'!" I said out loud, my body stiffening with indignation.

"I know yo punk ass was down here trickin' with some bitch!" She yelled and continued to bang on the door, "so open the door you trick-bitch-ass-nigga!" The knocks on the door became louder. "Now you wanna play like you ain't in there!"

"Fuck!" Pharaoh scuffed. He searched the room for a place to hide.

"You can run but you can't hide," she threatened in a husky voice. "You and that ugly heifer from the bar. I got something for you too, bitch!"

"Oh no, she didn't!" I yelled, moving toward the door.

Pharaoh grabbed my arm to stop me. "Chill, shawty!"

"I ain't no bitch!" I yelled loud enough for her to hear me. "Let me go!" I struggled against his grip wanting to rush to the door and give ole girl a serious beat-down. "Who the fuck is that?" I asked again.

"It's Lisa, my baby's mama," Pharaoh whispered.

"You're just like any other nigga," I said, pissed.

He frowned at me.

"Pharaoh Greene, I'm counting to three and if you don't open dis door I'ma burn dis muthafucka down!" She began counting. "One!"

I grabbed the sheet from my bed and wrapped it around my body.

"Two!" She continued to count.

"Go answer the door. Tell her I'm not here," Pharaoh begged.

"Is that your plan?" I asked sitting down on the bed, pissed.

Pharaoh sucked his teeth in disgust. "Go on. Hurry up!" he commanded.

I nearly stumbled over the sheet as he shoved me toward the door. I looked over my shoulder at him, considering whether or not I should lie for his ass or curse him out.

"Niggas ain't shit," I said aloud before I opened the door.

"Three!"

# Chapter Six

In front of the door was a pile of men's clothes about three feet high. A thick chick was hunched over with a yellow lighter in her hand. The vacillating flame accentuated her brown eyes in a maniacal way. This bitch looked crazy as hell. It occurred to me that I might need a knife for this ho; that was, if I decided to fight her. Sizing her up and seeing how incensed she was, I wasn't certain a knife would stop her. Plus, I wasn't no stupid bitch. There was no doubt in my mind that she was about to ignite the clothes and probably the entire hotel as a result of it. I looked to the left and to the right down the hall; every occupant on the hotel floor had their head out the door watching her, and now me. "What the fuck are you doing?" I asked.

"Who the fuck are you?" The crazy, full-bodied chick with a pretty face asked.

"Look, this ain't no ghetto hotel. You can't be in here causing no damn problems. Put that damn lighter down."

"Excuse me," Lisa said, sucking her teeth with attitude as she pushed past me. Her long, black hair spilled over her face.

I started to tackle her ass but I wasn't about to fight over no nigga that wasn't mine. Besides, Lisa was bigger than me and a bitch knows her limitations.

"I know goddamn well my man bet not be in herrr!" She lamented with a southern drawl.

She stomped to the middle of the room looking around for him. Her large breasts swelled as she huffed. Surprisingly, Pharaoh was gone. Lisa walked over to the closet and flung the door open so hard that it broke off the hinges.

"Look, bitch!" I said, "Don't come in here destroying shit. I didn't do anything to your ass."

She turned toward me and rolled her eyes, a loud exasperated breath escaping from between her large lips.

"Where is he?"

"I don't know who you're talking about," I said, playing dumb, wondering where Pharaoh had disappeared to.

"Bitch, I'ma beat both of y'all asses if I find him in here," Lisa threatened taking a step toward me.

I didn't move. I looked around the room for something to hit this ho in the head with.

"Bitch, you ain't gonna tell me where he at?" she demanded.

I balled up my face up at her. Without waiting for a response, she frowned back at me and began to search the room. While Lisa searched my room better than a cop with a search warrant, I saw Pharaoh's shoe peeking out through the ruffle in the bedskirt. Tired of the whole situation, I decided to dime him out. I wanted them both out of my hair. I snapped my fingers at the frantic girl who was now rummaging through my closet. She turned to look at me.

"Under the bed," I mouthed and pointed downward.

She grimaced at me and looked at the bed, pulling up the skirt.

"Muthafucka, wha'cha doin' hiding under the bed!" she screamed.

Pharaoh muttered, "I dropped my contact lens."

"You don't wear contacts, asshole!" Lisa said grabbing him by his leg and pulling him out from under the bed.

Pharaoh hollered in pain from the rug burn he received as a result of Lisa's anger.

"Let me explain—" he pleaded.

Instead of hearing him out, Lisa reached back with her fist and cold-cocked him dead in the face. Big mistake. All the thugs that I have ever known would kick the bone out a bitch's ass, and he was no exception to the rule. Pharaoh picked her big ass up and slammed her ass to the floor so hard, it vibrated. Amazingly, the chick got back up on her feet, a little wobbly, but they went at it again, toe to toe.

"Open up! Police!" A voice bellowed from the other side of the door.

My eyes rolled. "Fuck! This is just what I needed."

*Innocent*

# *Chapter Seven*

## IC MILLER

A public announcement system cackled inaudible names as feet shuffled by on antiseptic floors. Cold and shivering, I laid face down, soaking wet in a pool of my own blood. Barely conscious, I recognized the sights and sounds of the hospital. I gurgled and choked on my own blood, wincing in pain, as I tried to focus my swollen, blood-ridden eyes on the murky images ahead of me. I was in so much pain I could hardly breathe. I heard angry footsteps coming my way and a crowd of angry cops huddled over me.

"Boy, we need ta know why you kilt that girl. We need a confession out ya. If you don't ya might die right hurr on dis hurr flo."

This was their plan, their "Quid Pro Quo". Either I confess or die. My mind was in a fugue as I continued to drift in and out of consciousness. At the time I would have confessed to killing the Pope if it would have gotten my ass some help and gotten me away from these crackas. Just as I opened my mouth to speak, I saw the blur of tiny feet in small white shoes approaching, then came a high-pitched voice.

"What the hell do you think you're doin' to him?" a voice

called out toward my direction.

"We need to ask him some questions," spoke a brusque reply.

"No! Not on my damn shift and not in this damn hospital. No way, not fuckin' today!" the voice replied coming closer.

Instantly, I recognized the voice of a black woman. It reminded me of Big Mama. The woman shoved the racist cops out of the way and I heard them grumble as she bent down to examine me, being careful not to step in my blood. Her voice was soft and soothing. "Ohmigod, he's a teenager!" she gasped.

"This here is a suspect. He killed and raped dat gurl in the Dairy Queen robbery," one of the cops said.

The nurse turned and glowered up at the cop. "So what y'all plan on doing? Letting him die right here like a fucking dog to make it even?"

"Listen, we just need to talk to him a little while longer. Now you need to go on 'bout your business."

"This is my business!" The nurse raised her voice in defense. "Doctor Ferguson! Doctor Ferguson!" Her voice carried through the busy corridor and within seconds a doctor appeared through the emergency room doors. He looked tired and disheveled. A light tint of gray hair ringed his hair around the temples.

Dr. Ferguson pushed his glasses up on his nose. He paused momentarily. Shock registered on his face.

"What's going on here?"

"They're trying to torture a confession out of this child!" She pointed her finger at the cops accusingly.

"We're just tryin' to talk to him. He's a suspect in the rape and murder at the Dairy Queen," a familiar voice advised. It was Officer Burns.

Dr. Ferguson reached inside his white coat pocket to retrieve a pen light. Bending down he checked both of my eyes. "Can you hear me, son?"

I gurgled, "Yes."

To his right, I could see the nurse whispering something in his ear.

Irate, the doctor stood upright. "I want the handcuffs taken off of him immediately and I want him moved to the Emergency Room!"

"But he escaped—" the cop tried to explain.

The doctor challenged each one of them. "No, each one of you can, and will, be charged with murder if this man dies in my hospital. I will personally see to it." The doctor bellowed, "Bring me a stretcher!"

Pressing her lips together, the nurse wiped the blood from my nose. "You're gonna make it. I have a son at home about your age. You're strong, you hear me?"

The rancid smell of my own blood was in my nostrils. The nurse's hand touched my cheek as I continued to lie on my stomach. It was a struggle to just breathe much less respond to her. I could feel the handcuffs being removed as I went in and out of consciousness. I was lifted onto a stretcher and rushed into the emergency room, not sure if I would make it out alive.

*Innocent*

# Chapter Eight

When I woke up in the hospital I was shackled to the bed. I was cold and shivering; my only cover was a single sheet thrown across me. The nightmare was all too real because of the pain that rocked my body.

With a dry mouth, I tried to swallow, but my effort was useless. It felt like my tongue was stuck to the roof of my mouth. I tried to speak, but my voice was hoarse.

I lay in the bed shivering, trying to figure out why they had chosen me. To my right, I heard the rustling of clothes and saw movement. I turned my head gingerly and there was a white, tall and muscular man in a wrinkled gray uniform.

His dark beady eyes were pushed way back into the sockets. His large forehead, bushy eyebrows, and scruffy beard gave him an uncanny caveman appearance. I noticed his right eye twitch uncontrollably. As he approached me, he frowned. "What 'cha looking at boy?" he snarled, showing rotten teeth.

Startled by the large pistol in his hand, I half-whispered, "Who are you?"

"I'm your worst nightmare, boy." He placed the muzzle of the gun on my chest and did a slow crawl upward. He nestled it under my chin and pressed hard. "You's one of dem niggers dat likes to rape and kill white gurls, huh?"

I carefully shook my head, afraid to open my mouth to speak. I didn't want the gun to go off.

His eye twitched as he hissed at me. "Try to take my gun! Try to resist me, boy and I'll blow yo goddamn brains out so help me God." He began to reverse the movement of the gun down to my privates. "You robbed that restaurant, you blindfolded that gurl and raped her. Then you murdered her."

I cleared my throat. "No, sir."

He pressed the gun against my balls.

I vigorously shook my head. My heart beat fast and I knew for sure he was going to shoot me.

"Boy, you got three seconds to confess to rapin' and killin' that gurl. If you don't confess, I swear, I'ma blow your fuckin' balls off!" He removed a small tape recorder from his pocket and put it on the bed. He pressed a button. "Now talk!" He growled and continued to hold his gun against my balls.

I was shaking so badly that I could hardly talk. "I, I did it …"

The white man continued to probe me. He nudged the gun harder against my balls. "You did what, boy?"

Steeped in misery and fear I found myself confessing to a heinous crime that I didn't commit. "I, I raped her. I murdered her. I did it."

The white man's features suddenly changed as he beamed down at me with pride. He obtained what he had come there for. "I knew it all the time." He punched me in the chest.

Pain exploded through my body. My left arm jumped, toppling the IV beside my bed. I attempted to clutch my chest but with no such luck. With the air knocked out of me, I struggled to breathe.

Gasping, I struggled to catch my breath. "Don't hit me no mo."

The man looked at me and leaned forward. "Did that gurl ask you not to rape her no more?" With spittle dribbling from the corner of his mouth he reached back to hit me again.

The door swung opened and a nurse walked in. She looked startled by seeing another man in my room.

In one quick motion he put his pistol back into his holster and grabbed the tape recorder off the bed.

Sounding as country as the cops, she screeched, "Bubba Ray Nelson, what are you doing to him?"

The cop cringed and demurely stepped back from the bed.

With a straight face he lied, "Ms. Harvey, I just come to check on the boy."

I watched as the nurse's eyes turn into narrow slants. She looked at him suspiciously. It was obvious that she wasn't fond of him. "It's time for you to leave, Bubba Ray."

Bubba Ray held on tight to my taped confession as he rushed past the nurse.

"I can't stand that man. He's nothing but trouble," Nurse Harvey confided in me.

Nurse Harvey was a large woman with a caramel complexion and a pleasant face. She looked to be in her late thirties, but determination, dedication and experience had taught her not to take shit from nobody. I could smell her perfume as she stood over me, taking my vitals, noting in the chart at the end of my bed. "Mind if I take a look?" Nurse Harvey asked. She pulled back the sheet and I heard a gasp. "Child, you're bleeding!"

I opened my eyes and thought about telling her what the cop had done to me, but I thought better of it. What could she do to help? She would only make matters worse, reasoned.

*Innocent*

41

"What happened?"

No answer.

"Look here, I saw the tape recorder and the gun," she told me sternly. "Tell me what happened."

I grimaced and replied weakly, "Nothing happened."

She frowned at me. "He don't have no business putting his hands on you!"

As I exhaled, a sharp pain shot through my chest, forcing me to close my eyes.

I could feel Nurse Harvey's cold hands prodding, pushing, and pulling as she peeled the bloody gauze off of my chest, exposing my hideous, butchered and bruised body. I opened my eyes to watch her. She swallowed hard, trying to find answers to the questions looming in her head.

After cleaning my wounds, she covered them with fresh gauze, and spoke.

"If you let a white man hit you and get away with it, then all those years our people fought are useless. Eventually, you're going to have to fight back." She spoke very matter-of-factly.

I turned my head.

"Regardless of whether you tell me the truth or not, I'm letting

Dr. Ferguson know what I saw as soon as he gets in."

*Whether you tell me the truth or not,* echoed in my ears. I primed my lips, about to speak. This was too much for me to bear. It wasn't just about Bubba Ray. It was more, much more—unspoken words.

"Please help me. I ain't kill no girl. I ain't kill nobody. I need for you to call Big Mama."

"Who is Big Mama?" The nurse asked. Her voice was barely above a whisper.

"That's my gramma."

I focused on the nurse the best I could with my good eye. "Nurse Harvey, I could go to prison for the rest of my life for a crime I didn't commit." I felt a tear tug at my eye as I pleaded my case. There was no way in hell I was about to cry in front of her. I had just turned eighteen years old. I was a grown-ass man.

Nurse Harvey moved closer. "Son, they found a gun—plus, an eyewitness said they saw you leaving the scene of the crime."

"A gun? Eyewitness? Saw me? No, it wasn't me. I didn't kill anybody." I was getting upset and the machines began to make beeping noises.

"Calm down, honey," the nurse said somberly. She nodded her head, taking a timid step back as if to get a better judgment of me.

I reached out with what little strength I had and grabbed her arm. "I don't know nuttin' 'bout no gun. You gotta believe me. You said you have a son my age. You gotta call Big Mama for me. Please help me."

I noticed her swallow the lump in her throat. I was trying hard to convince her to help me. I was desperate.

She never took her eyes off me, nor did she try to remove my grip from her arm. She sighed deeply, "What's your grandmother's number?"

Groggily, I gave her the information. My mind began to slip back into a medication-induced coma. I began to have a nightmare, a cinematic horror film. I was lying on the side of the highway bleeding when a cop shoved a gun in my hand. It was a dream, though. It was real. The cops had set me up.

I fell asleep with the nurse watching me. I hoped she would make the decision to assist a black man accused of murder and rape.

# Chapter Nine

In the days that followed, the media parked outside the hospital while Bubba Ray was still up to his same old tricks. He constantly harassed me, doing everything in his power to make my life hell.

Finally, the day of my preliminary hearing came. It had to be held in my hospital room because of my injuries. I met my attorney, Andy Stromwich. He was dressed in a brown suit with large lapels, a red shirt and a blue tie. Several strands of gray hair were brushed over his bald spot, and he wore dark shades.

Several people carrying furniture strode into the room as my attorney introduced himself to me. "My name is Andy Stromwich. I'll be representing you in the event you can't afford an attorney."

Quickly my room filled to capacity. A table and some chairs were placed next to my bed and directly across the room from me. I watched as my newly appointed lawyer bumped into the table, scattering papers all over the floor. Then he knocked the chair over and damn-near fell. Some snickered, suppressing full-fledged laughter. It occurred to me that not only did the man look like a complete idiot in those damn loud-ass colors he was wearing, but he was also an idiot.

"All rise! The Honorable Ted Studebaker presiding."

The judge ambled in. He took his seat directly across from me.

The bailiff barked, "You all may be seated."

My lawyer went to sit down and completely missed the chair, falling to the floor. With assistance, he was helped back into his chair. He smiled with embarrassment. "Oh, shit, the man is blind!" I said to myself.

Furrowing his brow, the judge looked over the rim of his glasses, up from the paper he was reading. "IC Miller, also known as TC Miller, do you understand what you're being charged with?"

"TC Miller is my brother's name."

"Just answer the question with a direct yes or no," the judge replied sternly.

"Yes, I mean, no." I stumbled over my words.

My attorney whispered to me, "This is just a preliminary hearing. Just answer the question."

I looked up at him like he was crazy, pissed off that he didn't get it straight that I wasn't TC. He had a criminal record a mile long and used my name on a couple of occasions to get out of jail. This couldn't be happening to me. The judge looked at me angrily. "TC, you are being charged with six counts. Count one, murder; count two, rape; count three, robbery; count four, assault—"

"Assault!" I yelled. "I was the one assaulted!"

My outburst startled Andy. He appeared to be in over his head. I turned my head showing him that I was sorry for interrupting. He touched my hand in an attempt to get me to calm down.

"Do not interrupt me, boy," the judge warned angrily. "One more outburst and I will hold you in contempt of court. Do you understand?"

I looked at the judge and the unfair jury of my peers and quieted down.

"As I was saying," the judge continued, "Count four, assault and battery on a law enforcement officer; count five, resisting arrest; and count six, obstruction."

They had damn-near killed me and now they were charging me with all this shit.

The judge's stare dared me to make another outburst. He apprised me of my so-called rights. I could hardly understand one word of his legal terminology.

I leaned over to my attorney. "Are you going to say

anything?"

He sat in silence.

"How do you plead?" The judge asked me.

I squirmed, determined to control my anger. "Your honor, I am not guilty. I'm being set up and I don't know why." The words rushed out. "I was on my way to Georgia State University when I was stopped. I was beaten up, pistol-whipped, and shot for no reason. Just a few days ago an officer placed a gun to my head and made me confess to a crime that I didn't commit."

The judge banged his gavel.

Bubba Ray yelled out, "He's telling a lie!"

Still banging his gavel, the judge began to get angry.

"Again, I'm going to ask you, do you plead guilty or not guilty? If you feel that you've been harassed by the police, you need to take that matter up with your attorney." The judge nodded toward my attorney. "From the look of your criminal record, Mr. Miller, you've had a lot of experience with the courts. Now, how do you plead?"

I leaned forward. "How do I plead?" The handcuffs bit into my wrist. I was furious. I yelled at the judge and anyone that could hear me. "I was framed! I ain't kill nobody! You gotta believe me!"

"Your honor, my client pleads 'not guilty' and we intend to go to trial."

"Trial?" I asked, overwhelmed and tired by the day's events. I didn't want to go to trial at all, let alone with a blind, incompetent lawyer that was appointed to me.

"I think it's our only chance," Andy whispered to me.

"Your honor," District Attorney Staller began, "the state asks that Mr. Miller not be given bond or special privileges. He's a threat to society and should be moved to the county jail where he can be monitored in a more secure setting."

I stared at Andy.

"Mr. Stromwich?" The judge asked.

"I'd like to file a motion to keep my client, Mr. Miller, in this hospital because his injuries are life-threatening, sir."

I saw my chances for a normal life fly out the window.

"Your honor, Mr. Miller has a long list of criminal activity: attempted murder, kidnapping, assault on a police officer, suspected gang leader." The District Attorney was pulling out the big guns. He was reading off TC's criminal history and accusing me of all his violent acts.

I attempted to raise my hand. "Yo honor, that's my brother's..."

"Mr. Stromwich, please advise your client to keep quiet," the judge admonished.

Three people stood across the room from me, one of which was a woman that had been crying the whole time. I was sure she was the victim's mother.

The prosecutor continued as he took a step closer to me. "The defendant was also picked out of a photo lineup by an eyewitness that positively identified him as the black man she saw leaving the scene of the crime playing loud rap music in his car." He continued, "Your honor, we're pushing for the maximum punishment allowed by law."

The judge angrily looked at me, "As soon you're able to walk, you will be immediately moved to the county jail. You will not be given a bond and an evidentiary date is set for next month." He leaned over toward his clerk and looked at the calendar she held up. "June 10 is the date for your trial, Mr. Miller." The judge banged his gavel, "Court is adjourned!"

Nurse Harvey walked into the room before anyone left. She was in street clothes. She walked right up to my attorney and introduced herself.

"Sir, my name is Desiree Harvey. I'm a nurse here at this hospital. I'd like to be a witness. I had to force them police officers to allow Mr. Miller to get medical attention. I'm willing to testify or do whatever I have to do."

Two cops stood at the door and watched Nurse Harvey talk to my attorney.

For the first time, I felt a ray of hope.

# Chapter Ten

Two weeks had gone by and I hadn't seen Nurse Harvey, nor had I heard from Big Mama. Right after my preliminary hearing, my attorney had assured me that I could call her; but that had never happened.

Dr. Ferguson walked into my room. He seemed to be in a hurry as he meticulously took out my staples.

My inquisitive nature got the best of me. "I haven't seen Nurse Harvey," I told him.

As the doctor pressed his thin lips together, his mouth created a line across his face. I winced as he took another staple out.

A dark shadow cast in his eyes as he looked at me, then back at my wound. "She's on indefinite leave. About two weeks ago, her home was completely burned to the ground. Then just a few days ago her son never came home. He's presumed missing."

I felt my heart pounding in my chest and I wondered if all of that had happened because she had volunteered to be a witness in my case. There was no doubt in my mind that Bubba Ray's racist ass had something to do with what had happened.

"Can you walk now?" The doctor asked, shaking me out of my reverie.

"Uh, nah," I stammered a lie.

After the last of the staples were removed the doctor stared at me. He hesitantly glanced at the door, then back at me. "They might try to move you to the county jail today. In my report I'm recommending that you remain here and not be moved."

Humbled by his kindness I replied, "Thank you, doc."

I stared down at my boney chest. I had withered away to almost half the size I once was. With my one wrist still handcuffed to the bedrail I gingerly climbed out of the bed and did some calisthenics. Physically I felt much better. I had regained about ninety percent of my strength. I did deep knee bends. "One, two, three, four…" I gingerly flung my legs over the edge of the bed and stretched them. Even though I had regained most of my strength, I couldn't let them know that.

I heard footsteps on the outside of my door, and I quickly laid back down.

Bubba Ray walked in carrying a tray of food. On days like this, when some fool allowed Bubba Ray to bring me my food, I didn't bother eating.

I looked down at what was on the tray and frowned. "What is this shit?" I asked. The aroma of the unidentifiable and inedible food made my stomach turn as I thought about him seasoning the food with his shit and piss.

"Eat yo food, boy!" He grumbled.

I cut my eyes at him and snapped back. "I'm not hungry." Nurse Harvey and her missing son weighed heavily on my mind.

He set the tray down and looked at me. "So, you ain't gonna eat yo food?" Without cracking a smile, he opened his mouth to speak. "Wanna hear a joke?"

I turned my head to look at the sun shining brightly through the window. I answered, "Nope!"

"What do niggers in de electric chair smell like?"

I didn't answer.

"Just like fried bologna! Heee, heee, heee." He laughed at his own sick joke.

I snapped. "Fuck you!"

"Whaat!?" He jerked his neck around to look at me.

"Cracka, you heard what the fuck I said."

Bubba Ray walked over to me. A snarl was on his beet red face and a twinkling glare of mischief in his sunken eyes. Through clinched teeth he hissed, "It's because of you that black bitch got her house burnt down. Now her son is fish food." Then he did something totally despicable. He spit in my face and grabbed me by my throat. "Smart-mouth nigger, what you gon' do now, huh? The nurse ain't here to save yo sorry ass now!" He choked me harder.

I couldn't breathe and I was starting to see black spots before my eyes.

With his free hand Bubba Ray snatched his gun from its holster. "I'ma stop you from openin' yo big mouth forever, boy."

I struggled in my bed to wrestle his hand off my neck, but Bubba Ray was too strong. I began to lose consciousness.

The look in his eyes was that of a psychopath as he placed the gun to my head.

Suddenly, the door opened and in walked Dr. Ferguson.

Bubba Ray turned me loose as he turned to look over his shoulder.

I knew it was now or never. I grabbed for his gun. It went off.

*BOOM!*

*Innocent*

# Chapter Eleven

## TAMARA JENKINS

As soon as I opened the door to my hotel room, the scene was chaotic. Cops were everywhere. Hotel security and a host of nosey-ass guests gawked from their doors. The police rushed inside. Pharaoh and his chick were still going at it. The police quickly broke up their fight. Lisa looked a mess.

"Ma'am are you all right?" a short, thin officer asked her.

Instead of responding to him, she swung again at Pharaoh.

Thugs, baby mamas and police were always a bad combination. They began to argue about who had started the fight.

"Whose room is this?" the tall, chubby officer asked me.

It's mine, officer," I answered. The sheet was still wrapped around my naked body. "Look at what they've done!"

The hotel manager started in now. "Miss, I can assure you that you will pay for the damages to this room."

"Don't fuck with me!" I growled. "This is not the time!"

The manager took a timid step back startled by my reaction.

On the other side of the room an officer was handcuffing Pharaoh.

"Lisa, tell them this was just a misunderstanding," he pleaded.

"Girl, you know how we do!"

Pharaoh passed by me and his handsome face was a mask of anger.

"Please don't take him away. We was just playin'," Lisa pleaded to the cops.

Annoyed by her interference and ignorance, the police threatened to arrest her too.

As quickly as they had come, they all left. The entire ruckus moved out of my room and into the hallway.

The manager stood at the door. "Somebody will have to pay for this damage."

I slammed the door in his face. I sat alone in the quietness of my room, crestfallen and heartbroken. I thought about my two-year-old, Tyres. I thought about his father, IC and how he had abandoned us.

It's amazing all the damage a horny chick and a cheating man with a big stiff dick can do. I glanced over the broken glass and torn clothes on the floor. My eyes filled with tears.

The ringing phone startled me awake.

"Hello?" I answered anxiously.

"Ms. Jenkins?"

"Yes?"

"This is the hotel manager. We're asking that you be out of the room by 5:00 p.m. Today!" he spat rudely.

"But my room was reserved for three days; the entire weekend."

"Not any more. Your reservation has been cancelled and you will be held responsible for the damages."

"But I—"

"Five o'clock, Ms. Jenkins," he spoke curtly and hung up.

Damn! What was I going to do now?

Eventually, I managed to pick myself up. I tiptoed across broken glass like I was walking through a mine field. At the closet door I noticed my purse was wide open. My heart skipped a beat. I stuck my hand inside. Gone was the $127 I had brought with me.

"That bitch stole my money!" I screamed. My mind flashed back to Pharaoh's baby mama rummaging through my shit in the closet. I felt a throbbing headache coming. "What else could go wrong?" A suffocating feeling of despair began to come over me.

My mind ran a million miles a minute. I had never received the phone call I was so desperately waiting for. I didn't know a soul in Atlanta, and thanks to Pharaoh's baby's mama I didn't have a penny to my name. I didn't know where to go or who to turn to.

I searched for my shoes and found the ounce of weed I had stashed under the loveseat. With everything that had been going on I had forgotten all about it. Thank God the police hadn't seen it. As I reached for it, my cell phone and a shiny object caught my eye. It was wedged in between the cushions of the loveseat. I pulled it out.

"Sweet Jesus!" It was Pharaoh's platinum chain.

Instantly, my heart went to pounding in my chest like a bass drum. My hand trembled as I held the chain up to the light. It sparkled a rainbow of colors. The large jeweled pendant had twenty-carat baguettes that spelled out the initials PG. I was so excited that I started hyperventilating. The chain had to be worth at least a hundred grand or more.

"Cha-ching!"

Maybe today wasn't so bad after all. I turned and glanced at the door, half- expecting someone to come knocking, asking for the chain back. This chain was the solution to my huge problem. I was a broke and stranded bitch. I got back down on my knees to check to see if dude had dropped anything else.

My eyes bucked when I saw it. "Oh, shit!" It was a gun—a Glock 9mm. Pharaoh must have slung it under the couch when the police came. I put it in my purse with the quickness. I knew I could get rid of it. One thing about a chick from the hood, a bitch knows how to get her hustle on. I was prepared to auction dude's shit off because I wasn't about to be broke. I remembered seeing a pawn shop a few miles up the street from the hotel.

I quickly calculated how much money I thought they would give me for the chain. Of course, they would try to cheat me down to thirty or forty thousand. The chain didn't cost me nothing but a swollen coochie and a headache. So, fuck Pharaoh and his bitch. I needed money and I needed it bad.

# *Chapter Twelve*

I quickly threw on a sweatsuit and matching sneakers and decided to leave the hotel room. As I attempted to stride past the hotel desk, I could feel the weight of the chain in my pocket.

"Hey, you, where do you think you're going?" the hotel's manager asked.

I looked up and I felt sick to my stomach.

"I'll be right back," I said over my shoulder.

He continued to stare at me with a smug expression. I took a glance at my watch; it was 4:23 p.m. I had to be out of the hotel by five.

The crisp autumn air was tinged with smog. It chilled me. The cool breeze seemed to heighten my senses. I could hear the clamor of traffic noise and the congested streets were bustling with people from all walks of life. The sun was bright on my face but I was still cold. I headed for the pawn shop with the chain safely in one pocket and my fake identification in the other. I decided to leave the gun at the hotel.

I walked shoulder to shoulder with other pedestrians on the cramped sidewalk. I couldn't believe the streets were so congested. Out of the blue a dirty old man popped up from nowhere blocking my path.

"Baby girl, can you help me?" the old dude asked.

I took one look at him and frowned.

His skin was oily with dirt and grease. His beard was long and mangy. But there was something all too familiar about him. Maybe it was his eyes or his body language. I knew that look all too well. He was a crackhead.

"Look, I need to get to an appointment," I said annoyed, trying to get around him. "I can't help you!"

I crinkled up my nose at him.

He smelled nasty as hell. As I tried to get around him, he reached down to take something out of his pants. I was going to punch the shit out of him if he took his dick out. To my surprise, he pulled out a large yellow envelope and opened it up.

My eyes landed on the contents and he finally had my attention. The envelope was stuffed with cash—lots of it!

"I have to turn myself into the court today and they might not let me go," the bum said to me.

I gave him a sympathetic nod but the only thing on my mind was trying to relieve old dude of that paper.

"My name is Leon Blue," he said. He suddenly stopped talking and winced. Then he stuck his dirty hand back into his pants and scratched his crotch.

I took a step back.

He withdrew his hand and flicked whatever it was away with his long, yellow thumbnail.

"Ugh!"

He stepped closer. He glanced over his shoulder and then back at me. Then he continued to talk. "Here, take this and give it to my daughter."

I continued to plot, trying to come up with a plan.

"What?" I asked suspiciously.

"Take this to my daughter. She'll need it to get me out of jail if they lock me up." One thing about crackheads, they do dumb shit at times, but they're always deceiving and conniving. *This better not be no sting operation bullshit,* I thought, looking at the fat envelope and then back at all of the people passing by us. If it was a set up, he was about to get me.

I reached for the envelope and grabbed it quickly.

He wouldn't let go, as if he was having second thoughts. "How do I know I can trust you and that you'll protect it with your life?" he asked sincerely.

Leon Blue had completely caught me off guard. I could feel my heart pounding in my chest. It was the same anxious feeling you get when you're about to do something wrong. But you know you're going to do it anyway. I held my hands up like I was swearing to the Lord. I hoped the old dude was religious. "I swear to God, if you give me the envelope I'll protect it with my life. You can trust me." I grinned at him.

Maybe I was a little too eager because the expression on his face changed quickly. He must have sensed something. Shit! Greed is a terrible thing.

Leon Blue began to take the envelope back but I wouldn't let it go. I couldn't let it go if I wanted to. Our eyes locked as people hurried past us. Just as I was about to slug the old dude in his eye and haul ass with the envelope, I saw a cop car doing a slow creep in our direction. I cursed under my breath. "Shit!"

"Do you have anything, a personal item, a wallet or some money you can put inside the envelope? You know, something so that I know I can trust you?" the old man asked.

"Trust me?" I repeated as I spied the cop car passing from the corner of my eye.

"Yes, I'm trusting that you will give this to my daughter. If you put something in it too, then I know that I can trust you."

I reached into my pocket. "Look man," I told him, "what's in this envelope is nothing compared to how I roll." I pulled out the big diamond encrusted platinum chain.

The old man's eyes stared at the chain. He released the envelope and I saw handwriting on it, an address.

I opened up the envelope and dropped the chain inside. "See, you can trust me," I huffed. I put it in reverse and began to back pedal, bumping into a lady pushing a stroller and damn-near knocking her baby on the ground. The woman cursed at me in Spanish.

"Wait! Wait!" the old dude spat as he ambled up to me.

"I promise, I'll make sure your daughter gets it," I lied as I looked for a quick exit.

"No," he looked around with true crackhead paranoia. "You have to hide it so nobody will take it from you. Hide it in your pants, like this." He took the envelope from me and stuck it back inside of his pants, showing me how to conceal it. Before retrieving it he scratched in six different places then passed it back to me.

I imitated him and hid it inside of my sweatpants.

"Thank you, my sista."

"No, thank you. I'll make sure your daughter gets it." I gave him a reassuring smile.

"Meet me right here at five o'clock. If I don't show up that means they locked me up." Leon Blue uttered, flinching like he was trying to tame whatever it was crawling around in his pants.

"Okay. God bless you." I turned and walked away as fast as my legs would carry me. I glanced back one more time. The old guy was gone.

I walked into the middle of the street and waved my hands frantically. Cars screeched to a halt as I stepped in front of a cab. The Arabic-looking driver shook his fist at me as I walked around the car to get in.

"Lady, what are you doin'? I could 'ave kilt you!" He screamed in broken English.

I ignored him and gave him directions to the Four Seasons hotel where I was staying. He shook his head begrudgingly and with an attitude, he began to drive. Atlanta wasn't so bad after all. As I rode in silence, I thought back to Pharaoh and then to the crackhead.

Here I was, only seventeen years old, with a bankroll and an ounce of weed back in my hotel room. I couldn't forget about the iced out platinum chain worth a fortune and the Glock I could hock. I was that bitch who was paid in full. I began to laugh out loud as I reared back in the seat. The cab driver turned all the way around and stared at me.

I made a face at him. "Wha'chu lookin' at?"

My plan was simple. I would go back to the hotel, pick up my clothes, show my ass, curse out the hotel manager, and then go to Lenox Mall to splurge a little. After all I had been through a lot and I deserved it. I laughed and talked to myself some more.

The whole time the cab driver watched me in the rearview mirror. I glanced at my watch. I had thirteen minutes until five o'clock. I reached into my sweats and pulled out the envelope and opened it. I giggled to myself while the driver continued to stare. I reached inside the envelope and pulled out a large wad of neatly cut newspaper.

"Newspaper?" I screamed out loud. The money was gone. The chain was gone. I did a double-take, looking inside the envelope. It was all newspaper. The old crackhead had run game on me. My mind flashed back to when he showed me how to hide the money in my pants. That must have been when he made the switch on me.

"Oh, my God!" I cried. There's only so much a bitch can take. I was past the emotional breaking point. I broke down and cried like a baby. The cab driver shot me a befuddled look. Now he was certain I was crazy as hell. He tilted his neck back to get a better look at me. I was a mess. A ball of snot rolled off my top lip as tears streaked my face. Suddenly the cab came to a stop in front of the hotel. The cab driver looked over his shoulder at me apathetically.

"Dat will be ten forty five."

"Ten forty five?" I scoffed. If it had cost a penny for oxygen I would have suffocated. Teary-eyed I glanced at my watch as I wiped the snot from my nose. It was 4:56 p.m. I faked like I was going into my pocket for the money.

"How much did you say it was again?" I asked.

When he turned his head to look at the meter, I flung the door open.

"I'll be right back," I told him. Then I busted out running.

"Ay! Ay! You! Come back with my money. Police!" he shouted, jumping out of the cab. He ran behind me. It was a foot race.

# Chapter Thirteen

After making a mad dash with the irate cab driver still on my heels, I rushed into the hotel lobby breathing hard. I placed the hoodie on my head, trying to look as inconspicuous as possible. I briskly padded across the marble floor and looked up at the clock on the wall. There was one minute until my eviction. I was expecting to be accused by the hotel manager of trying to skip out on the bill as I passed the front desk. In ran the cab driver nearly stumbling and falling. Directly in front of me the elevator dinged open. I dipped inside.

The cab driver yelled, "HEEEY, YOU!"

The door slowly closed just as he was fast approaching. "Lord, help me," I mumbled.

Full of apprehension and gloom, I trudged back to my room. I expected my card key to not work or worse, the police to be standing there waiting for me. But instead a black maid, about my grandmother's age, stood at the door. She looked at me grimly.

"Child, look what you did to this room. Didn't your mama teach you any better?" she chastised me.

I could do nothing more than look down at the floor.

She continued, "You need to be ashamed of yourself. Y'all young people are somethin' else."

I wiped my eyes and responded, "Ma'am please, you don't even understand what's going on in my life. I'm a single mother, trying to make a way for me and my son. I came here for a job fair. I was supposed to get a call for an interview, but the call never came. Then a chick stole my money. I'm being kicked out of the hotel for something that's not my fault and I'm stranded with no place to stay." Tears welled in my eyes. "And that's not even the half of it."

After listening to me the old woman took a step forward. I saw something wash over her face. Placing a placating hand on my shoulder, she spoke in a more empathetic, motherly tone. She reached into her purse and pulled out some crumpled bills and placed them in my hand.

I looked at the bills then I looked back to the woman and extended my hand to her. "I'm sorry, I can't—"

"You can and you will," she told me sternly. "The day manager should be off duty now. I'll tell them you're gone. They'll believe me but you gonna hav'ta be out by eight o'clock in the morning, suga."

"Thank you," I stammered. I looked at the money in my hand then back up at the old woman.

"God bless you, you hear?" The old woman mumbled as she ambled off, pushing her cleaning cart. As she walked away I noticed a large hole in her pantyhose. It made me feel bad. I knew she probably needed the money more than me.

I walked back inside the room. Other than the bed being made the room was still a mess. I stopped and looked at my jagged reflection in the broken mirror. Something about my face in cracked glass sent a chill up my spine. I began to take off my clothes right there. I needed something to help relax me so I rolled a blunt from the weed that I had gotten from Pharaoh and poured myself a drink from the wet bar. After a few hits of the bud and a sip of my drink I was feeling just right. I ran a hot bubble bath and lit one of the peach scented candles that were in the bathroom. I sat in the tub to marinate in the delicious aroma.

It was picture perfect—relaxing with a drink in one hand and a smoldering blunt in the other. I was getting my grown woman on. I closed my eyes and enjoyed the sensation of the tiny bubbles that tickled my body. Just then, Innocent's face appeared in my thoughts. Who in the hell was he to invade my dreams, my intimate thoughts, after he had walked away from his child and me? Fuck him! I blamed him for everything that went wrong in my life.

I took another sip of the wine and eased further into the tub, wanting to escape my thoughts, but the familiar sound of Kelis came from nowhere. "I'm bossy! I'm the bitch y'all love to hate. I'm the chick that's raised the stakes..." Then I remembered that I had brought my cell phone into the bathroom. I didn't know if I wanted to answer it. Kelis continued to play and I decided to answer it. It could be my mom. Maybe something had happened with my baby. "Hello?" I spoke into the phone

"May I speak to Tamara?"

Hesitantly I replied, "This is she."

"Haaaay gurrrl, it's me, Kanisha!"

"Kanisha?" I remembered the name, but it couldn't be who I thought it was.

"Yeah, Kanisha Williams!" she caroled excitedly.

Kanisha used to be my girl. We had lived next door to each other in the projects until her mom moved. After that, we lost contact with each other. As a young girl I tried to emulate her. She was a few years older than me, but not all of my memories of her were good.

Kanisha was one of them kind of chicks that used her body to seduce dudes for money. That's where the trouble started and it always seemed to follow her, no matter where she went.

I was curious about how she had found me, but at the same time I was happy to hear a familiar voice. Guardedly I asked, "Girl, how did you get my number?"

"I called yo mama. She told me yo ass had quit that dead-ass job and was down here in the A doin' da damn thang." Kanisha exclaimed loudly. "I done stepped up too. I got my own business, gurl. Nothing like two successful young black chicks in the A!"

My silence hummed awkwardly and my throat tightened as I somberly replied. "My whole life is fucked up." I took a long sip of my wine and managed to tell Kanisha everything that had happened.

Kanisha said, "Look gurl, we're gurls. I'ma come over there and swoop you up in about an hour. You can stay with me. I got a nice crib in Sandy Springs but tonight we're gonna get tight and kick it at the club. Bet?"

"Bet!" I said, finally feeling a little better.

# *Chapter Fourteen*

An hour later I was dressed to finesse in a semi-sheer mini-dress with matching four-inch suede boots that complemented my long shapely legs. I tied a silk scarf around my slim waist making my plump ass protrude, enhancing my hourglass figure. Next, I pulled my hair back into a regal chignon, applied my make-up and a little cherry lip gloss. When I gazed at myself in the mirror I puckered my lips and did an air kiss, approving of the results. I was that young, fly bitch that hoes loved to hate.

There was a soft rap at the door and I sashayed over to open it. There stood Kanisha Williams. She was still drop-dead gorgeous. At school she was the only chick that I felt gave me a serious run for my money. Her skin was flawless and she was thick in the right places. However, Kanisha Williams had one major flaw other than the fact that her ass was flat. She was a self-centered, egotistical, arrogant, back-stabbing bitch with a big-ass mouth. She also happened to be bisexual.

"Haaay gurrrl!" Kanisha shrilled. She gave me the big sisterly hug I needed. She took a step back after our embrace.

Kanisha was hurtin' 'em in her fly-ass outfit. I also eyeballed the clutch she held in her hands. Her neck and fingers were tastefully bejeweled with diamonds. She had on a white gold and diamond embellished watch. It was shimmering on her wrist and it got my attention. Either ole' girl was doin' the damn thing or she was stuntin' with some fake- ass jewelry. With Kanisha it was hard to tell.

Kanisha's mother was a Brazilian beauty. Kanisha had inherited her mom's physical traits. Kanisha's father was an American soldier, Private Frank Williams, who'd had the misfortune of going into a massage parlor while on a tour of duty in South America. While there, he had met Tangela, who specialized in full-body massages with her mouth and hands. Private Williams began to make regular visits to the massage parlor, requesting Tangela every time. The massages became more important to her because she knew that he was her meal ticket out of her life of poverty. After a couple of sessions, Tangela began to relieve Frank of his semen with her pussy instead of her mouth. Tangela was so gifted, she was able to hold Frank's cum inside of her for a long time. This was her plan all along when she saw that he was an American. Frank had gotten caught up in her beauty and lost the sense he had in the process. Not too long afterwards, Tangela got pregnant with Kanisha. Frank did the right thing by marrying her and moving her to the States. But everybody knows you can't turn a ho into a housewife. Unfortunately, someone should have told Private Williams that. One day he had returned home to the army base early to surprise his lovely, pregnant wife with a box of chocolate candy and a bouquet of roses. And surprise her, he did.

When he had first pulled into the base and drove up to the barracks, he had noticed a line of men that looked like they were standing at his front door. When they had seen him approaching, they scattered. Frank thought that was odd. He had walked inside his apartment to find his loving wife in a very compromising position—butt-naked on the living room floor, riding one dick, while another dick was pounding her from behind, in the ass. The third, she deep-throated like the pro she was. To make matters worse, the men were three of Frank's closest friends. Tangela had a painful scowl of ecstasy on her face when he walked in on them.

In a rage, Frank had brandished his pistol. He killed one man and seriously wounded the other two. Kanisha's father was sentenced to life in the Atlanta Federal prison. Tangela had never gone to visit him or send pictures of their child because, truth be told, she wasn't sure who the father was.

I stepped aside, allowing Kanisha into the room. I was glad that she didn't mention anything about the mess, but instead, she helped me gather my things.

"I like your hair. It looks good long."

Kanisha had what black folks called "good hair". When we were younger, she was always cutting it off.

Kanisha tilted her head and smiled at me with a nostalgically wicked grin. "Gurl, I see you still killin' 'em with the bangin' body. What I wouldn't do to have a big ole butt and a tiny waist like that."

I saw something mysterious in her eyes, but couldn't tell what it was. One thing was for certain; she had made such a quick appraisal of my body that it, somehow, made me feel eerie.

We gossiped and giggled like school girls but in the back of my mind, I relived a memory of when I was about twelve. Kanisha had taken me to this old man's house. He used to pay her fifty dollars to eat her pussy. When we had gotten there, he had a friend there. He was a much younger dude. They had gin and weed ready for us. We smoked and drank with them and I waited while Kanisha went into the room with the old dude to turn a trick. That's when things went crazy. The other guy tried to push up on me. He said he had already given Kanisha a hundred bucks so he could have sex with me. I told him I didn't get down like that. He got mad and tried to rip my clothes off and rape me. With my panties around one of my ankles and his head between my legs I managed to grab hold of the gin bottle, and I smashed it across his head knocking him out cold. I ran out the door half-naked and crying.

The next day at school, I had confronted Kanisha.

"I don't know what you're talking about." Kanisha smirked in my face. "But, you want to make a quick hundred dollars? Dude wants to see you again." She laughed.

I almost punched that bitch in the face. From that day on we only spoke casually.

Years later, I was curious as hell to know if she had changed. Over the phone she had told me she had her own business. I wanted to know what kind of business it was.

"Come on girl, let's go." She hoisted up a few bags. "Time's money."

I grabbed the rest of my bags and followed her out the door, wondering if things with her were as perfect as she made them seem.

Outside, dusk was starting to set in the starry horizon. A cool, light breeze played around us as our high heels echoed across the full parking lot. Kanisha walked to a raggedy car. I immediately knew she was on some shit. If she had her own business and had come up the way she claimed she had, she wouldn't be rolling in no raggedy-ass whip. Kanisha had the nerve to reach in her purse to grab her keys and chirped the alarm.

Right then and there, I decided that she was still fake and so was her jewelry and designer clothes. I could only imagine how her crib would look.

Kanisha passed by the gray pile of junk and walked toward an exotic, sleek-looking car sitting next to it. It was a pearl white on white Ferrari 599, trimmed in gold, and it sat on chrome Giovanni rims.

"There's my baby," she crooned and chirped the alarm again.

I dropped my luggage, astonished, and walked all the way around her whip. I was mad buggin' when I peeped the license plate.

"Pimpstress?" I asked. "Daaaamn!"

Kanisha caught me staring at her tag and smirked impishly.

I tried to play it off.

"This ain't but one of my toys," she bragged. Kanisha pushed a button on the remote and the entire roof slid back and the trunk popped open. "I been neglecting her for a while, so I decided to let her out tonight." She patted the car like it was an exotic animal. "She was priced in the high two hundreds and can go from zero to 65 in 3.7 seconds, so we can definitely get from one spot to the other tonight." Kanisha teased.

I laughed.

That night we cruised the town with the top down. We listened to music and smoked blunts. I allowed my young mind to fantasize about the city and the people. I wondered where Kanisha was getting all of her cheddar. I also wanted to know if I could get some of it.

While it was still early we stopped at a sports bar, dined on grilled shrimp, drank beer, and watched a basketball game. It seemed like every dude in the bar knew Kanisha. I left that night with a phone full of numbers and a new understanding about how to lure a man. Now I knew to catch the big fish—you have to know which ponds they're in.  But that's not all Kanisha would teach me.

# Chapter Fifteen

Back in Kanisha's whip we sped through the naked city as if taunting it with the top down. The system was bumpin' and our hair was swirling. On the expressway we passed cars at breakneck speed as if we had been propelled out of a slingshot. Daringly, Kanisha reached speeds of over 100 miles per hour. Her rambunctious laughter was contagious. I watched as she reached into her purse and pulled out a stack of pills that looked like fruit-flavored candies and popped two in her mouth before offering me one.

"Here, take a coupla these!" Kanisha shouted above the music. Her hair played in the wind.

"Nah, I'm good," I replied as the road seemed to race toward me and the city held me spellbound.

Kanisha surprised me by placing her hand on my leg. "You scared?" she asked.

"No, I'm cool with this." I frowned at her and waved the blunt wedged between my fingers at her. I had heard some stories about Ecstasy, but the way Kanisha looked at me reminded me of the time she had asked me to go with her to the old dude's house.

We ended up at a slammin' club. Outside the club, the streets swelled with excitement. I had never seen so many beautiful cars in my life. There were stretch limousines, Lambos, Bentleys, and Porsches.

The line to get in was all the way around the corner. There were people everywhere. We valet parked and I watched Kanisha tip dude a hundred bucks. I thought she was out of her freakin' mind. Like super models we strutted all the way to the front of the line, ignoring the stares from the haters. Two huge, muscular bouncers stood at the door. One of them was baldheaded.

I was nervous as hell. Perhaps it was because my day had been so fucked up. I was certain that something else had to go wrong.

The baldheaded dude beamed broadly as soon as he saw Kanisha. "What's up girl?"

His partner flashed his gapped-toothed grin.

"Shit, just out there tryna make that dolla," Kanisha said back.

The men grinned and exchanged pleasantries with Kanisha but I noticed both of them ogling my body like I was eye candy. Kanisha and I brushed past both of them and continued walking through the metal detector. I glanced over my shoulder and caught them looking as I jiggled my ass in my short dress.

The club was jammed packed. I started dancing as soon as we walked in. Jay's new joint, "Dig a Hole", was bangin' hard, pulsating through the speakers with so much rhythm I could feel it reverberating through my body. The club's décor was off the chain. The pungent aroma of weed permeated the air. I soon noticed that the chicks outnumbered the men. My competition was fierce. Most of the females were scantily dressed with nice bodies like mine.

Kanisha and I made our way toward the VIP section.

"Hey, hey, baby." A couple of guys called to me, completely ignoring Kanisha.

I know she had to notice.

Outside the door of the VIP, a chick with flaming red hair wearing a tight-jumpsuit with matching heels, stood with a clique of chicks about Kanisha's age. She was vehemently arguing with one of the bouncers. Kanisha walked right into the fray.

Always seeking to get attention, Kanisha snorted arrogantly, "S'cus you!" She flashed a black card at the bouncer and pointed behind her to me and said, "She wit me."

Sucking her teeth, the chick arguing with the bouncer turned and looked at Kanisha. She spat, "Who dat bitch think she is?"

Kanisha whirled around. "I'ma be dat bitch who buries her foot in yo ass if you don't get da fuck outta my face, biiitch!"

The bouncer stepped in between them. The girl took a step back and began to remove her earrings. Kanisha and the chick continued to curse at each other as I squeezed my ass on by. As far as I was concerned, I was neutral. Plus I realized that Kanisha was dead-ass wrong for stepping to that girl like that. I couldn't help but feel an allegiance with the hood chicks. They were just like me, trying to come up on a nigga with some cheddar. If we have to con our way into the VIP without paying, then so be it. I had been in their shoes before. Hell, I still was in their shoes.

VIP was plush and full of palatial splendor. Leather and velvet recliners with matching tables, red carpeting and long shiny poles with gorgeous women dancing on them were everywhere.

Kanisha caught up to me and we navigated our way to a table. It seemed like just about every stripper and baller in the joint acknowledged her. She returned their gesture with a subtle nod or wave. A tall, bowlegged, dark-skinned chick with blonde hair and a ghetto-booty waved at Kanisha. I was entranced by her ability to make her butt cheeks do a thunder clap. Even chicks were having a ball throwing money at the strippers.

*Innocent*

73

"Aye, yo! Kanisha!" A guy stood and called her name.

"Hey boo!" she waved and hollered.

When Kanisha turned her back, I waved at him too. He was fine. I looked around in awe. I had never been in a place where a sista could come up so quickly. Kanisha watched me closely, and that was when she decided to try and school me about this club scene.

"Listen Tamara, you need to be cool...starin' and shit like that. We not in Cabrini Green housing projects no more. This is the big league with major players, seven-figga niggas. In the ATL, this is common. Celebrities, ballers, trap star dope boys and other shot callers, you know."

My eyes started to roam the club again. I was checking out all the ballers and fly chicks. A waitress appeared and placed a bottle of champagne on the table.

"Thank you," Kanisha acknowledged, looking over at the handsome dude across the club who had sent the bottle.

Kanisha leaned forward and her ample breasts pressed against the table. She poured me a drink. "Never forget this," she said dead seriously as grabbed my hand. "Niggas with money always want and desire more even if what's available is less. A woman's flesh will always be a sacred and cherished commodity, but first you have to learn how to manipulate and make them want to give you money without them knowing what you're doing."

I nodded my head like I got it.

"The key is not so much your body, but your brains. You have to create the illusion of the chase by acting unimpressed by their wealth." A smile spread across her lips. Then she released my hand and crinkled her delicate nose at me.

To my right I watched a chick get down on her knees under a table and give a dude some head. Kanisha summoned the chocolate chick with the gorgeous body who had been dancing on the pole when we walked in. She came over to our table and gave Kanisha a lap dance. That shit blew my mind! The chick had a navel ring connected to a gold belly chain that hung from her curvaceous waist.

"Tamara, take the pill, gurl." Kanisha motioned to my hand.

I opened it.

I stared at the colorful pill in my sweaty palm. I tried my best not to stare at Kanisha and the girl, but I couldn't help it.

"Take it gurl," Kanisha's mellow voice cajoled like the devil.

I looked around. There were nude chicks, ballers at the next table and dudes making it rain. And then there was the broad who was still on her knees sucking dick. Suddenly, the music changed and the speakers screamed, *"Rich boy selling that, all them haters wanna check, pimp tight no flex, just bought a Cadillac. Throw some D's on dat bitch!"*

"Oh, shit, that's my joint!" I hollered. I tossed the pill in my mouth and washed it down with some champagne.

Kanisha placed a hundred dollar bill in between the chick's bald pussy lips. I danced to the music and ten minutes later it felt like an electric current hit my ass. The chick with the bald pussy was still dancing in front of us. There was perspiration on her perfectly plump ass.

There was a lot of commotion at the entrance to the VIP and people parted like the Red Sea. I stretched my neck to get a better view. In walked a small posse of thugs all dressed in black. They were draped in jewelry, and a few wore dark stunna shades. The lights stalled. I stared with my drink in my hand while the stripper chick continued to dance, her ass cheeks clapping in front of me.

When Kanisha saw who the posse was, shock registered

on her face. Every chick in the VIP section rushed over to the entourage—even the chick who was giving dude head under the table. It was the last dude in the entourage that really caught my attention. He was dressed in a Versace sweatsuit and had on a crazy iced-out platinum chain. There was an aura of mystery and something gangsta about him. That shit turned me on. He was fine. I took a gulp of my drink and continued to stare. I realized my pussy was moist. I couldn't sit still in my chair.

"Who da hell is dat?" I asked Kanisha dreamily. The pill had kicked in and I started to feel crunk. I placed my hand on Kanisha's arm. I was bouncing to a rhythm, and it wasn't just to the music.

"That's Bleu Baptiste, but everyone calls him Haitian Bleu. He's from Haiti. He's an ex-drug dealer and he's a crazy-ass nigga. Some say he's worth over a hundred million and I believe them."

"Word?" I asked.

She nodded her head. "Yep, this nigga is doin' it! Doin' it!" she exclaimed. She wasn't paying any attention to me rubbing her arm, but she never took her eyes off Haitian Bleu's crew as they took over half of the VIP section. "Last week one of his dudes got popped by the Feds in an RV right here in Atlanta. They found one thousand bricks of high quality cocaine and ten million dollars in cash. It was the biggest drug bust in the history of the ATL."

'Daamn," I droned.

"Of course he denied having anything to do with the coke. Says he's a legitimate business man. He owns Silky Records. He got a chain of funeral homes and he makes caskets."

"Caskets?" I repeated.

"Yep," Kanisha said like it was no big deal. "I just wish he had not showed up here tonight." Kanisha looked down at my hand on her arm. "Girl, what the hell you doin?"

I moved my hand and sat down. I watched Bleu take a seat. Prancing like peacocks in front of him, chicks clamored for his attention. He flashed a dazzling smile as he opened up a duffel bag and passed out stacks of money to his boys.

The DJ announced, "BHM is in da building, they bought the bar out, drinks on the house." The club went wild.

I leaned toward Kanisha. "What does BHM stand for?"

She made a face and replied, "Black Haitian Mafia; and gurl, them niggas is gangsta fo-reel! They came to town about a year ago and niggas in da game been droppin' left and right. The police

*Innocent*

75

had to create a special task force just to concentrate on them."

"Shit, I like that gangsta shit; it's part of my nature." I looked over at their table.

Kanisha nudged me. "Gurl, you staring again."

"My bad." I shrugged her off, but actually I was doing more than staring. I was drooling. My mouth was wide open and my panties were wet.

I couldn't help it. I glanced over at Bleu's table. He was passing out big stacks of money.

Someone screamed, "Dem niggas making it rain hundred dollar bills over derr."

I sprung forward almost leaping out my seat. I wanted to get in on the action.

"Calm down." Kanisha pulled my arm.

I tempered down. Just then a dude popped out of nowhere "What's up, baby?"

I cringed. His breath smelled so bad I had to duck to get out the way. I turned to look at his face. "Nigga you oughta be ashamed to come out smelling like that," I spat at him.

"Baby girl, you so fine," he said with his hot breath wafting in my face. "These bitches in here ain't got shit on you. Yo ole fine ass. You must be a fo-reel model." He reached out and tried to touch my shoulder.

I flinched.

"Let's get our freak on out there." He motioned toward the dance floor with his head.

I exhaled deeply and replied with a curt sigh, "I don't think so," and fanned the air for him to keep moving.

"Well fuck you then!" He barked, and walked off to find his next victim.

I laughed and turned my eyes back to the prize—Bleu Baptiste.

"Gurl let's get the hell outta here. These niggas are wildin' out too much for me. And look at them bitches. Stank hoes!" Kanisha pointed.

I continued to focus on Bleu's table. The women were ankle-deep in money and seemed to be having the time of their lives. Just then Bleu stood and headed for our table.

Kanisha cursed under her breath. "Oh, fuck!"

# *Chapter Sixteen*

I watched Haitian Bleu's brazen swagger. I felt his thug charisma. He was the kind of dude that would always stand out in a room full of people.

Kanisha reached over and grabbed my arm. "If Haitian Bleu stops at our table, I need you to jet for a minute. I need to talk some business with this nigga. It's important."

Before I could question her, he was in our faces. Up close he was even more handsome. Everything from his neck to his wrists were icy. I looked up at him. I felt my heart pounding and my nerves racing.

"Yo, wuz up Kanisha?" He spoke in broken English. It didn't sound like he was all that pleased to see her.

Kanisha bolted from her seat. It seemed like she was surprised to see him in the club. Her large breasts nearly came out of her blouse as she reached to hug him. He didn't even attempt to hug her back.

I noticed him glance down at me as he pulled away from her. I turned away pretending to be interested in something on the crowded dance floor. I felt the effect of the pill crawling around in my brain like a fugitive. My senses tingled, my teeth grinded and my mind plotted. I had to have this nigga.

I watched as a member of his crew took a stack of bills and hit a chick in the face with it so hard that she damn near fell. Though she was slightly dazed, the broad loved it. She and her friends scrambled to pick up the money. All I could do was shake my head in disgust. There was no way in hell I would let a nigga disrespect me like that.

"Shit, why dun't you call mi about mi muddufuckin moni!" Bleu said, raising his voice above the music. The large vein in his forehead bulged. The diamonds in his ear sparkled like a chandelier.

"That's why I came here tonight to find you. I'll have the money in a few days." Kanisha abruptly stopped. She seemed nervous.

Bleu tilted his head to look at me.

"Dis one of yurs?"

"Uh, Tamara, don't you have to make a phone call or something?" Kanisha asked with grit in her voice.

I didn't pay her the slightest bit of attention. In fact, I crossed my thighs seductively, one over the other. That damn pill had me on another level. I felt like I was the official diva in the club.

A chick with long black hair and lots of ass and tits walked up, boldly invading my space. She whispered something in Bleu's ear. Kanisha shot the chick a venomous glare. Whatever she said made Bleu smile. I was filled me with envy. I watched as he reached inside the duffel bag and handed the chick some bills. She did the happy dance making her breasts jiggle for him.

Kanisha rolled her eyes at me with contempt. I could tell she didn't want me at the table either, but I wanted this nigga and I was going to get him.

I was in that zone and decided I was going to do whatever it took to get with this nigga named Bleu Baptiste. I turned in my chair and hit him with a stare. I puckered my lips and eyeball-fucked him. I pretended like I was adjusting my dress and leaned back in my chair, showing off the spread of my generous hips and thighs. There isn't a chick in the hood that doesn't know how to flirt with her body. I had learned that shit when I was twelve years old.

I heard Kanisha mention something about owing Bleu money and that she would pay soon. He ignored her, but continued to stare at me. The music changed. A Kanye West joint, "Can't Tell Me Nothin", came on.

"That's my shit!" I got up and started shaking my butt. I

acted like I didn't notice my dress rise above my thighs.

I heard Bleu exclaim, "Goddamnitmon!"

I bent over and gave him a glimpse of my satin thong, home of the fat monkey. When the song was over I sat back down.

Bleu was still staring at me, and Kanisha was still chirping in his ear.

Grabbing her bag, Kanisha rose from her seated position, "Bleu, I gotta go."

Bleu ignored her and I seized the moment. Taking a sip of my drink, I pretended to spill some of it on me. I wiped at the invisible stain, exposing my young, succulent breasts. I teased Bleu, showing one supple brown nipple at a time.

Bleu watched me like a cat watched a caged bird.

Kanisha turned to see what had captivated him.

"Bitch, pah-leez!" Kanisha squinted her eyes at me. "This nigga out of yo league."

Bleu reached for a napkin and handed it to me. "Luv, yo surre I dun't know yu from sum werr?"

I furrowed my brow at him. "No."

As I took a sip of my drink, I stared at him over the rim of my glass and winked.

Bleu did a double-take.

I smiled again. "Do you like what you see?"

He nodded and grinned at me.

The club had been getting more and more crunk as free drinks flowed like water. I could feel the pill kick into another gear. It mellowed me out.

Bleu playfully leered at me and he sparked up a blunt. He blew smoke in my direction.

I frowned and fanned the smoked out of my face and looked at him annoyingly.

Kanisha tugged at Bleu's arm to get his attention, but he pushed her away. He then reached into his duffel bag and tossed a sack of money in my lap. The moment stalled as I was sure that he realized that I was the one chick in the club who didn't seem to give a fuck about him or his money. I glanced down at the wad of cash wrapped in a rubber band and remembered what Kanisha had said, *"Create the illusion of the chase by acting unimpressed by their wealth."*

Coolly, I tossed the money back at him like I was unimpressed. "Don't try me like that." I had thrown the stack back at him with more force than I had intended, though, accidentally knocking over his glass and spilling his drink on him.

Kanisha's mouth flew open.

Bleu jumped up from the table with surprising quickness.

I sat there scared to death. It seemed as if the music stopped and all the people stared.

Frantically, Kanisha tried to wipe at the stain on his pants.

I stood with my hand over my heart.

"I, I am so sorry!" I apologized.

# *Chapter Seventeen*

Talk about a bitch with bad luck.

I wanted to crawl my ass under the table and disappear. I looked at the large wet stain on his sweatpants. I thought this nigga would beat my ass.

Bleu whispered something to one of his boys and pointed at me.

"Bitch, you did it now!" Kanisha growled and made a face.

Bleu stalked over toward me.

I braced myself.

"Ya see whut ya did ta mi!" he yelled.

I nodded my head like a small child who had been scolded. "I, I am so sorry."

Bleu's expression changed and he smiled. He took my hand and led me to the dance floor.

"Luv, da least yu caan du is give mi a dance," Bleu laughed.

I couldn't help but smile. I felt so relieved.

Kanisha was watching me as I shook my ass on the dance floor. Her expression was smug. After a few minutes, she glanced down at her watch and signaled that she was ready to go.

I wasn't.

Jazzy Pha's and Sammy's new joint, "You Should Be My Girl," came on. The chick next to me was trying to out dance me.

There wasn't a bitch on the planet that could out-dance me. I was the reason why they didn't allow seventeen-year-olds in clubs. I knew how to pop that coochie on the dance floor. I rocked my hips, shook my ass, and danced all up on Bleu. He stood there with a devilish grin.

"Why you ain't dancing?" I asked over the loud music.

"Mi neva dance. All mi do is dis." Bleu nodded his head and snapped his fingers.

"Cute," I said with a smile.

Bleu eased up on me and placed his hands on my hips. He challenged me with his stare. I dropped my ass to the floor and bounced, popping my coochie with my face near his crotch. I sprang back up and shook my ass.

The chick dancing next to me stopped. She looked at me and walked off the dance floor. I bent over and pressed my ass against her man.

Kanisha was standing with her hands on her hips, watching me in disbelief.

I was crunk and having the time of my life. That pill still had me feeling electrified. The feeling was intensified by the music and the fact that this fine-ass nigga was standing in front of me. With a pixie smile I ambled up to Bleu. "Thanks for the, uh, dance."

He grabbed my waist and pulled me close, pressing his body against mine. He moaned in my ear.

I wanted him right there on the dance floor. I leaned forward and melted in his arms.

"Not only are yu beautiful, but ya soft as a muddafucka," Bleu whispered in my ear and his mustache tickled my neck.

I giggled. I pressed forward, grinding against his manhood. I could feel his erection. *"Niggas with money always want and desire more even if what's available is less."* Kanisha's words played in my head again. With all of the strength I could muster, I reached back and peeled his hands off my ass, holding his hands with my own. I nestled close, and rode the ebb and flow of our closeness.

He whispered in my ear again.

This time I tried my best not to giggle.

"Luv, I throw ay stack'a hundred dolla bills in yo lap, yu throw'em back. Damn, yu feisty, not like de rest of these hoes," he said earnestly.

I smiled and reached up to caress the nape of his neck. I

continued to press my body against his, slow fucking him on the dance floor. I heard a soft moan escape his mouth indicating that his desire for me was building.

Kanisha tapped me on my shoulder. "Gurl, we gotta go!" She had a look of petrified horror on her face. "Shit finna pop off. PG and his boys just walked in."

I frowned at her until it dawned on me what the fuck she had just said.

"These niggas beefin' big time on some drug turf war shit. We need to go!" Kanisha said adamantly.

I looked up only to see Pharaoh Greene.

"Oh, shit!"

My heart slammed against my chest so hard that it made me gag.

Pharaoh was mean-mugging the shit out of Bleu. My legs turned to rubber. I needed an escape route and quick! I positioned myself behind Bleu and hid.

Kanisha chirped in my ear, "Let's go!"

I tried not to panic as Pharaoh Greene and his henchmen headed straight for Bleu. Their confrontation was inevitable.

*Fuck! Think fast! Think fast!* My brain churned.

Pharaoh edged closer. His men pushed and shoved people out of the way.

I wanted to run but that would have only caused more attention. Suddenly, I had an idea. "Baby, don't look now. This nigga Pharaoh is comin' up behind you. I used to be his chick, but now he's sweatin' me to come back. "I don't—"

Before I could finish Pharaoh and his men were up on us.

Haitian Bleu's posse had peeped the move as soon as PG and his boys hit the VIP section. The situation had quickly turned volatile.

Here I was on the dance floor, high on Ecstasy and intimidated with fear. I had no way of knowing what was about to go down.

Pharaoh called out to Bleu like he knew him. "Yo, Bleu!" He continued calling his name until he had walked up on him.

My mind went into frantic overdrive as I tried to hide my face. I was so scared, I felt my legs trembling.

The crowd began to chant in jubilant unison. Someone bumped into me hard. I ignored them and focused my attention on getting the fuck out the club alive.

Bleu replied to Pharaoh, "Wuz up?"

Pharaoh reached into his pants.

Bleu continued. "De woman dun't wun't nuttin'ta du wit'cha." He stepped out of the way exposing me.

Pharaoh's eyebrows arched and our eyes locked.

I attempted to walk away even though I wanted to run.

A circle had formed around us.

"Bitch where's my muthafuckin chain at?" Pharaoh yelled above the music. He reached out and grabbed my arm. He reached back to punch me. With feline quickness I scratched him and drew blood.

Bleu grabbed his hand and spoke forcefully, "She don't wunt you."

Seeing the commotion, both camps rushed over. Pharaoh held onto my arm and with his other hand, he pulled out a gat and fired at Bleu.

He missed.

There was a taunting look on Bleu's face.

One of Pharaoh's henchmen stepped into the fray. Pharaoh ducked out of the way. More shots were fired and people scattered. Pandemonium quickly erupted into mayhem and Pharaoh fired shots at Bleu, missing him again.

Bleu and his men escaped through an open door, leaving me alone in the chaos.

"Fuck!" I cried.

Pharaoh turned to me in rage. He grabbed my neck and lifted me off my feet. "Bitch where is my muthafuckin' chain at?"

It felt like his large hand was about to crush my windpipe. I could barely breathe and I began to see stars. I knew that he was madder about Bleu getting away than he was about me not having his chain, but I also knew that he would kill me.

Pharaoh placed his pistol to my head and cocked the hammer.

I began to cry. There was so much commotion going on around us that I couldn't focus.

"Yo man," someone yelled, pulling Pharaoh's arm. "Fuck that bitch. We need to bounce!"

I could see death in Pharaoh's eyes, and I could feel it in his iron clad grip around my neck. If I didn't tell this irate nigga something, he was going to kill me.

"Yo chain is in the car. I swear. I'll show you," I cried to Pharaoh.

He shoved me so hard I fell. I got up and stumbled toward the door.

"It better be."

He dragged me past the security guards and bouncers.

Nobody even attempted to intervene. These were the same people who had let his crew in to murder Bleu. Since they had failed, they turned a blind eye as Pharaoh and his boys abducted me from the club.

# Chapter Eighteen

A crescent moon hung in the sky. The streets were congested with cars and people. I didn't know what to do next.

Pharaoh continued to yell, "Bitch, I swear if you don't have my muthafuckin' chain you'll wish you'd never met me."

"Dude, either chill on that shit or pop the bitch," someone said. "The cops are coming and we ain't got time to fuck with her!"

I prayed like hell the cops would hurry up. I didn't have any more excuses. We turned the corner to the parking lot. Kanisha's car was still where she had parked it. I remembered the gun in my luggage and I glanced over at Pharaoh. My heart was pounding in my chest. A crazy thought went through my mind and I wondered if I could try him and his goons with the gun in the car.

I looked around. They were at least forty deep with me in the middle. Even in all the chaotic madness there were still people loitering in the parking lot.

Out of nowhere two black SUVs pulled up in front of us and came to a screeching halt. Masked gunmen jumped out, heavily armed with AK-47s and Mac 10s. A spray of sparks and red balls of fire lit up the night as bullets passed my head. Bodies dropped and grown men screamed like women. The deadly ammunition roared like thunder. I screamed and tripped over a body and fell to the ground.

"Goddammit!" I muttered. The heel on one of my boots snapped.

I watched in horror as a dude with his face partially blown off frantically struggled to hide under a car.

One of the gunmen saw the man, raced over, squatted and leveled his gun to the man's head.

"BHM, nigga! BHM, nigga!" he shouted. Then he fired.

Directly to my right, a guy who looked just like Pharaoh kneeled on his elbows and knees and a dark pool of crimson blood formed underneath him. "Fuck! Fuck!" He cursed, pounding his fist on the pavement.

It was like The Vietnam War had been recreated all around us.

"Fuck! I let that bitch-ass Haitian creep me," the guy lamented.

Another gunman rushed over and placed his gun to the back of his head. He pulled the trigger. Blood, chunks of brain and gritty skull matter splattered on my face. I took off running as fast as my legs would carry me. In the distance, sirens screamed and bodies continued to drop. A black SUV swerved in front of me and I wondered if this was my turn to die. The doors flung open as it came to a stop.

"Hurry! Get in!" a voice screamed to me.

It could have been the devil calling me, but it didn't matter. I dove in headfirst. My dress tore as it got stuck on the door paneling. The vehicle sped off with my legs still dangling out the door. My dress was almost pulled up over my head with my ass out.

I screamed at the top of my lungs "Call an ambulance! Call an ambulance!"

The hooded figure in the front seat turned and looked at me. He casually replied,

"No, luv, dem dun't need an ambulance, dem need a hearse wit lots of body bags."

I did a double-take at the driver as the hood fell away from his face. It was Bleu Baptiste. His lustful eyes followed my exposed backside. He almost hit a car as he stared at me. He swerved back into his lane just in the knick of time. In the passenger seat next to him was Kanisha. Her mascara was smeared like she had been crying. Her face was ashen and ghostly pale and her hair was askew and wild. She looked like a hot mess. I had to blink twice.

I wiped at the blood and grit that had splattered my face.

"Luv, dun't worry. We goin' tu mi home. How 'bout a litta ménage-ah-trios," he suggested. Bleu reached back and palmed my ass.

I slapped his hand as I sat up. He laughed in a deep cackle.

Shivers ran up and down my spine. I looked over at Kanisha and got nothing from her. Looking out the window in dismay, I thought about the time I had almost gotten raped. *Menage-a-trois? What has this bitch gotten me into now?*

# Chapter Nineteen

## IC MILLER

After the gun had exploded, it propelled me backward onto the bed. Bubba Ray stood over me.

The doctor rushed over, and his eyes frantically searched to see who had been shot. His eyes opened wide as he gasped in horror at the blood, sanguine red, spewing on the white bed sheets.

The blood ran like a faucet from Bubba Ray's neck. He teetered, weaved, and staggered on his feet. Then he grabbed at his throat. His gun lay on the bed and he keeled over backward, hitting the linoleum floor in a heap.

My heart pounded fast as I looked at the bloody gun on the bed. I knew I needed to get out of there. I glanced at the door. I expected a platoon of redneck cops to come storming through the door at any minute. Without hesitation, I reached for the gun as the doctor hunched over Bubba Ray frantically trying to resuscitate him.

Bubba Ray struggled to breathe. He gurgled blood and panted. Then he moaned, "Help me."

The doctor looked up at me with a pained expression. His face had paled to the color of rotten fruit.

He would see no empathy from me for the dying cop, only desperation and fear. My trembling hand aimed the gun at Dr. Ferguson as I kept my eyes moving between him and the door.

Bubba Ray lay on the floor babbling for help like a small child.

"What are you doing?" the doctor asked.

"I, I'm getting the fuck outta here."

"But you didn't do anything. I saw everything. You acted in self defense. Don't be foolish. Put the gun down, please."

"Uh-uh." I shook my head waving the gun at him. "What would be foolish is staying here and trying to explain this," I told him.

"You're making a big mistake."

I eased out of the bed. "Gimme the handcuff keys off his belt. Take your clothes off and hand 'em over to me."

"Whaat?! That's outrageous!" the doctor exclaimed.

In a voice that sounded strange to me, I continued, "Doc, please don't make me kill you." My trembling hand aimed the gun at his chest.

"This is foolish!" he muttered, realizing that I was serious. He unclasped the keys off the cop's belt and passed them to me, then proceeded to undress.

I quickly changed into the doctor's clothes. The white coat was too big and the pants were too short. It didn't matter; I was determined to escape by walking out of the hospital. I tried on the doctor's shoes, but they were too small. I handcuffed the doctor to the bed then looked down at Bubba Ray's feet.

"I don't think this is a good idea," he warned.

"I don't care what you think right about now." I didn't feel the least bit of remorse as I removed the unconscious cop's shoes.

They fit perfectly. I strolled to the door with the gun in my hand. My palms were sweating and my heart was racing.

The doctor watched me. His mouth open wide. "Let's talk about this."

I noticed large beads of sweat had started to dampen his forehead as he continued to try to convince me not to go. I ignored him. My mind was focused on the door and making a quick exit. With my heart beating and nerves racing, scared as hell, I tucked the gun in the small of my back and opened the door.

The people traversing the halls caused me to hesitate and

exhale deeply. I glanced back over my shoulder and looked at Bubba Ray's languid body sprawled out on the floor. I mustered the courage to step out into the hall and close the door behind me.

It was on.

# Chapter Twenty

With a casual gait, and my head bowed inconspicuously, I walked through the hall. Ignoring all the gawks, I acted like I wasn't the inhabitant of brown skin, nappy hair and a tall willowy frame. So far it was working. I walked straight ahead with my hands in the pockets of the high-water pants. I was almost there. Thirty or so more yards to go and I would be free. I saw an electric door up ahead beckoning me as I continued to move cautiously with my eyes cast downward. I counted each step unknowingly, holding my breath. In my peripheral vision I saw the nurse's station to my right. Next to it stood two uniformed cops with their backs to me.

"Oh, shit!" I muttered under my breath. Laboring in jagged sips of air, I moved on the balls of my feet with my eyes alert and focused. My heart and pulse raced out of control.

Ten yards to go.

"God, please let me make it to the door," I prayed as I reached the double glass doors. They mechanically whooshed open, and hot air along with rays of sunshine welcomed me, beckoning me to freedom. I stole a glance over my shoulder at the cops still standing at the nurse's station and before I knew it, I collided with an old lady being pushed in a wheelchair. Her oxygen tank crashed to the floor and the wheelchair nearly toppled over.

"Haay, watch where you're going," the old lady shrieked in a high-pitched tenor. She shook a gnarled fist at me.

Both cops turned around and looked directly at me. One cop nudged his partner and a nurse knotted her brow.

Nonchalantly, I eased my hand out of my pocket onto the gun in the small of my back. I two-stepped around the old lady and several other people who were coming into the hospital entrance.

"Stop him! Stop him! He's got a gun!" I recognized Dr. Ferguson's voice coming from behind me. He was still handcuffed. Somehow he had managed to pull the bed to the door.

"Hey! You!" a voice yelled.

I turned around.

The cop was talking to me.

Visceral instincts kicked in, and I reacted. Jumping over the old lady in the wheelchair, I sprinted outside in haste. I didn't know where I was going or what I was doing. None of my actions were planned. All around me chaos erupted. People screamed and ran away from me like I was the devil in disguise.

A shot rang out as I ran blindly into the middle of a busy intersection. A hero in a mini-van tried to run me over. I zigzagged between moving cars and pulled the gun out with no intention of using it. My legs kept moving.

"Stop! Stop!" The police called out, continuing to gain ground on me.

I saw an old picket fence adjacent to a tall wooded brush of grass. It was at least one hundred yards ahead. I could hear the piercing shrill of sirens nearing.

I was in trouble.

# *Chapter Twenty-One*

Winded, I reached the picket fence. My lungs were on fire. My body was in no condition for all the rigorous exertion I was putting it through. I felt a sharp pain in my chest as I climbed the fence, managing to escape the cops. I tore my pant leg on a rusty nail and stumbled in the wild thorny bushes. I didn't care. I just had to hide. The landscape was brutal and the sweltering heat was unbearable. My legs ached and my lungs burned, but I continued to run.

I stopped to catch my breath and listen. My heart was throbbing in my chest and sweat burned my eyes. I squatted down in the grass.

"God it's hot!" I said out loud.

I took off the doctor's white coat. Somewhere in the deep crevice of my frantic mind I heard Big Mama's voice. "Boy, what have you got yo-self into?"

Then I heard something that made my skin crawl. Barking dogs and men were approaching fast. It was a cacophony of voices.

A voice bellowed, "Do you see him?"

I cringed in the brush. Frantically I looked around for a place to hide. That's when I had an uncontrollable urge to scratch. I looked down and most of my body was covered with mosquitoes feasting off the blood and hundreds of tiny cuts I got from falling in the razor sharp thorny bushes.

Near delirium, I began to swat at the bugs. I felt like giving up, but somehow I mustered the courage to bridle my sanity. The bugs continued to use me as their lifeline while the dogs were quickly approaching. They were onto my scent. I laid down in the grass, perfectly still. Out of nowhere a black helicopter appeared overhead. It's mighty rotors reverberated, swaying the tall brush. I was exposed. The search party descended toward me. Just when I was about to get up and take off running the helicopter veered to the right and swooped down like a large vulture. It headed in the opposite direction, away from me.

Still petrified, I let out a deep sigh. On my belly in swampy grass, bugs continued to bite me. Then something cold and slimy slithered across my neck. It was a large black snake. I shrieked in fear and flung it off me. I jumped to my feet in one quick motion.

All around me I could still hear the brusque voices of men yelling commands and dogs barking. I was so scared I didn't know whether to run or keep still. The persistent buzzing and stinging of bugs had started to numb my body.

I sat the gun down next to me in the tall grass. That was when I heard a low growl. It was sinister and menacing. I spun around and a huge German Shepherd crept toward me. His large canine teeth glistened. The large beast was about three feet away.

"N-nice...d-doggy," I stuttered. My hand fumbled around in the grass in search of the gun. I couldn't find it. The dog stared at me ferociously then lunged at my throat. I managed to throw my arm up as the beast landed on top of me. He knocked me backward and mauled my arm. It bit down to the bone. Its weight and strength overcame me as it continued to bite my arm. My left hand continued to grope the grass in search of the gun.

"Ole Yella got 'im boys! Over here! Over here!"

Continuing my frantic search for the gun, my hand finally found it. With meager strength waning I was somehow able to level the gun under the belly of the dog.

*Boom! Boom! Boom!...Click Click!*

The large beast howled a painful cry and collapsed on top of me in a heap. The animal's warm blood saturated my body. I shoved the dying carcass off of me and struggled to my feet. Standing directly in front of me was a young white boy. He had a rouge complexion with a face full of acne and scars. He was dressed in threadbare overalls. A mane of unruly blond hair partially concealed his eyes. He spoke with tears in his voice with his mouth quivering. "You kilt Ole Yella."

I took off aimlessly running again. My arm was badly mangled. I cradled it close to my body, willing myself to keep going. I ran until darkness descended on the earth. The crisp night air turned cool on my damp skin. I stumbled upon a brush of tall grass. Fatigue-ridden and tired, I couldn't go any further. I sat down with my arm throbbing painfully and listened to the nocturnal noises while hungry bugs once again used me as their lifeline.

"God, if you can hear me, please help me." I closed my eyes and prayed.

What seemed to be moments later, I was awakened by several luminous flood lights that shown bright as the sun. The lights sat atop pickup trucks and monster SUVs. All around me was caustic chaos. Was I having a bad dream? Blinded by the light, I groped for the gun at my side.

"We got 'im, boys! We got 'im!" an excited voice exclaimed.

As I struggled to get away from the thousands of hands that grabbed hold of me, I was subdued, pummeled and assaulted with crude clubs and fists. Blood streamed from my head and face. It felt like all the vigilantes, sharecroppers, farmers, and police officers were determined to get a lick in as I was being captured. It was payment for the hard work it had taken for all of them to catch me.

"So you like killin' n' rapin' white gurls?" a gravelly voice asked.

Another voice whined, "He kilt Ole Yella!"

Strangely I thought I recognized the voice. I looked up only to see the butt of a shotgun come crashing down on the side of my head. I reeled into perpetual darkness and welcomed it like a human soul that couldn't take any more abuse.

# Chapter Twenty-Two

### IC MILLER
### EIGHTEEN MONTHS LATER
### THE TRIAL

"The Fifth Amendment of the U.S. Constitution protects against self-incrimination; and, since the easiest way to solve a crime is to get a confession there is a thick body of law that governs police conduct during an interrogation. A confession obtained from an accused who has been threatened is not admissible in court," my lawyer said the first day of my trial.

I sat perched in a seat next to him. My entire body itched from the cheap seven dollar wool suit I had on. I watched the all white jury look at the grotesque photos of the sixteen-year-old girl that had been brutally raped and murdered. Her pink panties had been shoved into her mouth.

The pictures provoked shock and outrage as the State's star witness sat on the stand in a wheelchair crying hysterically. Bubba Ray Nelson was now a quadriplegic as a result of the gunshot he had suffered while tussling over the gun with me. He would never have the swagger or the pompous arrogance he'd once had. He elicited no empathy from me as he cried pensively.

The prosecutor retrieved the photos from the last juror.

I pretended not to notice some of the jurors' evil stares.

One old lady dabbed her eyes with a napkin as she looked over at Bubba Ray.

The prosecutor turned to him with a satisfied scowl on his face and asked, "Officer Nelson, could you please tell the jury, once again, exactly what it was the defendant told you on July 3rd when he confessed the murder to you?" For dramatics, the prosecutor leaned against the witness stand and moved the microphone closer.

"He, he told me he killed Betty Sue. He said he raped her and robbed the restaurant."

"You lying! You lying!" I was on my feet shouting so loud that veins protruded from my neck and forehead.

My lawyer grabbed my arm as my outburst caused a ripple of voices to stir in the courtroom. Two husky bailiffs approached me. I sat down, simmering in anger at my stupidity for making the outburst in front of the jury.

"Chile, be nice. You hear me, be nice," Big Mama's mellow voice warned.

Her voice quelled me as I rubbed my face with weary hands. My mind told me not to look up at Bubba Ray's crippled white ass on the stand. After all the shit he had done to me he had the nerve to sit there and cry.

Big Mama had taken a bus all the way from Chicago. Throughout the six-week trial she had sat three rows behind me in the midst of people who were repulsed by her persistent presence. Like most old black people, she had made it a ritual to show up to court early and read the Bible before trial started.

After Bubba Ray's tear-jerking testimony, Dr. Ferguson testified on my behalf. He was considered a credible witness and so was Nurse Desiree Harvey. I was glad to see her. Her seventeen-year-old son was still missing and presumed dead. With valor she testified, telling the court that on more than one occasion she had personally witnessed the police attempting to torture a confession out of me.

An eyewitness named Wanda Clark claimed she had seen me running from the restaurant. I don't know why she got on the stand and told such a bold-faced lie but for whatever reason, my lawyer decided not to cross-examine her.

Despite all of their false accusations, I still felt that I had a winning chance. Not only had I passed two polygraph tests but the only thing that could link me to the murdered girl was DNA.

On a rainy Friday afternoon on the eighth of April, the medical examiner and DNA expert took the stand. I watched the proceeding with a suffocating feeling, as if I were having an anxiety attack. This was the prosecutor's only hope in the case to send me to prison for the rest of my life or set me free.

There was an abated silence in the courtroom as the DNA expert, Steven White, with his neatly trimmed salt and pepper beard sauntered to the front of the courtroom. He looked like a college professor.

I cast a weary glance over my shoulder at Big Mama. It looked like she had aged ten years.

The prosecutor strolled over to the witness stand. This was his stage. He had come to perform the final dance. Everything hinged on this very moment. After the doctor answered questions concerning his profession and credentials, the prosecutor went into his theatrics.

Arms spread, he faced the jury box and gestured, "Could you please tell the jury of your findings from the DNA testing?"

Dr. White went on to explain how he had discovered eleven pubic hairs and two scalp hairs on the victim's body. "They did not belong to her." He tossed out words like "morphology" and "cortex". Everyone in the courtroom listened attentively while the doctor meticulously explained DNA testing. Afterward; he stopped talking and hesitated as if he was considering his words. Silence hovered and it felt like the air was being sucked out the courtroom.

"So, Dr. White, can you tell the court what your findings were?"

The prosecutor smirked with a gleeful gleam in his eyes, his chest swollen with pride.

My heart pounded vigorously as he delivered his findings. "In conclusion," Dr. White spoke with an aura of reliability that bolstered his credibility, "there is absolutely, positively no scientific way that the DNA found on the body matches that of the defendant." The doctor spoke emphatically as he pressed his thin lips together, nodding his head with certainty.

The sound of disgruntled voices rushed through the courtroom like a tidal wave. The prosecutor's face turned beet red as the jury looked on with pure shock and dismay.

"Hallelujah, Jesus! Hallelujah, sweet Jesus!" My grandmother hollered to the top of her voice. Her large breasts bounced as she praised the Lord.

I looked over at my lawyer. He twirled a pencil between his fingers as he sat stoic, but proud. I noticed that he smiled for the first time.

"Do you have any further questions?" the judge asked the prosecutor.

The prosecutor shrugged his shoulders. He was embarrassed beyond belief. "Oh, er, yes, um, I mean no your Honor," he stammered with his forehead knotted in disbelief.

"Mr. Stromwich, would you like to cross-examine the witness?" the judge asked my lawyer sternly, massaging the red warp on the bridge of his bulbous nose.

The noisy clamor in the courtroom quieted down. Everyone wanted to know what was going to happen next.

Clumsily, my lawyer arose from his chair. "No, Your Honor, I have no questions. The expert witness has said enough. Hmm, uh, at this juncture in the proceedings, I would like to request that all charges as they relate to the defendant be dismissed due to lack of physical evidence."

"That's preposterous!" the prosecutor yelled, hurling words across the courtroom. "Your client is a rapist and murderer and just because his DNA was not found at the scene, that does not remove his guilt from this case."

"If I'm not mistaken counsel, it's the jury's and the judge's job to decide my client's fate," my lawyer responded tersely.

Several of the jurors nodded in agreement. Some of their expressions had softened.

The judge banged his gavel. From somewhere in the back of the courtroom I heard a woman crying sorrowfully.

The judge's voice boomed like thunder as he looked at my lawyer and spoke. "I will consider your motion to dismiss the murder charges in its entirety as soon as it is filed with the Clerk of Courts. File it no later than Monday."

The judge turned to face the prosecutor and issued a stern caveat. "I suggest you substantiate this case with more persuasive evidence or try to come to some viable plea agreement."

District Attorney Staller nodded his head. He looked defeated.

"Court is adjourned until Monday. I would like to ask both

attorneys to meet me in my chambers," the judge announced before banging his gavel.

For the first time in what felt like years, I felt the urge to smile—even to laugh. The DNA had proven my innocence. I looked forward to Monday like a child who looked forward to Christmas Day. I looked back at Big Mama. She wiped tears from her face as she sat courteously with her Bible on her lap. *God, I had taken that old woman through so much*, I thought. Just as I started to wave at her, the bailiff quickly came and took me to a holding cell.

# Chapter Twenty-Three

I awakened to the sound of keys jingling as the rusty, old cell door squealed opened. Light shown brightly from a single light bulb in the hall. Ever since my capture and throughout my trial, I had stayed in the Douglas County jail. This was my corner of hell. There were three other occupied cells. I sat up in my bunk and placed my bare feet on the cold concrete floor.

The sound of keys resonated in my mind like a silent alarm. The silhouette of my grandmother made me blink in bewilderment. I had to be dreaming. People only came in my cell for three things: to intimidate, to interrogate, or to investigate. A large rat scurried across the floor and dived into a hole underneath the toilet.

"Gramma?" my voice cracked.

She was wearing a flowery skirt with large buttons down the front. In her hands were two plates of food. The delicious aroma of fried chicken, corn on the cob, and macaroni and cheese made my hungry stomach churn.

"Baby, I brought you something to eat and I got good news for you."

I looked past her to the doorway. I saw my attorney, the district attorney and two guards watching us closely.

"You got thirty minutes to visit with your grandmother," one guard said.

"We need to go over some legal formalities and try to bring this thing to a close, but your grandmother wanted to talk with you first," my lawyer informed.

The cell door slammed shut.

Gramma sat the food down on a dilapidated table ignoring the large cockroaches as they scattered for cover.

The light in the cell flashed.

She reached out for me and wrapped me in her arms. "How are you, baby?"

I inhaled the familiar scent of jasmine and hair grease. Gramma's unconditional love was heavy in my nostrils.

"Hmm, I'm taking my grandbaby with me," she said, squeezing me in her arms. "Boy, you skinny as a rail. You lost a lot of weight." With a sad face she reached down to poke one of my bony ribs.

I shrugged my shoulders.

She cast a long glance around the cell, pensively clasping her

arms around me as she shuddered. "How can you live like this?"

"Gramma, I don't have a choice."

"Humph."

I sat down at the table and tore into the food like I was starving.

Gramma sat on a wooden bench. She didn't touch her plate of food. "You passed the DNA test." She beamed.

"Uh, hmm," I said, stuffing my mouth full of food.

"You still got more charges but they want to make a deal with you so you can come home with me."

"What kind of deal?" I smacked with food in my mouth.

She frowned. "I don't know, exactly. They just came and got me from the hotel."

I stuffed a whole chicken leg in my mouth.

"They told me I could bring you a home cooked meal and talk some sense into you. They want you to accept a plea deal, so I cooked enough food for everybody; your lawyer, the prosecutor man, and the judge ... all of 'em. I just want to see my baby come home with me."

"Me too, Big Mama, I'm ready to come home." I grabbed another piece of chicken and inhaled its seasoned meat. I looked at my grandmother and asked, "You seen TC or Tamara?"

Big Mama frowned like someone had stepped on one of her

bad feet. Then she slapped the shit out of me. "Don't you be askin'
bout dat fast-ass heffa! You need 'ta be concerned 'bout this mess
you in, boy!" she scolded.

I rubbed the side of my face.

Just then keys rattled and the door squeaked open. In
walked my attorney and the prosecutor. Both men wore somber
expressions. They seemed serious and intent. The prosecutor
extended his hand for me to shake.

I didn't shake it.

Big Mama swatted my arm. "Be polite," she whispered under
her breath.

I shook his hand.

"Your grandmother has informed you of a plea bargain
agreement, correct?"

"The State is willing to make a plea," my attorney told me
with a hint of a smile tugging at the corners of his mouth.

"However, there is the troubling matter of the police dog you
killed," Staller continued.

"Dog?" I responded in shock.

He walked closer.

Gramma fidgeted as she smiled.

"Under Georgia State law you can be charged with
manslaughter for killing a police dog. They undergo special
training just like officers do."

"Whaat? Because of that dog I had to get forty-nine
stitches!"

"Also, you have the pending charge of assault with a deadly
weapon with the shooting of Bubba Ray."

"I didn't do nothing wrong. He pulled the gun on me!" I said,
raising my voice. "I was protecting myself. The doctor even told
you so."

He ignored me. "We may have this matter resolved if you'll
just plead guilty to all charges and accept ten years probation with
the condition that you'll never step foot in Douglasville, Georgia
again."

"You ain't gotta worry about that," I mumbled under my
breath, "but I still didn't kill or rape that girl and the DNA proves
it."

"No. The only thing that proved was that you were clever
enough not to leave any evidence," Staller shot back. "You still
have an eyewitness and a police officer who says you confessed.

"They set me up!"

"You want to let the jury decide that or do you want to walk out of here a free man come Monday?" This time it was my lawyer talking.

"But I didn't do nuthin'!" I scuffed sourly.

Big Mama reached over and grabbed my arm. "Listen boy, you gotta give these white folks sumpin' even if you innocent. They not just gonna let you outta here scot-free."

That day I signed the plea agreement as everybody watched: the DA, my grandmother, and my attorney. It felt like a large weight had been lifted from my shoulders. After almost two years I was finally going home. Monday couldn't come fast enough.

# Chapter Twenty-Four

Monday morning at nine o'clock they brought me into the courtroom wearing a secondhand suit and shackles. A large group of armed guards stood by while the courtroom quickly filled.

Big Mama was in her usual seat. She looked up from her Bible and waved.

The atmosphere was electrified. I could feel my heart pounding in my chest.

Once Judge Studebaker took his place, he lectured the spectators against making any outbursts.

My lawyer seemed aloof.

Across the room from me was the prosecutor's table. DA Staller was frantically scribbling something on a yellow legal pad.

Inside, I smiled.

"Let's get going," the judge began and banged his gavel. "The State and the defendant have reached a plea agreement. Is that correct?" the judge asked, looking up from the papers in front of him.

A hushed ripple of voices rose throughout the courtroom.

The judge grabbed his gavel and glowered out into the gallery of faces.

I held my breath.

I noticed several members of the jury staring at me suspiciously. Their jaws were slack and they appeared to be befuddled.

I did my best to look straight ahead.

"The defendant is pleading guilty to the following charges ..." The judge went on to rattle off the list of charges so heinous they would have made the devil blush.

I cringed in my seat while across the room the victim's mother began to cry.

"Is it correct, Mr. Miller, that you are pleading guilty to these charges?" The judge asked looking at me over the rim of his reading spectacles.

I nodded somberly and croaked out a dry, "Yes."

"Mr. Miller has your lawyer apprised you of the sentence as it relates to the plea agreement?"

I looked over at my attorney.

He stood up from his chair. "Your Honor, I have spoken to my client in depth about the consequences of his guilty plea. However, as you are aware, when in your chambers last Friday, we discussed the probability of a plea negotiation, in light of the expert's DNA findings."

The judge nodded his head and looked over at the prosecutor.

"Your Honor I have reviewed the law in this particular case, as it relates to the plea bargain and capital punishment, and all of this is perfectly legal."

I sat there stupefied on a wooden chair wearing a wool suit that made my entire body itch.

"Will the defendant please stand?" the judge ordered.

I didn't move. I didn't want to. I sat with unflappable calm. I scanned the many faces in the courtroom. There were no other black faces, other than mine and my grandmother's. I saw Bubba Ray in his wheelchair. His body had withered. The scout who had flown out to my grandmother's house to recruit me to play college basketball at Georgia State was in the courtroom, too. I also saw a host of other people that had taken the stand and lied on me. Even the jurors did a miserable job of hiding their prejudice against me.

Slowly, I turned all the way around in my seat. The shackles rattled. I looked at my grandmother, holding her Bible tightly to her bosom.

"Boy, get up!" Big Mama hissed through clinched teeth.

"Will the defendant please stand?" The judge asked again.

This time his voice was a little louder. The judge removed his specs and glared at me.

My lawyer whispered, "Stand up."

Finally, I did.

The judge leaned forward and stared down at me. "In light of the fact that this is an extraordinary case with special circumstances, I will accept your negotiated plea. I will hand down the following sentences." The judge cleared his throat. "I hereby sentence you to ten years probation for the assault and battery of a law enforcement officer."

The boisterous chatter of voices clamored.

I looked over at Bubba Ray. He was crying again.

The judge banged his gavel. "Quiet in the courtroom!" the judge ordered. He went on to sentence me for at least ten more charges. "Your years will run concurrent with the ten years probation."

When the judge got to the sentence for the murdered girl, he stopped, looked at me and frowned. A jagged line appeared across his face. "For the heinous, atrocious, and cruel murder you committed, for the purpose of your own sick, perverted reasoning, and because I feel there is a strong likelihood that you will kill again, and thus proving yourself a continuing threat to society; you shall be put to death by lethal injection."

The courtroom went silent.

I felt my legs wobble.

"Lawd, pleeeez…nooo…nooo!" Big Mama cried out loud enough for the heavens to hear.

"The judge sentenced me to death," I said to myself. I couldn't believe or understand the gist of what had just happened.

My grandmother continued to scream with fury "That's not what y'all promised me! Y'all said he'd get probation and that's why I agreed to help! Y'all dirty bastards!" Big Mama raged as she moved forward. The girth of her large body pushed past people as she struggled to make her way to the front of the courtroom.

I turned my head and cast a wondering glance at my lawyer, the judge, and then the prosecutor. "What the fuck! Ya'll set me up!" They had conspired to convict me and used my gramma to convince me to sign papers. I had admitted guilt.

Big Mama stormed down the aisle. She was headed for the judge. Her nostrils flared and her fists were balled tight. She took one more step and fell forward, face first. All of her three hundred pounds fell hard to the floor. "Oh my!" She shouted painfully and her King James Bible slid from her hand.

The judge looked over at the prosecutor with a conspiratorial smirk.

Someone in the courtroom laughed and then others joined in as the morose atmosphere turned festive.

Big Mama didn't move. She didn't even try to get up.

I stood there shackled, fettered to chains like a slave. "You sneaky son of a bitch!" I screamed. I snapped on my lawyer. I swung with all my might and hit him in the face. The blow sent him sprawling across the floor like he had been shot out of a cannon.

The laughter quickly stopped as the white woman behind me let out a horrified high- pitched wail. I looked up to see the bailiff running toward me, but before he could reach me, I picked up the chair next to me and hurled it right at the judge. The bailiff grabbed me just as the chair left my hand, sailing through the air like a precision missile. The judge's eyes bucked wide as he saw it coming, but the inertia of old age would not let him move fast enough. The chair struck him in his head, knocking him out cold.

Pandemonium erupted.

Almost instantly, I was pummeled, kicked, punched, and choked. I ended up on the floor close to my grandmother. Curled up into a fetal position with my eyes shut tight, I prayed it would all go away. By now I had become immune to pain, and the only thing that mattered was Big Mama.

Big Mama suffered a sprained ankle and a mild heart attack. My lawyer and the judge had sustained head injuries. The judge's was the most severe. He received seventeen stitches. And me—I was sentenced to death.

# Chapter Twenty-Five

Executions take place at the Georgia State Penitentiary Maximum Security Facility. About an hour before an inmate is put to death they are outfitted in light blue surgical scrubs and then secured to a gurney. The doctor attaches a heart monitoring device while a Deputy Warden stands at a small white podium and records everything in a notebook. Next to him is a phone just in case the Governor's office calls with a reprieve. When the formalities are done and the warden is certain there will be no last-minute phone calls the injections will start.

First a saline solution is pumped into a vein. Then the first drug, Thiopental Sodium, is administered, quickly knocking the inmate out. Another flushing of saline solution is injected and then the second drug, Potassium Chloride, is administered. This stops the heart. The doctor appears and checks vital signs. He'll then pronounce the time of death if the procedure is administered correctly.

I cringed as I read this. After I was sentenced to death, I was taken back to the Douglas County Jail and was given a pamphlet entitled, *Things to Know About Your Execution.* I decided after all that had happened to me, I'd rather die standing on my feet like a man. I'd rather fight back than lie down like some caged animal being killed at the hands of another man.

I had gone from being a promising college athlete to a condemned man. Fuck 'em! If they were going to give me a death sentence I was going to give them hell.

I flooded my cell and threw shit at the guards. I became the embodiment of a one-man wrecking crew. There was a white dude in another cell down from me. His name was Bruce Sinclair. He was a career criminal charged with kidnapping and statutory rape for taking a seventeen-year-old female across the state line and having sex with her. He had been sentenced to seven years and the Feds had picked up his case. He was about ten years older than me and was a monster of a man at six feet, eight inches; and he weighed at least four hundred pounds. He possessed a mischievous grin and a crooked smile.

Bruce taught me a lot. We invented ways to fuck with the guards and he even showed me how to make a zip gun out of a lid, paper, and toothpaste. Once I shot a guard in the ass because he always messed with my mail. My punishment was the removal of everything from my cell. They removed every piece of clothing, every sheet of toilet paper, my thin sheet from my bunk — everything. Afterwards, they roughed my ass up pretty good.

They gave me a thin paper gown, but that still didn't stop me from being a menace. I wreaked havoc on whoever crossed my path. Why shouldn't I have reacted that way? I was an innocent man about to be put to death for a crime that I hadn't committed.

I have to admit, the white dude, Bruce was cool as shit even though he was a redneck. We would talk into the wee hours of the night. He even made fun of my tricked- out Chevy and the fact that I liked to eat Oreo Blizzards.

As I waited to be taken to death row, I received cards and letters from Big Mama and my twin brother, TC. That made me feel good. My grandmother had been released from the hospital a few days after my sentencing. She took a bus back home and made it her job to get in contact with black leaders, support groups, and the media to help with my case. Despite her efforts, though, the most attention my case ever received was a small article in *Jet* magazine:

*"Condemned man, IC Miller, sentenced to death for the rape and murder of a 16 -year-old white female in Douglas County,*

*Georgia—long regarded as one of the most racist counties in the South.*

*There was suspicion concerning the evidence and the guilty plea.*

*Mr. Miller maintains his innocence."*

One day after I flooded my cell, I stood atop my bunk doing my best impression of a demolition derby bashing in the light fixtures with youthful impishness.

I tussled with a stubborn light fixture while trying to get the wiring out. I figured that if I could do that without electrocuting myself, I could place the wire in the shitty water. When the guards stepped in, it would electrocute the hell out of them.

With a grimace on my face, I strained to pull at the thick glass of the light bulb. Two white men boldly walked up to my cell. They both had on nice suits and I felt underdressed in my paper gown. It exposed my nudity, hundreds of horrific scars, and a gunshot wound, all courtesy of the good white folks of Douglas County. Both men stood with their shiny shoes in a pool of shitty water. I figured they must have been crazy as hell or adventurous to come stand their white asses in front of my cell.

In a giddy whisper I called Bruce's name. "Bruce! Bruce!"

I guessed Bruce's fat ass couldn't hear me. He often hid his medication when the jail nurse gave it to him so that he could stockpile and get high later. He'd sleep for days at a time. This was obviously one of those times.

One of the white men spoke in a congenial voice that sincerely sounded kind. "Mr. TC Miller?"

It stopped my movement. "No, I'm IC," I responded back. That was nothing new to me. It was the way he said it that was a problem.

He continued, "My name is Vincent Steel and this is my partner, Joe Ross. We're Federal Agents."

The once evil scowl on my face vanished.

"The Feds now have jurisdiction over your state case and you're being placed under federal custody."

"But I got a death sentence," I replied bitterly.

"Maybe, maybe not. The United States Supreme Court has a case before it right now dealing with cruel and inhumane punishment especially concerning guilty pleas in capital cases that carry the death penalty—cases similar to yours, Mr. Miller. Particularly cases with flimsy evidence that were mishandled by the arresting agency. Many of the cases amounted to bad police work and conspiracy on behalf of the judge and prosecutor. You're being moved to the Atlanta Federal Penitentiary's death row until your appeal is heard."

I looked into his blue eyes and felt some type of hope. Hopefully, there would be an appeal. I would finally get a second chance, but most importantly I was getting the hell out of Douglas County. It had been almost three years. I was so excited I extended my hand through the bars. "Thank you."

Fitted in chains around my waist, the infamous black box on my wrist, and leg irons, I shuffled my feet to a waiting car. To my surprise, Bruce was also escorted to the car. His massive body caused the car to sink down as he got in. For the first time I noticed how chalky white Bruce's skin was. I also noticed that he emitted a sour odor that made me appreciate the cool air conditioner, and a few inches of space. I saw a shadow of sleep in his face and crusted dry saliva on the side of his jaw. Still, I welcomed his company and the limited feeling of freedom as the car drove down a long isolated skirt of highway. The sun warmed my cheeks.

"You want a smoke?" one of the agents asked. He lit up a cigarette.

"Hell yeah! Is a pig's pussy pork?" I replied jokingly. I had never smoked a cigarette in my entire life, but I did that day.

The agents drove us to the nearest town. It was Spartanburg, Georgia where a large white bus full of convicts awaited us. Behind the bus was a chase car.

As Bruce and I boarded the bus, I saw nothing but dudes with hard faces. My pants sagged, and shackles could be heard scraping the floor. Bruce took a seat next to some white dude with a shaved head. I moved to the rear of the bus and sat next to a dude that looked like I felt—scared and uncertain. I was twenty years old and he appeared to be even younger. He looked over at me with a blank stare.

"What's up?" I said.

He nodded, but said nothing.

As soon as the bus pulled off, a cacophony of voices started up and hip-hop music resonated through the speakers. I looked out the window and did what convicts seldom do, and what they seldom admitted that they do—I dreamed of going home and being free.

"*Death by lethal injection.*" The judge's ominous words echoed in my head. I tried to shake them away.

From the chatter, I learned that the Atlanta Federal Penitentiary was the most violent prison in the United States. After snitches, the most despised inmate is a child rapist and someone who abused their mother. Those particular inmates are often singled out and assaulted, preyed upon by both staff and convicts with deadly intent.

From a distance I saw the infamous forty-foot, grayish-white wall. The loud ruckus of voices on the bus lulled into apprehensive whispers as we all stared in awe at the gigantic edifice. To me, it resembled a dark castle. We pulled into a cavity of the prison; I was overcome with a feeling of claustrophobic despair.

When the bus came to a stop a guard yelled, "Everybody out!"

The guards from the chase car had already formed a gauntlet facing the bus. Single file, we were hustled through a labyrinth of dimly lit halls. Steel doors slammed behind us as we stood in a line.

"You know the deal," a lieutenant barked while guards removed the shackles. "Strip!"

We complied.

"Run your finger through your hair."

We complied.

"Open your mouth and stick your tongue out. Lift up your dick and balls."

Again, we complied.

"Turn around, bend over and spread your cheeks."

I did so with a feeling of humiliation as the guard walked up behind me and looked at my asshole. In coming to prison I had relinquished a part of myself that no man should ever have to compromise—my free will over my own damn body.

I stole a glance to my right and saw that Bruce was the fourth person down the line from me. He had a smug expression on his face.

"TC Miller!"

My twin brother's name was called, but I was certain that they were referring to me. "I'm IC Miller," I responded.

No one seemed to care.

After a moment of hesitation, I stepped forward, still cupping my nuts in my left hand. A black man approached me. He had on a white shirt and tie. His bug eyes bulged out almost comically and he wore his hair short and cropped. He was built funny—muscular on top and little legs held up all his weight. There was nothing funny about him, though.

"Didn't you fuckin' hear me call your name?" He yelled in my face.

I noticed his eyes linger on the grisly scars on my chest, abdomen and arms.

"My name ain't TC, it's IC Miller," I responded with grit in my voice. I read the name on his badge. I felt a thousand pair of eyes bearing down on me.

His brow furrowed as he took a step closer. "I don't give a fuck what your name is. Get the fuck out of the line and stand over there!" He pointed toward the wall.

Four other guards walked up. I didn't budge. I had taken so much shit from them crackas at Douglas County, I for damn-sure wasn't gonna take no shit from this popeyed-ass nigga. I clinched my fist and held his stare.

"Captain Turner is there a problem, sir?" asked one of the guards.

"Is there a problem, Miller?" the captain asked, awaiting my response.

I moved, hesitantly, never taking my eyes off the captain.

"Oh," Captain Turner laughed, "you one of them bad muthafuckas. We'll see about that. This one here raped a poor, innocent little girl and now you wanna come in here and play tough!"

"I ain't rape nobody. All y'all got me fucked up," I retorted feeling my face flush with anger.

I stood there rigid and nude. I heard mumbling voices grow louder. The convicts looked at me with pure hatred.

"You'll see how fucked up we got you when we get your ass to death row," Captain Turner said haughtily.

In walked a platoon of guards, and behind them came Warden Scott. He was a tall white man—the ex-marine type. The warden wore blue jeans, combat boots and a sweatshirt. His wrinkled skin looked like weathered leather.

"Is this the inmate right here?" he asked as he walked up to me, flanked by at least ten burly guards.

The captain gave a subtle nod to his superior. "Take the rest of these maggots to R&D," the captain shouted. "It's time to get the girls settled into their new home," he laughed evilly.

I pressed my lips together.

Finally, in a thick baritone voice the warden spoke, devoid of emotions, almost mechanical. "Normally, I don't come and greet our inmates but in your case I had to make an exception. So," he hesitated, "you raped and murdered a—"

"I didn't—"

"Shut the fuck up!" The warden raised his voice.

The guards closed in on me.

"I talk. You listen. Understand?"

I gave him a cold stare.

"You seriously injured a police officer and left him paralyzed. You even killed a damn police dog." Warden Scott walked around me and stopped directly in front of me. "You even assaulted your own attorney." He paced one more time. "And you assaulted a judge!"

I stood and looked straight ahead.

"I'm going to tell you up front that the captain and I have a bet on you." He turned and looked at Captain Turner, then looked back at me. "Since your death sentence is on appeal it's up to me to decide if I want to keep you on death row or let you into general population where some psychopathic predator will make you his girlfriend."

All around me was laughter. It resonated in chorus in my ears.

The warden walked up to me and snarled. "Smart-ass, I placed my bet on you." He turned to his guards, "After he's finished in R&D, get him a bed roll and take his ass to C-Unit."

"Let's go! Move it!" someone spewed.

I felt a shove from behind, and I wondered what the fuck they meant by placing bets on me. I quickly tossed the thought out of my mind. All I wanted was to get myself a shank and crawl into a bunk and be left the fuck alone to sleep.

# Chapter Twenty-Six

After I left R&D I was given a set of dingy clothes: socks, T-shirts, and underwear. Twelve-deep with six guards on each side I was escorted across the compound. The institution had been shut down so they could move me.

Lieutenant Vice, a scrawny little guard with bloodshot eyes, continued to grill me. To my right, a taller guard snickered derisively. The steel door opened and fetid, musky air hit me in the face. We walked down a long corridor. I felt like I was going into the gallows of hell. Inmates were isolated in gloomy cells; it was Ramadan for the Muslims. C-Unit was eerily quiet, other than the constant mechanical whirl of electrical gates opening and closing, punctuated only by the litany of prayers resonating through the halls.

I heard a voice, an eerie voice. "TC, this is Betty Sue. Why did you rape and kill meee?"

I turned my head and a white man with tattooed arms, a bald head and bushy eyebrows blew me a kiss. The guards fell over themselves in giddy laughter.

Suddenly it dawned on me. They had been waiting on my arrival. A shudder of fear ripped through my body as I walked with my meager gear in hand.

The guards stopped at a small enclosed shower. "Welcome to your new home. You bathe around here twice a week, if you're lucky," the tall, slender guard chided with a gloating grin as he hiked up his gray colored uniform pants leg.

I looked inside the shower through a six-inch window. There was no privacy.

"You want your shower now or you want to wait 'til next week?" the other guard asked brusquely through heavy breaths. He was a short, fat man with sweat dripping down the sides of his face. He stared at me through thick glasses.

I noticed that he had a lazy eye. I wondered if he had ever really apprehended a suspect. I wasn't going to try to find out. I was already in enough trouble as it was.

"I, I wanna take my shower now," I stuttered as both of the guards looked at me with contempt.

"Good," the tall guard said with a smirk. "Take as long as you like." He removed my shackles and opened the shower door.

I walked inside and cringed when the door slammed shut behind me. I was alone. Silence hummed in the quietness. It had been a long time since I'd had a real shower, with both hot and cold water. A shower was a necessity that now felt more like a luxury. A hot shower with soap was one of the little pleasures that free people take for granted. Stepping into the shower, I let the titillating water cover my body. It felt so good. I closed my eyes and sighed deeply as steam rose around me like dense fog. Absentmindedly, my fingers traced my skin. I looked down at the permanently bruised flesh and hideously contoured skin. I had suffered a gunshot wound, a dog bite, abuse, and assaults—all at the hands of white men.

I closed my eyes again and thought about Big Mama. I had broken her heart. I thought about my brother and my girl, Tamara. I had abandoned her. She was pregnant with my child. I had never been a gangsta, not even a thug for that matter. I was just a young, gifted, high school athlete with a dream of going to college and then turning pro.

As I lathered soap across the jagged, scarred contours of my battered body, my index finger stalled inside of a deep, curved wound that reached from my collarbone all the way to my lower abdomen. The emotional scars were deeper than the physical scars. I had gone from a future at Georgia State University to Georgia Federal Penitentiary.

The steam continued to rise and the water covered my body. Then it happened. A choked sob escaped my mouth and reached a crescendo as it became a penitent howl. I couldn't help it. I broke down and began to cry. I was about to be put to death, executed for a crime I had not committed. Suddenly, I heard something. A cold wind brushed past my leg and a hand groped my ass.

Startled, I spun around. "What the—"

"Damn, you got a nice ass!" the pale figure said. The man was huge and had a wild look in his eyes as he began to stroke his erect penis.

I took a tentative step back.

"What the fuck's wrong with you?" my voice echoed.

"What's wrong with me? You da one in here crying, lil mama," the man spoke with a southern drawl. "I came in here to love you. Get a little shit on my dick." He began to stoke himself faster. His beady eyes looked too close together, too small for his big head.

"Get the fuck outta here, cracka!" My voice carried like we were in a tunnel. As torrential waters ran, I dropped the bar of soap that was in my hand and placed my back against the wall. I noticed two people standing outside the shower door, staring inside of the window; Warden Scott and Captain Turner.

My mind raced in a million directions. I thought about hollering for help. I thought about fighting back. I thought about a lot of shit.

The big man pulled out an object that resembled a huge dagger and continued to advance on me with fiendish, feral eyes. "Either I'ma get shit on my dick or blood on my shank, fuckboy. Which one do you prefer?" he threatened.

I looked around for something, anything to hit him with. There was nothing.

He drew his arm back.

I could already feel the piercing cold steel tearing through my flesh. For some reason, I resisted the urge to close my eyes. My voice lowered meekly. "Please, don't hurt me. I'll do anything you tell me to do."

The wild look in the man's eyes seemed to subside with my submission. "Turn around, bend over and pick up that soap. I'ma make love to you real slow." He made a grinding motion with his hips. "It'll hurt for a few minutes but after the first hour or so you get used to it." He laughed in a derisive cackle. "Afterward, in my cell, I'ma tattoo my name on your asshole." He laughed some more. Four hundred plus pounds of deteriorating muscle and blubber jiggled as he wobbled closer to me with his arms spread wide and his head slightly turned.

I hit him with everything I had.

The powerful blow sounded like wet wood smacking against concrete. The shank in his hand dropped to the floor. We stood toe to toe, nude, as the misty, ominous steam enveloped both of us. My next blow landed in his solar plexus and echoed loudly. Neither punch seemed to faze him.

Outside the window I heard raucous cheering and chanting.

He rushed me hard against the wall and pressed me up against the wall with all four hundred pounds of blubber. "Oh, you like it rough, huh, punk? I likes me a bitch dat fight back; best pussy I ever had." He grunted. "Yeah, I'ma love you in my cell and make you my wife. Ain't no better joy than a fat booty, black boy." He continued to cajole in a sing-song voice while he persisted to squish me against the wall with all his weight.

I couldn't move, couldn't breathe. "Get...the... fuck...off... me," I said.

He rammed me against the wall again—and again.

Now nearly unconscious, my eyes rolled to the back of my head. I was about to pass out. He looked over his shoulder. He looked at his audience with a giddy smile before turning back around. Inches from my face, he puckered his lips and prepared to kiss me. I opened my mouth and sank my teeth down to the bone and gristle at the bridge of his nose. I almost choked on the blood as a chunk of meat came out in my mouth. I bit down harder, grinding my teeth. Warm blood squirted, running down my chin.

The giant let out a blood-curdling scream. He shrieked like a bitch. He pulled away from me, and his hands flew to his face. I spit out the large chunk of his nose and kicked his big ass in his tiny nuts trying to crush them. "Take that motherfucka'!"

He howled and staggered in the pink, bloody water that flowed underneath our feet. Enraged, the giant tried to rush me again. I sidestepped him and drilled him in the face with a left, a right, another right, and then an overhand right.

He fell to his knees. Gasping, with his face covered in blood, he begged for mercy. "Stop! Stop, okay!"

Not feeling merciful, I hit him again and again. I kept hitting him until he keeled over like a beach whale. I sat on his chest and continued to pound his face. Even though my hands hurt and the skin on my knuckles was raw, I kept on pounding.

The giant lay motionless.

For some ungodly reason, I thought about fucking him in his white ass. Not for some perverted sexual need or desire, but just to humiliate him the way he wanted to humiliate me. In this macabre world of hate that I now existed in, humiliation was an aphrodisiac to be used and abused by the victor. The victim was a fuckboy—something I had no intention of becoming. I rose from his body, naked and bloody, walked over to the window and gazed out. "Let me out of here!"

The silhouette of two figures ensconced in the vaporous fog gawked back at me in awe.

"Whaat! Whaat!" I yelled, pounding my chest hard. The sound echoed loudly. "You got my body but you'll never kill my soul or my spirit! I'm fuckin' innocent! Innocent! You hear me? Hear me!" I raged. I felt infused with insanity. I had lost a bit of my humanity and learned quickly that this was the only way a convict could survive on death row.

The shower door flung open and in rushed the prison's Special Operations Response Team. There were twenty guards armed with plastic shields and heavy batons. They tried to subdue me, but I resisted.

"Get off me!"

Eventually they carried me out kicking and screaming past a smiling Captain Turner. The warden frowned bitterly and handed over two crisp bills to Captain Turner. He then walked off in disgust.

I knew that this was just the beginning. If I was going to survive on death row, killing would have to become a way of life.

# Chapter Twenty-Seven

Bleu Baptiste and his Haitian goons had just slaughtered at least ten dudes in cold blood in the parking lot of the club. I looked out the SUV window at a fuchsia colored dawn as the sun peeked over the horizon. I was still high from the pills, and I had been shaking since witnessing the horror of a bloodbath.

The caravan of whips arrived at a gated community with plush green landscaping. As I sat up straight in the backseat, I couldn't help but admire the splendor and wealth that we were entering. A large, brown-stoned mansion was up ahead.

Kanisha looked back at me from the front seat. Her mascara was smeared like some sad clown. She gave me an apologetic glance.

I rolled my eyes at her.

"Just make sure any witnesses are dealt wit," Bleu yelled into his cell phone before he slammed it shut. He checked his rearview mirror and looked at us. "Let mi tell both yu beeches sumthin'. Wha happened back derre is none of you business, understun mi!"

I looked down at the dried blood under my acrylic fingernails and nodded vigorously.

Kanisha cried, "We didn't see nothing, Bleu."

"Hush up! Yu hurt mi ears. Yu neva stop talkin'. Yu need tu get mi monee. Talk 'bout dat," he scuffed at her.

"Okay, daddy, I told you what's up. I got you, baby. Me and my girl finna look out for you now," Kanisha cooed, rubbing Bleu's arm.

"Ummm," I cleared my throat.

Kanisha turned around in her seat and looked at me.

I made a face at her and gave her a defiant stare.

She raised her brow.

"Humph," I huffed and sat back in my seat with my arms across my chest.

When the SUV stopped, I looked outside the window and saw a huge mansion three stories high. I counted six luxury cars, many motorcycles, and four white hearses.

I didn't understand why the hearses were there, and I didn't want to find out.

The Haitian posse got out of their exotic cars, rowdy and hyped. They ran amuck past us into the mansion with their weapons in their hands.

Bleu beamed. "Welcome tu mi home, luv."

Kanisha turned to look at me.

I couldn't believe what I was seeing: a huge Mediterranean-style mansion. I was in love. As we walked into the grand splendor, I spotted a white baby grand piano underneath a crystal chandelier, and decorative lacquered wood furniture with mauve, moquette upholstery. The furniture looked as soft as a kitten's kiss.

Just as I walked toward the baby grand, an elderly lady appeared out of nowhere. It was near dawn and I didn't expect anyone to be awake, especially anyone at her age.

"Um, excuse me, I'm just ..." I looked at her.

Bleu appeared. "Dis eer mi grandmudda, Delia." Bleu kissed her on the cheek.

She had pleasant eyes and deep sepia colored skin. The flowing dress that she wore was yellow and brown with a floral pattern. She had a matching scarf on her head that partially covered her kinky, gray locs. The old woman nodded her head at us and kept it moving.

Kanisha cut her eyes at me as Bleu awkwardly took my hand. "In my countree, Haiti, mi grandmudda was highly respected in de...*art* of her religion. Dats why no harm can neva come tu mi. Delia caan werk meeracles."

The hair on my neck stood up. I thought about Pharaoh pointing his gun at Bleu at point blank range and firing—and missing. Everyone knew that Voodoo was regarded as a common practice in Haiti. Most practitioners of the religion didn't readily admit their involvement to outsiders, though. I raised an eyebrow at Haitian Bleu. "You sayin' your grandma know Voodoo?"

Instead of answering, Bleu mysteriously looked into my eyes and kissed my fingers. Foreign men were a trip, but I had to admit that his gangsta game was a big turn-on. I glanced back over my shoulder at Kanisha. That bitch had the nerve to roll her eyes at me.

We strolled out to the pool. The morning sun cast an aquamarine glimmer on the tranquil water that shimmered like jewels. The pool was big as shit. There was a wet-bar on the side and a Jacuzzi. We sat poolside next to a barbecue grill.

I tried to relax while Kanisha sat in the lounge chair a few chairs away from me. As I grinded my teeth, I tried to put the scene of the massacre out of my mind. I tried to digest information; but most importantly, I wondered how I was going to pull Bleu's fine ass and get that cheddar.

*Innocent*

131

"Pssst!" Kanisha hissed, disturbing my plotting.

I looked over at her.

She frowned. "I know what you doin'. You don't know what you're getting yourself into. Bleu ain't no good for you."

I made a face at her and thought about her ill whip and all the expensive iced-out jewelry she was flaunting. The ho was hatin' from the sideline. -

I was about to holla at her when a big shadow fell over me, blocking out the sun. I looked up to see a nigga who looked just like something right out of *The Night of the Living Dead*. He had a missing eye with a grisly hole where it used to be. Dude scared the shit out of me! He had nappy, ugly blond locs that fell in his face. He was muscle- bound and terrifying. He was at least seven feet tall.

I screamed, "Oh shit!", and scrambled from my chair, damn-near falling as I tried to run to the other side of the pool.

I could hear Haitian Bleu laughing as he walked up. He had changed into a simple pair of Prada knee length shorts and leather thong sandals. "Luv, Boss is haarmles. He mi cousin. Say hello tu de ladies, Boss."

"Ha-yah," the big dude said as he scratched his head.

I glanced over at Kanisha whose arms were crossed over her breasts. She smirked at me.

"Boss got de mind of a 12-year-old. Him albino. Dats why him skin so white. He died once, but him wuz brought back frum de dead." Was Bleu being serious? If he was, I couldn't help but wonder if it was Delia who had brought Boss back from the dead.

I watched the big man amble off and felt a slight shudder with Bleu's words. I walked back to my seat and sat down. How tall is he?" I asked.

"Seven-feet-tree," Bleu replied, still smiling.

"Da-yum!" I droned.

Bleu passed me a tall frosted glass. The drink looked like a milkshake with large strawberries on top.

I took a sip from the straw. Ambrosia! The drink was off the chain! My throat was dry and the sun was starting to make my breasts perspire. I smacked my lips, then looked over my shoulder at Kanisha.

Bleu hadn't brought her a drink. She rolled her eyes at me and laid back in her lounge chair. I stared up at Bleu and admired his chocolate colored skin. He reached down and gently wiped at the sweat between my breasts. His nimble finger lingered leaving a trail.

As the birds flew over head it looked like his head was up in the clouds.

"Sit down," I told him.

Our eyes locked. Boldly, he pushed my legs far apart and copped a seat between my thighs. My fat coochie was exposed for him to see.

At first I tried to hide it with my hand but with my legs spread it was no use. I stopped resisting.

Bleu pulled out a bag of Purple Cush and rolled a blunt.

I took a sip of my drink. "This shit is good," I said loud enough for Kanisha to hear.

Bleu lit the blunt and inhaled. He turned and looked down between my legs. A cloud of smoke ringed his head. He passed me the blunt and held me with his eyes. His hands took a slow trek up my inner thigh as he looked at me with them sexy-ass eyes. "Yu are bootiful," he cooed, licking his lips.

I sucked on the blunt and couldn't say a word.

He leaned forward and kissed me on my smoke-filled mouth.

My pussy danced to its own beat.

Bleu's tongue played in my mouth while his hands unbuttoned my shirt.

I wiggled out of all of my clothes, except for my thong. I peeked over at Kanisha, who was playing like she was asleep. I set my drink on the ground. Looking down at the crotch of my thong, my pussy was soaking wet. I was embarrassed. My hard nipples stood at attention and my taut flat belly awaited Bleu's touch.

Bleu removed my thong and looked down at my twat. "Pussy fat like de mumps, wumon!"

I smiled. "It's all yours, baby."

He reached down and grabbed a big strawberry out of my drink and placed it delicately inside my wet pussy.

I shuddered and moaned an old song as I nibbled on my bottom lip.

We both looked down to watch the strawberry and his finger disappear inside the succulent mounds of my wet flesh.

"Mmm. Ohhh." I trembled at his touch as the hot sun beamed down on my skin.

Bleu lowered his head between my legs and spread my pussy lips expertly with his forefinger and thumb. Flicking his tongue, he sucked on my engorged clitoris and ate the strawberry at the same time.

"Da-yum! Oooh, ooh shit! Keep it right there, right there! Yes, right there!" I crooned, spreading my legs wider. I continued to thrust my pelvis in his face, feeling a steady stream of warmth running down my ass-crack.

Bleu picked one of my legs up and placed it high on his shoulder giving him more access to the pussy. "Wumon!"

I felt his tongue do its dance inside of my hot tunnel causing a fire to erupt inside of me. I screamed. "Damn it's good! Oh shit, muthafucka! Oh, yes, yes, that's it!" It was hard to keep still. "Sweet Jesus!" I shouted out.

I dropped the blunt on the ground as seismic convulsions rocked my body like I was having a seizure. I came repeatedly. I was surprised at how much release I needed.

He slurped up my juices, licking me like I was sweet licorice.

Bleu finally came up for air and wiped at his lips and mouth.

I continued to grind and undulate my hips. "Don't stop,

baby," I begged. I was aggravated that he had stopped. I needed to be fucked hard and long to put out the fire that roared deep inside me. "Fuck me! Fuck me!" I chanted repeatedly, sticking three fingers inside my dripping wet pussy and then sucking the juices from them.

Bleu stood up and took off his shorts. He had hairy, scrawny legs, but had dick for days.

"Ooh shit!" I muttered, playing in my pussy.

The Haitian nigga's dick was thick, long and black as night. It had a pink mushroom head wide as a damn doormat.

It was also the most beautiful dick I had ever seen—if there was such a thing. It was elegant in its length, standing straight up at full mass. It was so long I could have done pull-ups on it. I admired it while the sun gleamed in my eyes and beads of sweat cascaded down my body. I grabbed his dick with both of my hands, squeezing it to make the gigantic pink mushroom head swell. I looked up at Bleu and then I swung around in the chair and placed both feet firmly on the ground to concentrate on the task at hand.

"Suck it, luv! Yu know yu wan tu," Bleu croaked dryly.

"Oh, daddy," I groaned. I continued to stroke and kiss his dick lovingly, as if it were a small child. I smiled up at him and then deep-throated him.

Standing on his toes, Bleu whimpered and groaned as if he were caught up in the rapture. He grabbed my head. "Goddamn wumon!"

I looked up at him. I knew my dick-sucking game was tight, so I began to suck on this nigga's dick like a starved Ethiopian. I began deep-throating him with a rhythm and pace that sounded like sweet music. The suction cup in my mouth commanded him to deposit his semen down the back of my throat. I bobbed my head faster, taking him deeper. I almost gagged. But I never stopped.

Bleu threw his head back howling like a wolf. He rolled his shoulders and began to curse in French. His body became rigid. "I'm 'bout to cum, wumon."

I pulled my lips off his dick and let him deposit his skeet in my face, my hair, and on my breasts. He came like a faucet.

I massaged his lubrication into my skin. "Pah-leez give it to me from the back, doggy-style," I begged. I fingered my pussy, and cum dripped down my hand like honey.

Bleu obliged as he bent me over the pool chair. He tried to ease inside of me, but he had more dick than my young, horny ass could handle. He knew it, so he held tightly to my hips so that I couldn't move. He eased inside of me. Palming my ass, he plunged a few inches deeper.

I bucked and quivered, biting down on my lip and squealing with delightful pain. "Oh, my God!"

Bleu thrust inside of me so hard, my eyes closed. I held onto the back of the chair so tighly that my knuckles turned white. I started to feel another erogenous sensation. Pure ecstasy began to consume me. Something was vigorously hitting my clit just the right way while Blue continued to pound inside of me. The feeling was too damn good and I had to see what was happening. I opened my eyes and looked down. "Oh, sheeeit!"

Kanisha had somehow managed to position herself between my thighs. Lying on her back, she had my clit in her mouth. Her long, pink tongue was like a small dick. It licked my clit while Bleu's balls banged against her chin. She was devouring and savoring each lick.

The scene should have been illegal. I was so mad at Kanisha for invading me. I wanted her to leave me alone but my body begged for more. Bleu filled my pussy while Kanisha's tongue was bringing down yet another orgasm.

I wanted to scream, but feminine growls escaped.

In a duet of feral lust they fucked and sucked on my young body until I couldn't stand it anymore. I begged for more. I looked up and I noticed Boss across the pool watching us. With his dick in his hand, he was frantically masturbating. It felt like I was making a porno film.

Finally, it happened—a catalepsy climax exploded in my body. My cum gushed in all directions. My legs went wobbly and bucked uncontrollably. We all collapsed on the chair in a heap.

Bleu laughed a deep, throaty cackle.

Kanisha screamed. "My neck. Y'all hurtin' my neck!"

"Bitch, dats what yo sneaky ass get," I said panting. I could feel her head awkwardly beneath us. I glanced back across the pool and Boss was gone.

# Chapter Twenty-Eight

After my first ménage a trios, I laid back in my chair feeling totally satisfied. The combination of dick and tongue at the same time was what a bitch had needed. Kanisha could eat some pussy and that Haitian nigga knew how to lay pipe like a plumber. Together, they had taxed the shit out of my young ass. My pussy was "on swole".

As I sat poolside, hot sun beaming down, I found myself still enraptured by all the extravagance of this nigga's crib, his baller lifestyle.

Kanisha leaned toward me in her chair. "Look girl, we gotta get outta here. Dis nigga ain't right."

"Ain't right?" I retorted. "Yo ass was the one told dude *we* gonna look out for him. You was the one wit dat freaky shit. I looked down and yo sneaky ass got yo head between my legs," I reminded.

"Bitch, whateva, you ain't stop me." Kanisha rolled her eyes at me. "But I know we need to be gettin the hell outta here."

As she continued to talk, Bleu and another dude stepped out of the house. They walked toward us.

I eyeballed Kanisha. Instantly I recognized the dude with Bleu from the club. He had braided hair and feminine features.

He was too skinny for me. Plus, I didn't like the way he had his hair trimmed and brushed down the side of his face like baby hair. I liked thug niggas, not pretty boys. I grabbed my shirt off the ground and placed it over myself, but Kanisha boldly laid there nude.

Bleu tossed me a brown paper bag. "Dis mi nu artis, Lil Phazzy."

I looked at the bag and then at them, using my hands to shield my eyes from the sun. "Hello," I chirped politely.

Lil Phazzy looked hungrily down at my thighs, then his eyes traveled over to Kanisha's nude, bronze body.

She opened her legs showing him an eye full.

He bugged out and unexpectedly blurted, "Shawty, what wrong wit yo face?"

Kanisha wasn't expecting that. She closed her legs and sprung straight forward. "Nigga what de fuck you mean, 'what's wrong with my face'?"

"Look like a nigga been shootin at you wit one of dem paint ball guns."

I hollered.

Kanisha jumped up and ran toward the house with Lil' Phazzy following closely behind her.

With them gone, I took a long sip of my drink.

Bleu sat down next me and bent over to kiss me. "Look into de bag," he said with an impish grin as he kissed me again, squeezing my titty.

His touch made me purr like a kitten. I looked inside of the bag. "Good lawd! What, what you want me to do wit this?" I stuttered.

He smiled as he caressed his mustache with his index finger as if considering his next words carefully. His dick was on hard as he spoke, the thick mushroom head slightly peeking from underneath his shorts. His next words blew my mind. "I wunt yu tu promise mi dat yu wun't work for Kanisha at M&Ms and dat yu'll consider bein' mi lady."

"M&M's? Your lady? Promise?" I sat straight up. A large cloud blocked the sun. I could see his face. I knew this Haitian nigga was catching feelings so I had to be careful not to crack it. "Look Bleu, I don't know nothing 'bout no M&Ms and as far as being your lady," I eyeballed his sexy body and cradled the bag of money in my hand, "you never know what the future holds."

I reached out and grabbed his Mandingo dick and continued on a softer note in my most sultry voice. "But I can promise dat Kanisha and I will spend the entire weekend with you."

Bleu moved closer.

My hand expertly pulled his shorts down and guided his dick into my wet and waiting mouth. One thing about being a hood chick I knew when a nigga was sprung and from the way he was staring and drooling at me, this nigga was sprung. I delicately licked at the oval rim, slowly sliding my tongue down the shaft then I nibbled on his balls. I gently blew on them as I pumped his dick. I pulled on it like it was a Vegas slot machine.

Bleu's rhythm increased.

"I want you to cum in my mouth." I dragged my lips and tongue up and down the side of his dick.

"Awwh, Godummit wumon, what yu du tu mi?!" Bleu moaned in ecstasy.

I put my mouth vacuum on his dick and swallowed all that nigga's babies. -

Kanisha and Lil Phazzy walked up just as Bleu was putting his dick back into his shorts. Kanisha's amber complexion looked clean and refreshed. She had washed the smeared makeup off her face and was now dressed.

Kanisha held her purse under her arm, "I'm ready to go, Tamara."

"Yo, Bleu, I gotta go to the studio. When you get a chance, peep the news about the shit that popped off at the club last night," Phazzy told him.

Bleu gave him a nod and they dapped.

Phazzy stole a glance at my titties before bouncing.

"C'mon, Tamara," Kanisha spoke.

"Nah, girl, we staying the weekend!" I told her.

She arched her eyebrows at me.

Bleu turned and caught her scowling. "Wumon, take yur clothes off. Yu stayin' de weekend."

Kanisha looked back and forth between me and Bleu.

"Take off yu clothes. Dun't let mi ax yu no mo!"

Kanisha fidgeted and smiled like cracked glass. She removed her clothes.

"Beech betta hav mi moni," Bleu continued to mutter loud enough for Kanisha to hear.

Kanisha put on a fake smile and sat down next to me.

"Wunt tu watch de Haitian soccer game?" Bleu asked.

Rubbing my throat, I frowned and politely chirped, "Nope baby, but you can give me some more of that good weed and something to drink. My throat's kinda dry."

Bleu laughed at me hilariously.

I looked over at Kanisha. Her face was flushed and I could tell from the way her nostrils flared that she was pissed off.

I didn't care. I was getting what I wanted.

# Chapter Twenty-Nine

The entire weekend, Kanisha and I partied at Bleu's fabulous mansion. I met members of his posse and we got fucked up on "X" and "Purple Cush". He snorted coke and drank Patron. I had myself a good time.

On Monday morning, Kanisha woke me up early. "Tamara, wake up. Let's go."

I rubbed my eyes. "I'm coming. Damn."

Kanisha and I moved quickly around the room, careful not to awaken Bleu. We took our showers and got dressed. Bleu snored lightly with his Glock underneath his pillow. He was one of them weird dudes that slept with his eyes partially open and I was the chick to fuck with him, waving my hand in front of his face just to be sure he was sleeping.

Kanisha hissed, "Gurl, leave that nigga alone. You gon' wake him up!"

I glanced down at him again and his mouth was slightly open. I padded over to the dresser and began to search through his things.

"Tamara, stop it!" Kanisha screeched.

Bleu stirred in his sleep.

I stalled in silence.

As soon as I heard his soft snoring again I picked up a stack of hundred dollar bills off the dresser and deposited them in my purse.

Kanisha peeped the move. She rushed over to me and she grabbed my arm. "Put it back!" she snapped.

Pulling away from her, I retorted, "Bitch, this Mandingo-dick nigga done fucked me raw and came in me all weekend long! I ain't on no damn birth control. Fuck his ass. His ass payin' pussy taxes."

"Put that nigga's money back," she ordered through tightly clenched teeth.

"What the fuck is wrong with you? Are you tryna play Captain-Save-A-Nigga? Bitch, please! Nigga gets no refunds, period!" I was tired of Kanisha's bullshit.

"Let's go," Kanisha said as she stomped away.

On our way out of the mansion, I clutched my purse and the paper bag full of money. Kanisha didn't say a word as she navigated the way. I thought about Kanisha and Bleu. It was obvious there was something between them, and it wasn't chemistry. Bleu was serious about the money she owed him; and what the hell was M&Ms? I walked as best I could with a broken heel. I was just about to take my boots off when I heard a melodic chant, followed by a drum beat and a blood-curdling scream.

I damn-near jumped into Kanisha's arms. "What de fuck was that?" I exclaimed, grabbing Kanisha's arm.

"I dunno," she retorted with a shrug. Without exchanging another word, we started in the direction of the bizarre noises. We followed them to the rear of the mansion, and to an interior room. The door was closed, but Kanisha silently signaled for me to open it. I shook my head. Kanisha sighed and slowly twisted the knob herself, pushing the door open just a crack. "L-look ..." Kanisha whispered as she stared back at me with wide eyes and nodded toward the room.

I craned my neck to peer over her shoulder. Inside of the huge room, I saw people with painted faces dancing nude around an open fire. The room was full of white caskets. I saw an old woman, also dressed in white, chanting incantations. Her body rhythmically swayed to the drum beat. I recognized the old woman as Delia. Someone screamed again.

"I have to pee real bad," I said to Kanisha.

Kanisha ignored me, but then whispered, "This is Voodoo. They're giving a sacrificial offering to one of the spirits."

I could feel her arm trembling badly. "A what? A sacrifice?" I asked, dumbfounded. "How do you know?"

Just then Boss stepped into view. His pale skin was aglow in the hue of the fire light. He held something small in his large hand, then he pulled out a long butcher knife. The serrated steel gleamed off the fire.

"Is that a baby?" I whispered to Kanisha.

The malevolent chants grew louder and the drumbeat faster. The old woman began to dance like she had been possessed.

I was terrified.

The drum beat.

Boss violently shoved the butcher knife into the infant's throat.

My eyes bulged and I opened my mouth to scream but Kanisha clasped a hand over my mouth.

The old woman placed a silver cup under the baby's neck to catch the blood. They danced in a zombielike trance with each step more dramatic than the first.

Kanisha whispered, "They sacrificed a monkey."

"A monkey?"

"Oh, shit!" Kanisha cursed.

I looked up and saw Boss heading in our direction. We took off running.

Even with one broken boot, I passed Kanisha's slow ass. I accidently dropped the bag of money going out the door.

"Leave it there!" Kanisha hollered.

"Fuck that," I retorted. I turned around and ran past her to get it. I hopped my one good boot-wearing ass right back down the hall and got what was mine.

Outside, the air smelled like rain. The marble stone was slippery as hell. I almost busted my ass coming out the mansion so fast. I grabbed hold of Kanisha. I could still hear the drums or maybe it was my own fluttering heartbeat.

Kanisha fumbled frantically in her purse.

"Where your car at?" I asked.

Before she could answer, Boss came out of the front door growling.

Kanisha pointed, and I followed her finger. Her Ferrari was parked three cars down. She chirped the alarm and we took off running.

Boss ran directly toward us.

The doors to the car were open and we hopped inside. Kanisha fumbled with the ignition.

"Hurry up! Hurry up!" I begged.

Boss's muscles flexed. He jumped clear over a white Maserati. His big ass was up on us now.

"Girl, hurry up!" I yelled again.

By now Boss was in front of the car.

Kanisha finally started the engine and the car roared to life.

The goon placed his hands on the hood.

Kanisha punched the gas. She tried to run his ugly ass over.

Boss dove out of the way.

The velocity of the powerful engine pressed me to the seat as Kanisha sped away. I held on to the bag of money.

She shifted gears, zig-zagging around cars.

When we passed through the front gate I sighed in relief. We rode in silence for a moment with the soft whir of the exotic motor humming along.

"Nisha, what tha fuck was that about back there?" I raised my voice angrily.

She looked at me and replied cryptically. "It is what it is."

"What the fuck you mean 'it is what it is'? You have to do better than dat," I screeched, still holding the bag of money. "What the fuck you got me into?!"

Kanisha sped through traffic, changing lanes like she was on a race track. She pulled over on the shoulder of the expressway and narrowed her eyes. "Bitch, lemme tell yo dumb ass somethin'. If it wasn't for yo stupid ass trickin' on Bleu ..."

"You saw how that nigga was sweatin' me at the club?"

"Humph, is that what you think?" Kanisha looked at me, and her top lip curled in disgust. "Looked more like *you* was sweatin' him, dick-teasing and shit. You still did that shit after I warned you to leave dude alone."

"Hold up! Hold the fuck up!" I slammed my fist down hard against the dashboard.

Kanisha looked at me like I was crazy.

"*You* was the one who took me to *that* damn club."

"It don't matter now," Kanisha spoke. She put the car in drive and eased back onto the expressway only to make a sharp right at the next exit.

I was starting to get a splitting headache.

"Tell me something," I said, "what is M&M's, and why did

Bleu keep talkin' shit about you owing him money?"

Kanisha sighed and pulled in her bottom lip. Her knuckles tightened as she gripped the steering wheel. "I'm in a little trouble, Tam."

"What kind of trouble?"

"I owe him seven-hundred thousand," she told me wearily.

Kanisha fiddled in her purse and pulled out a Newport and fired it up.

I cracked my window for air.

"M&M stands for Meat Market."

"You run a store?"

"Well, kinda," Kanisha responded, taking a long drag on her cigarette. "M&M is a catering service I run for men."

I let my mind marinate on what she said.

"So, you run a whorehouse?"

"It's not a whorehouse," she replied peevishly. "My girls are top of the line dime- pieces, sho-nuff stunnas."

My cell vibrated in my purse. Without looking at the Caller ID, I answered it. "Hello?"

The familiar voice startled me.

"That's all you have to say, is '*hello*'?"

It was my mother. For the entire weekend I had not called her to see about my child.

"Um, hi, Ma."

"Hi ma, my ass!" she answered back. "You ain't grown yet. You could have at least called to ask about your son."

I had to take the phone away from my ear because she was yelling too loudly as she gave me her 'you ain't grown yet' sermon. I could hear my son in the background. It sounded like he was crying.

Kanisha stopped the car on the side of the road. "Aye, I have to holla at somebody for a sec."

She hopped out of the car. I followed her with my eyes. Kanisha walked over to a parked car, and it looked like she was talking to a white man.

"Tamara! Tamara!"

"Yeah, Ma?" I responded, keeping my eyes on Kanisha.

"Girl, you hear me talkin' ta you?"

"Yeah, Ma, I hear you."

"Since I ain't heard from you, tell me you got some kinda job or something. This boy needs more clothes and shoes."

I didn't answer. Kanisha was still talking to the white man in the car. She stomped her feet in disgust. She was apparently in a heated argument with dude.

"Tamara, you remember you sent them people at the Bureau of Prisons your resume and application?"

"Yeah, what about it?" I asked, still watching Kanisha.

"Well, the people called here and said they had a position open in Leavenworth. They got positions in other cities, too; and Atlanta is one of them. When I told 'em you was down there, the man suggested that you go by the prison there."

Kanisha stalked back to the car, her large breasts bouncing. I noticed several men in cars gawking at her as her skirt blew up in the wind, exposing her thighs. She got in the car and slammed the door.

"Mama, I don't know if I can work in a prison." I held onto the car door handle as Kanisha burned rubber, pulling off into heavy traffic.

"Girl, a monkey can do it," my mother continued to chirp. "All you do is turn keys. Shit, you need to do somethin'. Either do somethin' wit yo life or come home and get this damn baby!" My mother said with grit in her voice.

I could hear my baby bawling.

I clutched the bag of money to my bosom. "I'll be home soon, but I'll send you some money."

"How much?"

"A few grand."

"Good lawd!" she exclaimed. "Where you get money like that? On second thought, I don't even want to know."

"The money will be there tonight. Kiss Tyres for me." I hung up and looked over at Kanisha, "How far is the Federal Prison from here?"

She jerked her neck at me like she had been slapped. "Up the street. Why?"

"I got a kid to take care of, Kanisha. My ass needs a job."

"What if I can get you something that'll be worth your while and it pays well? You can have anything you want." Kanisha showcased her jewelry and patted the dashboard of her car.

"I don't know, Kanisha." Her offer was tempting, but I wasn't sure. "Can you just take me by there?"

"If that's what you want, but you know that shit ain't for you."

I sat quietly as she drove. We all do stupid things we regret when we're young but experience through trial and error would be my only teacher.

# *Chapter Thirty*

By the time we arrived at the prison, Kanisha hadn't stopped talking. She didn't want me to work at the men's prison, and she gave me every excuse why I shouldn't.

We rode through the archaic gates into the fortress. It seemed that the sun refused to shine on the place. I changed my clothes in the car.

Kanisha nudged my leg and pointed. "Look!"

I saw picket signs and a parade of media people. The guards paced back and forth in front of the prison.

Kanisha parked the car. "You sure you want to do this?"

I took all the money out of the paper bag and put it into my handbag. I nodded my head. "I have a kid to support." I got out of the car, and with a brisk pace, I headed for the concrete stairs. I read one of the picketer's signs as I walked. It read: "Atlanta prison is a blood bath."

At the top of the steps I heard a guard tell a reporter, "The warden don't give a damn about the safety of his administration here. The prisoners run the prison."

I walked by, taking the pyramid steps two at a time and entered the building.

The vestibule was cool and the marble floors had been waxed

to a high gloss. The smell of cheap disinfectant and decaying varnished wood tugged at my nose.

"You have to sign in," a guard at the desk informed me once he saw me.

"I'm here for an interview," I replied.

"You still need to sign in." He pointed toward an old log book that sat at his desk. "Who are you here to see? Lieutenant Vice?"

"Um, yeah," I replied. I had no clue who I was going to interview with, so at least now, I had a name.

"Go on over there to that booth. She'll get the lieutenant for you."

I pushed myself forward, ready to manipulate the truth for the sake of a job I didn't want. Inside of the booth sat a mammoth of a woman with her back to me.

I approached. "Um, excuse me."

She didn't respond, so I knocked on the bulletproof glass.

"Is Lieutenant Vice available?" I spoke loud enough for her to hear me over the murmur of voices in the lobby.

The woman turned around to face me. Her numerous chins sagged. A few seconds passed and finally she grunted and pointed her meaty finger down the hall.

I turned around and looked in the direction she was pointing. There stood a short, austere man with his hands on his hips. His bloodshot eyes were strained from alcoholism and lack of sleep, and his clothes were disheveled and wrinkled.

I walked to him maintaining a professional manner. "Lieutenant Vice," I extended my hand, "I'm Tamara Jenkins."

"Tamara Jenkins, what can I do for you?" he asked. His clothes were tinged with the smell of cigarette smoke and cologne.

"I'm here to talk with you about a job. I was supposed to interview for a position as a guard in Leavenworth, but I was told that you're hiring here too."

He looked at me, knotted his brow and stepped closer to me. "You've already applied through the Federal Bureau of Prisons?"

"Yes sir," I replied courteously. I could still hear the chant of the picketers outside.

"Follow me," Lieutenant Vice said stoically. He abruptly turned and walked off.

Heavy steel gates eerily clanged behind me as I entered a world within a world.

My high heels echoed across the marble floors and my

heart did somersaults in my chest. The long hall was filled with convicts—hundreds of hormonal, horny, sex- starved men. All around me I heard salacious drones and wicked cat calls.

"Dayum, shawty got a fat ass!"

A Spanish convict with a mohawk and a big-ass Cuban flag tattooed across his forehead yelled something in Spanish and pointed at my ass as I passed.

I feared no one. Maybe it was because I was from the hood and could identify with the thugs, gangstas, drug dealers, and killers.

"Put those damn cigarettes out!" Lieutenant Vice yelled to a group of men in front of us. They ignored him. They stared at my breasts as they strained against the soft material of my clothes, bouncing with each step. The contours of my ripe nipples must have looked like smiling faces because I saw a lot of dudes, with their hands in their pockets, smiling back as if they had stripped away every layer of my clothing.

After walking through a secured area, we came upon a woman sitting at a desk. She had on a blue suit coat with a matching tie and a white shirt.

"Morning, Lieutenant."

He grunted his greeting. "This is Tamara Jenkins," Lieutenant Vice said to the woman. "She says she wants a job here. She says she already applied. Of course, we'll have to verify that. Can you take care of that for me?"

The woman's eyes shot upward as she eyeballed me. I could tell she was checking out the way I was dressed. I sat back as she excused herself and exited the room. I assumed that she was making sure that my story had checked out, and was collecting vital information on me. Almost twenty minutes later, she finally returned.

I realized I was holding my breath.

"Secure the compound! Secure the compound!" a deep baritone voice said from the institution PA system. I saw inmates moving in a hurry.

The chick skirted around her desk and reclaimed her seat, "We're going to need you to fill out some forms, such as life insurance coverage, health benefits, W-4 for your federal taxes, and a G-4 for Georgia state taxes." She rattled off her rehearsed speech and handed me a stack of forms to sign.

"That's it?" I asked.

"We do need to get this position filled." The woman glanced out of the window. "As long as your background check comes back clean, we're prepared to take you—on a probationary period, of course."

I heard a commotion. The footsteps of marching men. I turned and look outside into the hallway. Guards appeared escorting a tall, slender inmate in an orange jumpsuit who was shackled and fitted in leg irons.

When the inmate looked up, my legs buckled and my heart sledge hammered in my chest.

"Innocent," I said to myself.

The lady at the desk stood up and looked out the door "That's a new inmate. He's goin' to death row. He raped and killed a girl."

"Whaat?" I shrieked. My mind refused to believe what I was hearing. What was I seeing? God, no!

"You look like you've seen a ghost," the woman said with concern.

"No, no, I'm okay," I lied.

"This job ain't peaches and cream and it sho ain't for the faint of heart."

I gave her a warm smile and sat down to fill out the paperwork.

By the time I made it back to the car I was numb from my head to my toes. It was like I had just witnessed a death in the family.

Kanisha quickly ended her call. "What happened? Did you get the job?"

I shrugged my shoulders and felt my eyes rim with tears. A riveting pain and despair gnawed at me. "Yeah, I got the job," I told her as she started the car.

"You don't seem happy," Kanisha continued. She backed the car up and began to drive away.

"I saw IC in there."

"IC?" Kanisha looked at me quizzically. "Yo baby daddy, IC?"

"Girl, yeah." Kanisha's mouth dropped open as I continued. "He's on death row for rape and murder." My voice cracked in disbelief. My bottom lip trembled as I fought a losing battle with my emotions.

"Get the fuck outta here!"

"I'm serious. It looked like he had aged ten years."

"Wasn't he going to college for basketball? He was scouted, wasn't he?"

"Yeah."

"How do you go from being a promising ball player to being a death row inmate?" Kanisha asked sarcastically.

"I dunno."

"Gurl, you don't need to work there anyway. All them niggas do is fuck each other in the ass and try to trick bitches to bring drugs in."

As she talked, I cut my eyes at her with disgust. I wished she would shut the fuck up. Finally, she did.

I had loved that nigga ever since I was eight years old. His grandma was the neighborhood candy lady. I would get money from boys I let feel on me and I would take that money to the candy lady to satisfy all my cravings.

Kanisha must have heard my sniffles. She affectionately placed a hand on my thigh. "You don't need that nigga. Fuck him and that job. I'm gonna take care of you. I'll give you what you need. Right now you need a nice fat blunt, a drink, a couple pills to mellow you out and some lovin'," she cajoled while caressing my thigh. Kanisha made a right turn at the light.

I nodded my head in agreement and wiped the tears from my eyes, "Yeah, you're right."

*Innocent*

153

# Chapter Thirty-One

I sent my mother two thousand dollars.

Thirty minutes later, Kanisha drove us through an affluent neighborhood full of nice mansions with luxury cars parked in the driveways. She pulled her car into the circular driveway of a beautiful, beige mini-mansion set ensconced in a wonderland of verdant green splendor. There were purple lilacs, red geraniums, snow white magnolias, and beautiful pink Japanese magnolias lining the brown stone walkway.

"Welcome to M&M's," Kanisha said with a mischievous glint in her eyes. She killed the ignition.

I could hear music bumping from inside of the house and Kanisha heard it too.

"This is not the ghetto," she said through gritted teeth, getting out of the car. Extending her hands outward, she continued, "This is my crib and these are my whips."

I looked and nodded my head with a raised brow. "Nice," I chimed. "I'm impressed."

We grabbed my luggage from the car and walked toward the door. The place nearly took my breath away. White shag carpeting, lots of exquisite crystal, and elegant furniture donned each room. It had elaborate, high cathedral ceilings, and it was furnished in mahogany, with gold accessories. In the living room sat four exotic-looking chicks. They were all drop-dead gorgeous except for a chubby, white chick that sat at the end of the couch munching on something.

Two of the girls were watching BET's 106 & Park on a large 72-inch plasma television. A black chick was perched on a velvet love seat recliner with her long shapely legs tucked underneath her as she read a magazine. One of the girls watching BET looked up at me with sad Asian eyes. She had a tall, svelte figure, long, shiny, black hair, and small perky tits. She actually resembled a younger version of Kimora Lee Simmons. Standing next to her was a Spanish-looking chick with lots of ass and hips, thick thighs, a taut waist, full breasts, an angelic face, and a cute mole next to her nose. I noticed they all were wearing sexy see-through lingerie that flaunted their bare essence. *So, this is Kanisha's M&M's, a meat market,* I surmised, feeling slightly intimidated.

Obviously, they had not heard us come in because the Spanish chick stood looking at a video, shaking her hips. Kanisha rushed over and slapped the cowboy shit out of her, making the side of the girl's face turn red.

"I told y'all bitches 'bout playin' loud fuckin' music!" she ranted. An angry green vein protruded from the middle of her forehead. "And you fat bitch!" She pointed to the chubby white chick sitting on the end of the couch blissfully eating a Krispy Kreme donut. Kanisha rushed over and grabbed her hair lassoing her fingers through her long, corn silk tresses.

The girl eeked out a muffled scream then Kanisha slapped the shit out of her, too. The Asian chick placed her hand over her mouth and giggled. Amazingly, the white chick never lost the donut that was in her hand. The black girl casually looked up from reading her magazine, unabashed and unafraid of Kanisha's dramatics. She barely batted her long pretty eyelashes. I couldn't help admiring the soft, velvety texture of her skin, dark as coal, a sable black hue. Her brown eyes were hooded in something I couldn't read. She looked at Kanisha the way an exotic cat might look at its master. "Y'all bitches got me fucked up if you think I'm finna go for dis bullshit, loungin' round and shit. Y'all bitches better have my muthafuckin money right!" Her demonic eyes challenged each girl in the room.

"I left for two days, on purpose, to see which one of you bitches was going to short my money," Kanisha lied. She began to take off her earrings like she was about to start kicking some serious ass. Kanisha stepped to the Asian chick, who winced. "Bitch, what? You see something funny?"

Kanisha slapped her ass, too. "Where my money at?" Kanisha demanded.

She shot me a sly, coy grin, as if to say, *watch this.* Sure as shit, the Asian chick reached down into her purse and pulled out a wad of hundred dollar bills and handed them over to Kanisha.

"How much is this?" Kanisha asked.

"Four thousan, sic hundrayed."

"Four thousand six hundred," Kanisha corrected her. She moved on to the next chick. "Ho, break yo-self!" Kanisha snapped.

The Spanish chick reached into her purse and retrieved a sizable wad of cash and gave it to Kanisha.

The black girl and the fat white chick both contributed money. It didn't look like it was nearly as much, but it was enough.

In high heels and diamonds, with her arms loaded with cash, Kanisha strolled to the middle of the room with the presence that read, *y'all bitches better respect my gangsta.* For the first time, I had to admit, she had indeed come correct—she was a true Pimpstress.

"Let me introduce you to y'alls wife-in-law," she told the ladies. "This is my homegirl, Tamara."

They all gave me blank stares. The tension in the room was so thick you could cut it with a knife.

Kanisha pointed. "That's Ebonyze." The cute black chick looked at me, expressionless. Her beauty set the entire room aglow. "That's Kim Wu. She's from Korea." Kanisha pointed to the Asian chick. Kim's exotic dark beauty was flawless. She stood tall and regal in splendor. Next to her was Carmen, a Spanish beauty with more body than the others. Her curves were crazy. She had a long mane of curly, blonde hair that cascaded over her delicate shoulders and down her back. I looked at Amanda and tried to figure out how she fit into the equation. She stood out like a sore thumb. Looking at all of the girls, I could tell there was something terribly wrong; but I just couldn't put my finger on it.

Suddenly, the doorbell chimed and all hell broke loose. The girls made a mad dash to the door, stumbling over each other.

Kanisha strolled toward the door. She composed herself before she looked back at the rest of the women.

Everything seemed rehearsed. Kanisha swung the door open with all the elegance and grace of a supermodel, but she squealed in delight when she saw the visitor. She called his name in a high-pitched, fake falsetto tone.

I craned my neck to look at the door. I damn-near fainted when dude walked in; it was the same dude that had sent over the bottle of champagne the other night at the club. He was wearing a black Nike sweatsuit, and his hair was freshly braided. His diamond stud earrings were blinding. Kanisha closed the door behind him.

Dude wordlessly waltzed in and began to eyeball Ebonyze. His eyes travelled down her body to her midriff, and then to the neatly trimmed fur between her thighs.

His solemn composure changed as he touched himself. He tore his eyes away from Ebonyze and looked at me and Kanisha. His handsome eyes never wavered, nor failed to take notice of each girl's beauty. He even sniffed the air, closing his eyes momentarily as he stopped at Carmen.

She greeted him with a lascivious sigh that sounded like an interlude to a moan. Carmen pushed her voluptuous breasts forward. He touched one of them, gently pinching it like a titty connoisseur. "Hi, Papi," she purred, licking her bottom lip so that it shimmered with saliva, letting him know that she sucked dick real good.

He demurred, raising his dark silky brow then moved onto Kim. I saw Carmen pout and stomp her foot. It dawned on me that he was choosing a chick to freak with; and from where I was standing, it appeared that I was next in line. I noticed an enormous dick print in his pants as he stood in front of me. Our eyes locked and I found myself holding my breath as I inhaled his cologne. I blushed, but my smile suddenly died, leaving me in ruins as I watched him walk over to Amanda. He looked at her momentarily, laughed then walked back toward me. My heart beat fast. He reached past me and grabbed Kim's hand, pulling her out of line.

"Will that be cash or credit?" Kanisha asked, rubbing her hands together.

"Black Card," he retorted. His eyes were filled with lust as Kim held onto his arm. They both walked past me.

They stopped at an antique bubble gum machine that took hundred dollar bills.

Dude stopped, adjusted his dick to a more comfortable position in his pants and withdrew money from his pocket. He fed the machine and pulled the lever. Dude took a bright colored candy from the slot.

He and Kim walked up the stairs with his hand under her chemise palming her round ass.

"Lemme give you a tour," Kanisha said to me jovially. As she led me away, she looked over her shoulder and told the girls, "Take her luggage to her room."

Kanisha gave me the royal tour. "The mansion is 12,000-square feet. We have a pool, spa, and a meditation and massage room." She pointed as we passed all the amenities. "In all, there are ten bedrooms." We walked into another area and my mouth dropped. "This is the lounge area. I have custom granite counter tops and a full service wet-bar. You see I have a stage and stripper poles. If you feel like getting your dance on, this is where you do it."

"Day-um!" I said out loud. "You got some freaky shit going on in here."

I had to give Kanisha her props. She was into something big.

Finally, we stepped into her lavish office. It had a cozy fireplace with a bar and lots of custom wrought iron features. The handsome hardwood walls were adorned with pictures of Kanisha cheesing from ear to ear with all kinds of celebrities.

I was star-struck.

Kanisha slid open a gray panel door. Inside was a safe.

Slyly, I tried to look over her shoulder as she dialed the combination.

I had to hold back a gasp when I saw what was inside. She removed coins and paper money to get to what she was actually looking for. When she turned around, I pretended to be fascinated with the décor of the office. "Girl, everything is off the chain!" I told her.

Kanisha just nodded, then threw five stacks of money at me. One of them landed on the floor at my feet.

I picked the money up, loving the feel of it in my hands.

"That's yours," Kanisha told me. Her voice was a soft breathy timbre.

"For what?" I asked, still holding the money.

"Well, Tam," Kanisha spoke as she walked up next to me. She pushed a wisp of hair out of my face. "I want you to be a part of this, us, me, wife-in-law, in my world. Work for me?"

"Work for you?"

"Yep. That prison ain't gonna do shit for you but damn-near get you killed with them inmates tryna get that ass." She took a deep sigh and continued. "I know yo baby daddy is there and you probably got feelings for that nigga, but remember he walked off and left you pregnant and for a bitch that he ended up raping."

My face turned somber when I thought of IC behind bars.

"Work for me," she said again with passion. "Work for us." She threw her arms up. "All of this and more can be yours." Kanisha walked back to her leather chair, reared back and smiled at me.

Everything she said to me was working and she knew it. I reflected on how Innocent's square ass had abandoned me and his baby. "Let me think about it." I told Kanisha, placing the money in my purse. I wanted to give that bitch her money back, but greed is a terrible thing. I needed it so I kept it.

We drank Grey Goose, smoked Purple Cush rolled in philly blunts as we reminisced about old times. We told stories about dudes we used to let hit it and niggas we had wanted to hit it. Kanisha admitted to me that she had let every cute boy in school get some pussy. They had even paid for it.

"Tam, you know damn well you like this city. You know you like these ballin' outta control niggas, my ill whips, and this fly-ass mansion." She smiled at me. "I need you on my team. I need you in the worst way. You see, Haitian Bleu and the rest of these niggas are my millionaire meal tickets. I live off their crumbs. I get a hundred grand or two a month while they're making millions in that same amount of time." Kanisha put down her drink and then frowned at me. "Trust me, a lot of these niggas ain't gonna be around long. That's why I'm beatin' them for their paper. I want you on line, wife-in-law status ya know." Kanisha picked up her drink and took a long sip. Then she put her glass down.

I could tell by her eye contact that, although she was fucked up, she was in perfect control of what she was about to say next.

"Don't take that job at the prison. You know what's up, and I don't have all day for you to make up your mind. I will send you back to Chi-town on the first thang smokin'."

I had to admit she was starting to look more and more like a Pimpstress. Then it occurred to me that our earlier laughter and reminiscing had been her way of priming me, setting me up to this point to pressure me. I thought about the seven-hundred grand she owed Bleu and the safe behind her full of dough. "Look, I need some time to think about it," I said meekly, feeling intimidated.

"Good." Kanisha smiled at me wickedly. "That's my girl."

There was a soft knock at the door before three scantily clad women walked in. They wore lots of hair and make-up, and their sweet perfume filled up the room. Their chatter was boisterous and they spoke as if they were old friends. These women were call girls, professional prostitutes. They all had big breasts, big asses, and even bigger mouths.

I sat there and watched as Kanisha joked with each of them. One thing that I did notice was that they were all serious about their paper. I watched, astounded as each girl gave Kanisha two hundred dollars to work the evening shift that night.

For the next few hours we sat in Kanisha's office drinking and smoking. In and out came more girls, the cook, two security guards, lots of dudes, and a few prominent community officials.

I found myself admiring Kanisha. At twenty-one years old, she was a young genius.

*Innocent*

# Chapter Thirty-Two

When we walked out of the office, I had a drink in one hand and my purse in the other. I was fucked up—high and drunk like a muthafucka.

The mansion was crowded with wall to wall people. Lights played on the walls and music pulsated in heavy rhythm. The mansion had been fabulously transformed into an elegant nightclub. A lot of gorgeous chicks pranced around in lingerie and six-inch stiletto heels. It was off the chain. I caught a whiff of fried foods, crab legs, and hot wings.

Kanisha and I squeezed through the sea of people. Mostly men filled the room. A dude and one of Kanisha's chicks got butt-naked. They walked through a door and disappeared.

I nudged Kanisha. She was talking with a tall, handsome brother who had a mohawk. I pointed to the door where the security guard was standing and shouted above the music, "What's dat?"

"That's the 'Boom Boom Room'," she yelled. "That's where there's a free-for-all fuck fest. Once they're in there, the girl can't turn down any sexual demands. Believe me, they be wildin' out. Sometimes it's three dudes on one chick or three chicks on one dude. Shit, anything goes. You'd be surprised what a bitch will do for five grand."

*No, I wouldn't,* I thought as we kept on moving. I spotted the bubble gum machine. It was already half empty.

Kanisha stopped to chat with some broad. While I waited, I dug in my purse and peeled off a hundred dollar bill. I placed it in the slot and pulled the lever. Two pills dropped. I placed them both in my mouth, and I chased them down with my drink. Within minutes, I was feeling good.

The music began to affect me. I was snapping my fingers and rolling my neck, bouncing my shoulders and moving my butt to the rhythm. A dude approached me. He was fine as fuck.

"You wanna go in the 'Boom Boom Room'?" He handed me a token.

"How much is that?" I asked in a high-pitched tone.

"Five G's, baby. I got more if you can handle more."

Curiosity was getting the best of me; but before I could answer, Kanisha walked over and pulled me away.

I continued to gawk at dude. There were so many celebrities, rappers and ballers. I was feeling the spot.

Kanisha whisked me up the stairs, down a hall, and into a bedroom suite.

It was a sanctuary for lovers. It had a fireplace, mirrors, and a push-button large screen plasma TV.

"Girl, I have to pee and bad," I told Kanisha. "Where's the bathroom?" She pointed behind me. I kicked off my shoes and darted to the bathroom to handle my business. "This is the shit!" I screamed out.

I noticed a big-ass whirlpool tub and a walk-in glass-bricked shower. I couldn't pass up the opportunity to be surrounded by luxury. So without a second thought, I ran a hot bath, stripped naked, and slid into the luxurious bubble bath. I sipped on my drink and played with my coochie. The X pills had me horny as hell. I marinated in the bubbles; and my mind, like a sixth sense, was churning. It was telling me something was wrong, but I figured that I'd deal with it when I figured out what it was.

After I bathed I put on a pair of panties and climbed onto the bed with my purse. With my legs spread eagle I dumped all the contents out. I loved the wads of cash. Some of it I had stolen, some had been donated, and some I had worked for. There was the gun, Pharaoh's gun, and the rest of the weed which I had really forgotten all about. I rolled a big blunt and began to count the money, placing it in neat stacks of 20s, 50s and 100s.

"Dayum, I'm killin'em!" I exclaimed out loud blowing smoke into the air.

There was a soft rap at the door. I scrambled to shove all the money back into my purse. No one could tell me nuttin'! I hid my purse underneath the bed and sashayed to the door in just my panties.

Kanisha walked in with a bottle of Alizé. I noticed that she had changed into a royal blue silk sarong, and she had a black bag tucked under her arm. Her lustful eyes traveled down my thighs.

"Where'd you go? I was talking to you when I was in the bathroom."

"I had to take care of some business." She walked past me and put the bottle down next to the bed. Kanisha turned and looked at me. "Damn, you got a beautiful body."

I felt my nipples knot up hard. I stretched out next to the gun. I had forgotten to put it back inside my purse. I saw both fear and panic in Kanisha's face.

"Oh God, what you doin' with a gun?" Kanisha's voice raised an octave as she took a pensive step back, petrified.

I picked it up.

"Put it away. Please, put it away!"

"Okay," I said, putting the gun in the nightstand and making a mental note of how she had reacted to it.

After the gun was out of sight, Kanisha seemed to calm down. "Did I disturb you?" she asked.

"Naw," I replied.

I watched her pour the drinks.

"Kanisha, you know I ain't really into none of that pussy bumping and grinding shit." I sat on the bed.

"Don't knock it till you've tried it." Kanisha handed me a glass.

I thought about how she had eaten my pussy at Bleu's crib and I started rubbing myself.

Kanisha sat down next to me. I could see that she wasn't wearing panties or a bra. Her large breasts looked soft and succulent. I wanted to touch them, but I stopped myself.

Kanisha sat the black bag on the floor.

"So how do you like it?"

"Like what?" I asked, gulping down my drink.

She smirked sheepishly as if she was eavesdropping on my thoughts.

"How do you like M&M's, my business?"

"I like it. I like it a lot," I told her, glancing at the black bag on the floor.

"I started the Meat Market from the ground up when I discovered mama's little black book full of elite, rich clients about a year after we moved here. It had phone numbers and everything in there."

"Kanisha, about your mother, I'm—"

"Don't," she told me, cutting me off, waving her hand as if she was trying to erase my words and her memories. Kanisha bit down on her bottom lip and her voice cracked with emotion.

"My punk ass daddy is doin' time right here in the federal pen and he didn't even send condolences to me when mama died. Then the nigga gon' write and have the nerve to ask me for money. I wrote back and told that nigga to sell some ass and suck some dick like his wife and daughter was out here doin'!"

"But that's your dad, Kanisha. You can't blame him for your mom's death," I said in a quiet voice. I reached for the partially burnt blunt in the ashtray.

Kanisha stared at my breasts and then looked away. "Shit, if his ass would have just walked away instead of killing that dude, maybe he would be in my life today. Maybe my mom would still be alive. That's why I don't accept his calls, write or visit him."

"I understand, Kanisha, but you still can't blame him. He's still your father and the only parent you have left."

She frowned at me and hissed, "Like hell I can't blame his ass. People just don't know the shit we went through living in the PJs with my mama fuckin' to survive. She taught me how to hustle and survive; but shit, it was still hard as hell."

I had to agree with her on that. I blazed the blunt and continued to listen to Kanisha's mind change lanes, zooming from one subject to another with her mouth in overdrive. "We family here, Tamara." Kanisha smiled taking a drink. "Did I tell you how I came up with wife-in-laws at the M&M's?"

I opened my mouth, but I shrugged my shoulders instead of speaking.

Kanisha continued. "To be wife-in-law, it's all about rich clientele and special treatment. Wife-in-laws work the day shift exclusively. Their pay is much, much better, with less competition. You can average about five grand a week and also spend quality time with me," she cooed, caressing my arm.

"So, where do I fit into this wife-in-law equation?" I asked, failing miserably at keeping the sassiness out my voice.

"Ah ha." Kanisha was stroking my clit.

I enjoyed it.

She continued. "Every night I sleep with a different wife. Sometimes I sleep with two or three and we do all kinds of freaky shit. What I love most about it is I don't have to pay them hoes shit, nothing, nada."

"Why is that?" I asked naively.

Kanisha's tone changed. "It's a long story and trust me, you don't want to know. Besides, half the time, them hoes can't stand my ass. That's why I keep my foot knee- deep up in they asses."

I took a pull from the smoldering blunt and studied her face.

Kanisha's mouth opened to speak, but this time, it was in a kinder tone. "Tamara, you're different. You're my homegirl." She took the blunt from my fingers and licked the paper where it was loose. Then she took a long drag. Her eyes were heavy. Kanisha leaned forward and she tried to kiss me.

I turned my head, giving her my cheek.

With her lips planted on my cheek, Kanisha reached down and grabbed my breast.

I felt a jolt of electricity. I tried to pull away, but I couldn't move. A soft sigh escaped my lips.

Her other hand eased between my thighs. Kanisha smiled.

"Kanisha," I said softly, even thought I didn't pull away.

Kanisha positioned herself between my legs and planted more soft kisses on my neck, and like tiny feet, her lips walked across my body. It was tantalizing, titillating, and exhilarating; my mind knew it was wrong, so wrong. But it felt so right.

Kanisha put one of my nipples in her mouth and sucked on it affectionately while she pushed me gently back onto the bed. Her tongue devoured and caressed me with sultry velvet licks. She moved down past my navel and at the same time she removed my panties.

I lifted my hips to help her as I allowed her to seduce me.

I couldn't move as her mouth travelled downward. My body was paralyzed. I swallowed, gulping air like I was drowning— drowning in a sea of my own promiscuity. I moaned, "Fuck me, Kanisha. Fuck me."

Kanisha's fingers sensuously seduced me while her mouth dove into my womanhood, spreading my pussy wide open. "You like it, don't you?"

My legs automatically spread like wings, answering her question. I soared high in ecstasy.

She sucked between my thighs.

It became too much to bear. "Ohhh, shit!" I reached down and caressed Kanisha's head as my simmering juices spilled over. "I'm cumming." And I did, right in her mouth. She was making me feel better than any man had ever made me feel. Tears welled in my eyes and I writhed and thrusted in the bed. I came again. "Oooh, God! Shit!" I screamed in a high-pitched tone.

Kanisha held me captive with her feminine tongue. "You taste so good. Can I do it again?"

Unable to get the words out, I just nodded for her to continue. I was enraptured in torrid passion. Gently she consumed me and our soft moans filled the room.

I couldn't help myself and couldn't take it anymore. I closed my eyes tightly as I felt her three nimble fingers and deft tongue plunging, exploring in and out of me.

I laid there with my eyes closed while Kanisha's mouth lapped up my juices like I was sweeter than honey. My eyes popped open as I came again. My body convulsed and shook in spasms. "Oooh, yes!" I praised her until finally she stopped.

Through hooded eyes, Kanisha looked up at me. Her hair was matted to her forehead and her mouth was ringed with my cum. Slowly, Kanisha rose and disrobed. The gown fell away from her body showing her large breasts and her nipples were aimed right at me. Kanisha moved slowly, but purposefully, as she reached in the black bag on the floor. She removed a thick, twelve-inch dildo and a tube of lubrication.

I sat up on the bed like a puppy waiting for a bone and watched with anticipation and excitement as Kanisha squirted the lubricant all over my body.

I helped her rub it into my breasts and between my legs.

Her focus was on my engorged pussy lips. Kanisha expertly strapped on the dick and eased on top of me. She licked her fingers and rubbed my pussy. "I like your shit. It tastes so good."

"I aims to please." I smiled at her.

"Have you ever done this before?" She inserted the tip of the toy into my dripping wet pussy.

"It feels so good," I moaned, not answering her question.

"Fuck, yeah."

We slithered, slippery in each other's arms.
Kanisha fucked me for hours.

# Chapter Thirty-Three

Afterward I lay next to her in the still of darkness. I was still high and my body was alive and tingling. I closed my eyes and Innocent's face flashed before me. My mind wouldn't stop racing. I thought about the plan I had to trick Kanisha out of the five grand she had given me. I had to take the job at the prison. I was young, but I wasn't stupid. There was no future in prostitution and I needed that legit job, not just for myself, but for my child too.

Kanisha stirred next to me. She sat up and lit a blunt. "You want a hit?"

I counted to ten in my mind preparing for what I was about to do. I had to find out if Kanisha was as petrified of guns as she appeared to be. I sat up in bed next to her. The humid scent of our sex permeated the air.

She smiled at me. It was the same smile I've seen dudes wear after a round of good sex.

I reached for the gun inside of the nightstand.

Kanisha's smile faded into fear. "What are you doin'?"

"Just thinking." I looked solemnly at the gun. I placed it on my chest and ran it down to my pussy.

"Put that gun away!"

"Why?" I asked, playing with the heavy, shiny steel.

"Because I don't like guns." She squirmed.

"Hmph." I attempted to hand it to her.

She jumped. "Please, Tamara, put that thang away."

"You know, I've been thinking," I spoke, still playing with the gun, "and um, I think its best that I take that job at the prison. I know you wanted me here, but I just can't do it. If I do anything here, it's on my own terms. Cool?"

In swift jerky motions, Kanisha nodded her head in agreement like a puppet.

I got up and put the gun back inside of the nightstand. Then I went to the bathroom. I knew that Kanisha wasn't going to fuck with it because she was scared as shit. "So what's up for today?" I asked her, walking out of the bathroom. "We hangin'?"

Kanisha's demeanor had changed. She had grown the balls that would have gone well with the dick she fucked me with last night.

"What?" I asked.

"Where's the money I gave you?" She was serious.

I couldn't believe she went there. I marched over to the nightstand and retrieved the gun again. "Bitch, you got this all wrong!" I told her, pointing the gun at her. Thoughts whirled in my mind as I plotted to countermine Kanisha's scheming ass. "You want me to work for you in your whorehouse. Be your damn *wifey-in-law*? Not to mention you had the nerve to damn-near suck my fallopian tubes out and fucked me with a foot-long dildo. Now you're askin' me for your fuckin' money back!?" With every word, I raised my voice.

"Nooo! No! No! Lord, no! That's not what I was saying!" Kanisha cowered.

"Well, what are you saying?"

Kanisha looked at me, then at the gun, then back at me before she spoke. "I was asking you where the money was because I can put it in my safe downstairs. You don't need to be walking around with all that shit on you." She was scared. "You can have whatever kinda schedule you want here, too. You can have part-time or shit, whenever you want." Kanisha smiled nervously.

"You got me fucked up. I'm not giving you my money."

"Will you give me some of that again?" Kanisha pointed toward my pussy, trying to change the subject.

Her request caught me off guard, but I nodded my head because I was still high and horny as hell. I walked back over to the bed.

"Come on," Kanisha begged nervously, "put that thing away." She nodded toward my hand.

I looked down and saw the piece tucked away in my hand. Remembering how expertly Kanisha had used her lips and tongue last night, I walked to the nightstand to put it away. Sauntering back to the bed, I laid on my back and spread my legs wide.

Kanisha smiled and climbed in between my legs. While I puffed on a blunt she ate my pussy like it was a four-course gourmet meal.

An hour later, after Kanisha had finished sexing me like a professional, I laid alone with my thoughts whirling. I still had that gnawing, intuitive feeling that something was wrong, and it caused my mind to push rewind.

I thought back to the day at the hotel when I was about to get kicked out. Something wasn't right. Kanisha had called my cell phone. How did she get my phone number? I remembered her saying that my mom had given it to her when she called, but my mama wouldn't give my number to just anyone, least of all, Kanisha.

I reached for my cell phone and dialed my mom.

She picked up the phone on the fourth ring. "Hello," she answered groggily.

"Hi, Mama, it's me."

"Hey, baby. It's early. Are you okay?"

"Yeah," I answered hesitantly.

I heard her yawn. "Thank you for the money."

There was a pregnant pause.

"Oh, yeah, uh, Mama, did Kanisha call you about a week ago?"

"Who?" she asked, stifling another yawn.

"Kanisha Williams, the girl that used to live next door to us. You know, her mama was Brazilian."

"Oh, yeah, I remember her. No, what would she call me for?"

"Just asking, Ma."

"Nah, you gotta be careful wit that child. You know her mama was something else."

I changed the subject because my mom was long-winded. We talked a little more and I told her that I'd call her later to talk to my baby.

I hung up the phone, fuming at Kanisha. That bitch was up to something. I remembered the gun in the nightstand, and I thought about stepping to her ass with it, demanding an answer from her. I fought to control my breathing and my sanity. I decided to focus on the prize, which was my desire to beat her at her own game. I was going to stack enough money, dip, and get my own place with my own legit job at the Bureau of Prisons. But if my mom didn't tell Kanisha I was in Atlanta in that hotel, then how did she know and why had she lied?

The Federal Penitentiary wasn't but a few miles from M&M's. On Monday morning, I drove one of Kanisha's cars to the gig. The inside of the car smelled like mildew and rotten fish. I could tell that the car had not been driven in a long time by the amount of dust that had collected inside. I switched on the radio.

A dude called in to give Kanisha's Meat Market a big shout. I couldn't help but smile at that.

Lieutenant Vice was waiting for me inside the front gate. Today, he was just as disheveled as the first time we had met, and he still smelled of cigarettes and whiskey. His hound dog eyes held me with reproach. It didn't matter because I was determined to do my job.

On my first day I was required to go through a rigorous training process. I learned how to frisk an inmate and how to search a cell. They also gave me an inmate rule book and five sets of guard uniforms.

"These inmates are not to be trusted. They are less than human. They are the scum of the earth and that's why society placed them here," Lieutenant Vice adamantly expressed to me. "They are merely caged animals."

I had a problem with what he said and I'm sure he could see it on my face. I saw young black men, my own people, when I looked at those prisoners. Some of them just happened to be victims of circumstance. Many brothas were around my age and were going to either die in prison, or spend most of their natural lives there.

After my training period, I was assigned to the D-Unit with two experienced male guards, so that I could "shadow" them. It was the most dangerous section of the prison. Over 233 extremely violent, dangerous convicts were housed there. I was scared to death, but I couldn't let the inmates know it. This is where being from the hood came in handy. I could relate to them.

I was surprised how kind some of the convicts were toward me, even the white ones. I got the feeling they could sense my apprehension and discomfort.

I made my rounds on the tier of D-Unit. All eyes were on me as I strutted past convicts. I didn't care. If it tamed them and made them happy to see me strut by, so be it. I continued to walk, and saw inmates up ahead quickly disperse. I was on alert and my senses tingled causing the hairs on my neck to stand up. I was determined not to look into the cell, even though I had been trained to do so. I was told some inmates found that disrespectful. I passed a cell and saw that there was blood on the door and floor. I picked up my pace trying to ignore all the convicts playing the wall.

Before I knew it a cell door behind me swung open and a convict ran out with his entire body on fire. Then I saw a hand reach out of the cell and stab a white convict in the face. Instantly, a commotion started like a wild stampede. The dude on fire ran by me, and I rushed back to look in the cell.

"Oh, my God!" I screamed out loud. It felt like a giant fist was squeezing my chest. I couldn't breathe. I couldn't move. I just watched as the other guards descended on the mayhem. There he was, stretched out on the floor in a pool of blood with a painful grimace on his face as his eyes held mine.

It was him. It was my baby daddy. It was Innocent.

# Chapter Thirty-Four

## DEATH ROW
## IC MILLER

I sat alone in a cell. It was my own corner of hell. All around me, the caustic clamor of rage echoed. I was nude, shivering and wet. I had just killed a man in the shower before the guards carried me away kicking and screaming.

The Muslims continued to chant eerily, "Allah is great."

I could feel my body shaking. I was trembling, and goose bumps covered my bareness. My arms and hands were raw and bloody. I was scared, alone, and about to be put to death for a crime I had not committed. And now I had just killed a man.

Down the tier, I could hear someone scream in agony. Terrified, I flinched. I tilted my head to the side, listening.

The Muslims kept chanting. The screams and the torture all resonated on my brain. It echoed around my cell, my steel casket. I realized my heart was pounding in my chest fast. I began to sweat profusely as the confines of the box were suddenly too small. Maybe I was claustrophobic. Maybe I was about to give up my sanity. I felt a scream growing in the back of my throat. I cupped my head in my hands raking my fingers through my nappy hair. I felt like I was on the fringe of lunacy.

I heard someone call my name in a strained whisper. "IC Miller. IC Miller."

I raised my head, listening. It could have been the devil calling my name. I was confused. I got up and trudged over to the cell door to look out on the tier.

Someone called my name again. "IC Miller. IC Miller."

It was the guy in the cell next door. He shoved a mirror out of the cell bars. This allowed him to watch everything happening on the tier.

"They was expecting you," the voice said.

"Whaat?!" I retorted, pressing my face against the bars.

The voice was slightly inaudible, as if whoever it belonged to was talking out the side of his mouth. "The warden and his captain told the cons you was comin' to the row. Said you had raped and murdered some young white child. Then, you attempted to kill a policeman. They said you kilt they dog and assaulted the judge in the courtroom." The voice stopped talking and began to laugh in a dry guffaw.

Absentmindedly, I held on to the bars and shook my head from side to side.

"You's a hell raiser," he spoke again.

"How you know my name and why is the warden and captain after me?"

"I heard the warden tell the white cons you was comin'. He said he was going to give a carton of cigarettes to whoever got to you first and made you they bitch. Him and the captain are just two sick sons of bitches."

"A carton of cigarettes?" I yelled bouncing on my toes, straining to see next door. All I could see was the mirror aimed at the tier.

"Yep. What they can't control, they fear. It fascinates them like death or dying. In your case, it's because you a killa. You haven't noticed? There ain't nothing but killas all around us."

"So why am I being singled out? Why me?" I heard my voice quiver, and I hoped he didn't notice.

"Because this is a sick game to them. The warden and the captain thrive off violence, mayhem, and murder. Kill or be killed, my young brotha."

I pondered over what he said. "What's yo name?"

"They call me Half Dead. I been on death row for three years, six months, two weeks, four days, and about seventeen hours. Twice already they tried to kill me. My execution date is set for next month on the 28th, it's my third one."

"Third one? You got appeals?" Hearing that he was never executed gave me hope.

"Nah." Half Dead got quiet.

There were so many questions I wanted to ask him. There were so many things I wanted to know, needed to know.

The ruckus continued and Half Dead lit a cigarette. The smoke billowed from behind the bars. I got the feeling he was marinating in thoughts with death as the motive.

"What was all that noise about? Why was you being brought in by the SORT Team?"

At first I demurred. I didn't want to tell him what had happened in the shower but I needed somebody I could talk to. I needed somebody I could trust, so I told him everything, including the way the white dude had tried me.

"Aye," Half Dead spoke, "what the white dude look like?"

"Big, crazy-looking white dude. Beady eyes and a big-ass head."

"Daamn!" Half Dead laughed. "You done kilt the warden's boy, Mark Hudson. He a bitch-ass snitch."

I put my hand up to my head in disbelief. I couldn't believe what I had just heard. "They gon' give me mo time for it?"

"Fuck nah, nigga. You ain't on the streets; you on death row. The judge and jury is the warden and his fuckboy captain. They sent him at you and you won fair and square. Same if the cracka would have kilt you. It's a game they playin' wit people's lives man."

"Yeah, it's a game and we ain't winnin'."

"Right," Half Dead interjected, "but the warden and his fuckboy ain't the ones you have to watch out for. It's them damn ABs."

"ABs? What's that?"

"Aryan Brotherhood. It's a white supremacy gang. They da most savage prison gang ever formed. Dude you kilt was part of them. The Dirty White boys and a bunch of mean-ass crackas that put in work on niggas on de regular."

I shook my head in disbelief, taking heed to what Half Dead had said. "Yo, man you got a sheet or sumpin? I ain't got no clothes, no nuttin'."

"Hold up a sec!" Half Dead hollered.

I stood there, nude, pondering my fate. A battery attached to a line of dental floss slid in front of the cell door.

"You see it?"

"See what?"

"The string nigga, pull the string! This is called *fishing*."

"Oh."

I bent down to fish for the string and excruciating pain shot through my body. It felt like at least three of my ribs were cracked or broken. I pulled the line and attached to it was a T-shirt, a pair of new boxers, an *XXL* magazine, and a Snickers bar.

"You got it?"

I took everything off of the line. "Yeah, thanks, man."

Half Dead pulled his line back.

"Yo, I'ma lay down and catch some z's," Half Dead said.

"Aight," I responded, putting on the boxers. I was tired, too. Mentally and physically. I sat on the bunk and fell asleep dreaming about freedom, basketball and my ex-girl, Tamara.

An hour later I was awakened by a big burley guard who stood in front of my cell. His stomach overlapped his pants and he breathed heavily. "You wanna use the phone or what?" he questioned me with an attitude.

"Yes. Yes sir," I replied.

He sat a telephone down and walked off.

I tried to pick up the phone, but the cord was too short.

The guard appeared again. He passed me a tray of food this time, then shouted "Chow time!"

A million angry convicts yelled at the same time, eager to get to their next meal.

I looked at the food on the tray; fried chicken, mashed potatoes, and cornbread. After figuring out how to make the phone work, I sat on the floor and dialed my grandmother's number.

"Hello?" she answered. Her smooth voice was sweet to my ears.

"Hi, Gramma, it's me."

"Oh, God! Oh, God! It's you, my baby! Are you okay?"

I'm fine," I lied.

"Baby, where you at?"

"I'm in Atlanta Federal Prison on death row."

She gasped.

I thought about what them white folks did to my gramma at

my sentencing. My heart hurt for her.

"Oh, Lawd, nooo," she moaned pitifully. She sounded like she was on the verge of tears.

I clasped the phone. "Gramma, I'ma be a'ight."

"Innocent, baby." She called me by my name. She only did that when she really wanted my attention. "Baby, whoever you meet in there that has wronged you in the past, you have to forgive 'em."

"Huh? What you talkin' 'bout, Gramma?"

"Just don't you go get in any mo trouble on account of what happened in the past. Hear me?"

I nodded my head, still uncertain of who or what she was talking about. After hearing her voice, I didn't want to think about it anymore. I just wanted to think about the time we had together and we began to talk in rushed tones of endearment.

I heard loud talking over the phone. "Hold on for a minute, IC," Big Mama told me. "Yo brother wanna talk to you."

"Man, dats fucked up! It's fucked up what dem crackas did!" TC vented boisterously once he got on the phone.

"Don't curse in front of Gramma," I told him.

"Listen bro, if you havin' any problems in there, let them niggas know yo brother is TC, a shot-caller for the Chicago Black Gangstas."

"Look, one of us is already in trouble. We don't need both of us gone. You gotta take care of Gramma—"

He cut me off in mid-sentence. "Nigga, you ain't cut like that to be in the joint. You ain't never had a fight in your life."

If he only knew what I had been through in the past few years—shit, in the last few hours, even.

"You need a lawyer?"

"I'm supposed to get an appeal lawyer."

"Fuck dat! Dem crackas finna give you a college kid lawyer for you to be they guinea pig to practice on. Just like you had that blind-ass muthafucka. What kinda shit was that man? I'ma get you some real lawyers, na'mean? I'ma get you out of prison even if I have to die trying."

The phone beeped ominously indicating we had ten seconds left. A lifetime of communication squeezed into finite moments of time.

We talked in rushed tones until the line went dead. I held the phone in my hand until the dial tone got on my nerves. I banged my head against the bars in frustration. Hostile voices continued to erupt around me. My food sat in front of me, but I still had no appetite. I set the tray on the floor and crawled into my bunk. I attempted to sleep.

In the wee hours of the night, a radio screeched with static from somewhere down the tier. Half-awake, I saw something inch in front of my cell. I focused my eyes and saw that Half Dead had slid me a line. Attached to it was a note. It simply read: "*In the morning watch your back during rec call. Destroy this note.*"

I tore up the written warning and flushed it down the toilet. Lying down on my bunk I closed my eyes, and the images from my psyche began to haunt me. Demons, white faces, blood, carnage, and human wreckage stopped me from sleeping. The cop strangling me, the gun firing in the hospital, the gory blood flashed in front of my eyes. Then I was back in the woods where they had chased me. The police dog and more demons were everywhere. The memories of the judge, the jury, my so-called lawyer and a conviction disturbed me. I thought I'd never get to sleep. Next, I was in the shower drenched in blood. Then everything stopped. Silence hummed like a vacuum. My grandmother's words gnawed at my mind, "You have to forgive 'em."

I wasn't sure what she was talking about. I heard something in my cell, and my mind signaled my body to attention. I realized I was having a nightmare. Was I alone? I looked around my cell and saw no one. Nothing. The noise continued. I looked around until I finally realized the sound was coming from the floor. I looked down and saw a big-ass rat eating out of my tray of food. I threw a magazine at him, and he scurried off with a piece of cornbread in his mouth.

I sat up, wide awake.

I heard Half Dead moving around in his cell. "IC, you awake?"

"Yeah." I heard something hit the floor.

Half Dead threw me a line.

I pulled it, and to my surprise there was a shank attached to it. "Thanks, man."

"Thanks man, my ass. You can't have it nigga unless you intend to use it."

"I intend to." I put it down on my bunk and attempted to go back to sleep, but I couldn't. With thoughts rummaging through my mind, I was awake the rest of the night.

Breakfast came and went. I still wasn't hungry. I paced the cell nervously with the shank in my pants. The guards picked up the breakfast trays, and I could hear them asking the convicts if they wanted rec.

When the guard got to my cell, he shot me a threatening glare. "Bad ass, you goin' to rec this morning?" His question was a challenge.

The entire tier got quiet.

"Yeah, I'm going to rec." I said loud enough for the tier to hear.

The guard smirked at me and walked away. I looked up and saw Captain Turner. He had on brown Dickies and a gray Polo shirt. He was muscular, at about six feet tall, and his eyes were beady and sinister. "You sho you wanna go to rec?" he asked.

I raised my chin and said what my heart was feeling. "Yes!"

"You realize after that white boy accidentally fell and killed himself in the shower, his buddies probably plan to cut you from asshole to appetite," he joked. His mouth smiled and his bugged eyes held mine.

The three redneck guards who were with him laughed.

I thought of what Half Dead had said about the warden being both judge and jury. He had convincingly covered up the murder in the shower.

"You got balls," Captain Turner told me. "The warden wants you released to the compound and so do I. I'm placing all bets on you."

I stood stoic and looked at the guards. The black one was laughing, too. He was a bona fide Uncle Tom.

I felt my blood boil. It's one thing to take abuse from white folks but it was ten times worse from your own kind.

As they laughed, I raged inside. "Why you doin' this, man?" I asked, raising my voice.

"Doin' what? Lettin' you out? It's the warden that wants you released on the compound. Personally, I could give a fuck 'bout 'cha." He grinned and turned around to look at the other guards.

More laughter.

"I ain't talkin' 'bout that," I shot back. "I'm talkin' 'bout you, a black man helpin' these fuckin' crackas!"

The captain flinched and the other guards abruptly stopped laughing. All their faces turned red.

In the next cell I heard Half Dead yell, "Dat boot lickin' ass nigga know what he doin'. He's a fuckin' traitor to his own people for a government job."

Turner walked over to Half Dead's cell. "Oh, I see you got your voice back from all that cryin' and shit you was doing when we had to drag your ass to the chair. Now you wanna act tough."

"Fuck you, nigga!" Half Dead exclaimed.

The guards continued to grill me with their evil eyes.

The captain walked back over to my cell, then pointed a finger at me indignantly. "You better learn how to fuck or fight 'cause no one likes a child rapist and a murderer," he said loud enough for everyone on the tier to hear. He abruptly turned and walked away followed by the guards.

One of the guards took the time to give me the middle finger as he walked away.

I looked him square in the eye, cuffed my nuts and said, "Fuck you!"

The guards yelled, "Dead man walkin'!" as each convict shuffled by my cell fitted in chains. Most of them looked at me with wide eyes. I was able to easily recognize the evil glares from a few white cons.

When the guards got to Half Dead's cell, the sound of leg irons rattling and shackles dragging the floor seemed to heighten my anxiety. I anxiously waited to see the brother that had befriended mem but never judged me.

"Dead man walkin'!" The guards bellowed.

A cell door slammed shut. Half Dead was led by my cell and stopped in front of it. I took one look at him and I leaped away from the bars. His face was grotesquely disfigured and charred. His posture was severely hunched and his hands-damn near touched the ground

"You see what they did to me? Tried to execute me, but I won't die."

"Move it!" the guard barked.

"My nigga, when you hit the compound look for a cat named James. He's yo homie from the Windy." As the guards shoved him away from the bars, Half Dead yelled, "Keep the joint I gave you. Just send me some cigarettes and some trees!"

"I got you! I got you! I got you, Half Dead," I said vehemently. It was something about seeing him like that. Even though he was severely disfigured, he had never given up. Because of that, neither would I.

Moments later a guard was back at my cell. He tossed a bundle of clothes on the floor in front of me.

"Get ready. You're being released to the compound," he barked.

As soon as I put my clothes on my cell door opened.

The guard yelled, "Dead man walkin'!"

# *Chapter Thirty-Five*

Like a zombie in a trance I walked out of C-Unit with my gear in my hand and my mind scattered. My pants were four sizes too big. I tried to hold them up with my hand, while hiding the shank. I was moved to D-Unit. A guard gave me a card with my name and assigned cell on it. The guard opened the steel door, and I walked inside clutching my pants and belongings. The steel door clanged shut behind me and the roar of convicts hollering and moving around had my attention. I tried my best to look hard, not like it was my first time in prison and I didn't have a clue as to what was going on.

I passed a card table full of white dudes with brawny muscles. Their skin was embellished with obscene tattoos. Two of them stood facing me and I inched toward the shank in my pants. They continued to mean-mug me.

I glanced behind me while I ascended the stairs to the second level.

They were still staring.

I walked by a television room full of black inmates yelling loud, watching sports and gambling. Standing in front of the stairs was a tall inmate. He wore pink shorts and a matching halter top. Red lipstick outlined his lips.

"Haaay!" He caroled to me, frantically waving with an

effeminate hand the size of a baseball glove.

I ignored him and kept it moving up the stairs.

The third floor was pretty much the same as the first floor only more congested. Convicts were gambling, shooting dice at one table and playing poker at another. Directly across the unit was a telephone. The guy on the phone was having a heated argument. Queued in line behind him, convicts waited patiently for their turn.

I found my cell. I squeezed by all the inmates standing around and went in. The funk hit me as soon as I stepped inside. Dirty clothes were scattered everywhere. An old black man hunched over a table staggered to his feet, frantically attempting to steady himself. The scene would have been comical had I not noticed the syringe in his arm. "What cha doin' in here?" he stuttered.

"This the cell they assigned me to," I said, looking away.

He furtively turned and removed the needle. He frowned and hobbled over to me pitifully. Perspiration gleamed off of his wrinkled forehead. He was nearly bald with a ring of graying hair at the temples. His skin was mahogany like wrinkled wood. "Damn, I didn't know a bus came in today," he said rubbing his arm.

"It didn't. They released me on the compound from C-Unit, death row."

He removed discarded clothes from the top bunk and patted it with his hand, indicating for me to place my articles there.

"They call me Crip," the man said, introducing himself.

His skin was old, cold and clammy. I also noticed that his eyes were heavily-lidded. He was high off whatever it was he had injected into his arm.

"IC Miller," I said. "I'm from Chicago."

His lip curled into a snare. "You from Chi-town? You got a lot of homies here."

I nodded my head. I made up my bunk with a dingy sheet and an ancient wool blanket that had cigarette burns in it.

"You Vice Lord?"

"Nah."

"Cobra Stone?"

"Nah."

"Black Gangsta?"

"Nah, but my twin brother is a shot-caller for 'em," I told him.

"Youngin', a cat named Chill drives the Chi-town Black Gangsta car," Crip said with a slur.

I climbed up in the bunk. I didn't feel much like talking.

Crip went on to play the name-game. He named dudes on the compound that were from Chicago.

"Where can I find James at?" I asked with interest.

"When we go to chow I'll show you where the Black Gangstas sit. James ain't on count no more, but they still eat together. Cats respect him because he doin' time for murder."

I thought about what he said.

"Youngin', there's so many gangs in here—black, white, Spanish, Dirty White Boys, Latin Kings, Bloods, Crips, GDs," Crip said. "But the worst of 'em all is the warden. Now he's tha real gangsta." An unlit cigarette dangled from his mouth.

"Crip," I called out, "has anyone ever escaped from here?"

He ignored me. There was a hard knock at the cell door that caused us both to flinch. I bolted up on my elbows.

Three dudes walked in. Each one had on a baggy gray sweatsuit and skull caps. I had the feeling some shit was about to pop off.

The leader's name was Gee. He was tall and slim. He was about my height, and he had a dark skin complexion. He had long braids that hung from underneath the black do-rag he wore under his gray skully. Behind him was Meatball and J-Rock. I could tell that they were some grimy, cutthroat niggas. Each one gave me with the screw face, like mayhem was about to happen. They were from DC, the most treacherous dudes in the B.O.P, bar none. They were infamous for robbery, extortion, and for breaking into lockers. At the time, I didn't know that Crip was from DC too. He just didn't associate with his homies because they were grimy. "A nigga know Slim? Let a nigga hold a few bags of dat thang," Gee said with his hand in his pants. He inched closer.

Crip winced like he had a bad toothache. Suddenly, he wasn't high anymore.

"Gee, I ain't got nothing. You know how niggas be lying," Crip said, playing it off with a nervous chuckle.

He struck a match and lit his cigarette. Smoke curled from his nose and mouth like a dragon. The moment pulsed. I eased my hand in my pants for the shank. Meatball, Gee's homie, must have detected my movement because his eyebrows knotted up suspiciously. Meatball had a bad case of acne and dark, ashen, bumpy skin that only a mother could love. He pulled something long out of his sleeve. The other kid just stood looking out the cell window. I got the feeling their actions had been planned.

Gee grabbed Crip around the neck with his hand. "Yo Crip, where dat muthafuckin' dog food at?"

The old man struggled to release himself.

"Hold up, man! Hold up!" I yelled. I had to do something. They all turned to look at me as I climbed off the bunk. My shank was still hidden in my pants. I could feel my legs trembling. I was scared.

The guy, J-Rock, turned around from the door. He pulled out a long ice pick with black tape around the handle. As soon as my feet hit the floor, he was on me. His breath smelled like shit. It was hot on my face and his shank was aimed at my stomach.

Before I knew it, Crip had managed to shove Gee off of him and had pushed him into Meatball. Crip grabbed his shank and I grabbed mine.

"Hold up man! Hold up man!" I heard my voice rise in a brazen cadence of courage.

Meatball grimaced and drew back to stab me.

I continued to speak. "Man, I was just released off death row. I caught a body while I was there. I ain't lookin' fo' no drama, but y'all niggas wrong!" I made eye contact with each man.

"Who de fuck is you?" Gee asked.

"He's a Black Gangsta from Chicago down with Chill and dem niggas. His brother a shot-caller for BG in Chi-town," Crip answered. He threw five bags of dope on the floor. Meatball scooped them up with the quickness.

Gee squinted his eyes and focused on me like he was trying to read my soul.

"You be Black Gangsta, huh?"

I held my chin up and nodded. I felt my heart pounding in my chest and the shank was sweaty in my hand. I could tell they were ready to go get high.

"Get out! Get out!" Crip yelled.

"Dig, Slim, if I finds out you ain't official, I'ma come back and bust that ass, na'mean," Gee threatened.

"Nigga, save the rap. Don't get it twisted. I'm my own man and if you got a problem ain't nothin' between us but air and opportunity, na' mean!" I imitated his threat.

Gee's jawbone clinched tight and Meatball stepped back. This was not what they had expected. The cell door opened again and another dude stuck his head inside. "Dirty White Boys done stabbed a bunch of niggas in the TV room on the first floor. They on a search and destroy mission." Dude left and we all gazed out of the cell. People were rushing around as pandemonium was about to erupt.

The PA system announced, "Lockdown! Lockdown!"

Someone shouted, "Y'all better man up, them white boys slaying niggas downstairs!"

Convicts ran up the stairs with panic-stricken faces. My mind was in a frenzy as people rushed by. I abruptly turned and walked to my cell. I met Crip leaning against the doorframe with a wooden crutch under his arm and a lit cigarette in the corner of his mouth. He looked at my shirt. There was blood on it. "You gotta get rid of that shirt, young'in." He pointed and started to cough violently.

I had no idea how the blood had gotten there. I looked up to see Gee and his homies coming back up the stairs. Whatever was going on down there, they wanted no part of it.

As Gee passed, he gritted on me. It was a silent reminder that our beef was not over. I ripped the bloody shirt off and headed for the trash can outside the cell, but changed my mind when a SORT Team stormed the unit. They were armed with heavy batons, clubs, and big metal flashlights.

Crip flopped onto his bunk, out of breath. Again, the cell door opened. It was the warden.

He spoke almost mockingly. "Generally, convicts are a lot smarter in the sociological realm of this environment. I can see you're making your adjustment here quite well." His eyes slid down to the bloody shirt in my hand. "It's only a matter of time before they find out who you are and what you did, not to mention what you did to one of their own." Abruptly, he turned to walk out of the cell, but he stopped. He snapped his fingers and pointed at me. "Kill On Sight. Dirty White boys three, black boys one." He added as if having a second thought. "When they put you to death, if you don't get killed on the compound first, that counts as a point, too."

Crip sat up on his bunk. "What the fuck was that about? Is there something you ain't tellin' me?"

I shrugged my weary shoulders. I tossed the bloody T-shirt in the trash can. Glancing out the cell window, I saw the warden pointing at our cell. My heart skipped a beat. My legs felt weak as I climbed on my bunk with my shank in my pants.

In an angry tirade, Crip managed to stand on unsteady legs. "Young'in, what de fuck goin' on? Somethin' you ain't tellin' me, boy? What you in prison fo'? If it's something fucked up, I needs ta know!"

I closed my eyes. "Ever since I was a little kid I've been a gifted athlete. Even on the play ground no one could outrun me, jump—"

"What de fuck that gotta do with now?" Crip screeched.

"Hold up, dude."

"Get to the point."

"Okay, listen."

Crip grumbled something under his breath, lit a cigarette, and sighed.

"I was scouted by Georgia State."

"Uh-huh," Crip chirped.

"To make a long story short, on my way to school the police pulled me over and charged me with the rape and murder of a white girl. I got shot and they tricked me into pleading guilty. Said I was going to get ten years probation. They had my grandmother talk me into it." I swallowed the dry lump in my throat as my mind vividly relived the moment in pieces of memory, all of them painful, all of them a hellish nightmare that I still had not awakened from. "I pled guilty and they sentenced me to death. Man, I ain't never been in trouble before in my life." My voice cracked with emotion.

"Dayum, young'in, dats fucked up. You'll probably beat it on appeal, though," Crip drawled.

"You think so?" I asked.

"You better hope so, cause you been convicted of raping a white girl. You in here with this crazy-ass racist warden and all the white supremacy gangs they got runnin' round here; you lucky your brotha a shot-caller for the Black Gangstas. Them crackas gonna be trying to get at you. The Ayran Brotherhood is the most savage gang in the prison, and the warden intentionally keeps more whites in the institution than blacks. Just in case of a race riot, we will lose. That's what that 'Kill On Sight' mission was all about. Probably in retaliation for the AB you killed in the shower. Aryan Brotherhood members are required to kill on sight. In fact, it's part of their initiation. The Dirty White Boys, The Order, a Neo-Nazi group, are a few of the gangs that support the ABs in a badge of honor. Most ABs have the number 666 tattooed on their body. The three sixes represent the mark of the beast, the antichrist, or the son of Satan."

"Dirty White Boys three, black boys one. What does that mean? The warden said it earlier."

"It means three brothas must have got killed in the ABs Kill On Sight mission."

"When they start keeping score?"

"I don't know, but I've got a feeling it started when you arrived, and things are probably gonna get worse."

"You think the ABs know 'bout me?"

"Maybe, maybe not," Crip shrugged his shoulders, "but it's just a matter of time. What you got in your favor is your brother. But still keep yo eye out."

# Chapter Thirty-Six

The next morning I woke up with Crip yelling in my ear like a drill sergeant. "Young'in, when you hear dat door open you better get yo ass up! This the Dead Man Inn. This ain't no Holiday Inn. Now get up. I'ma show you your Chi-town homies, the Black Gangstas."

"I thought we were on lockdown?" I said, still asleep.

"Lockdown around here means long enough to move the bodies and clean up the blood. That is, unless a CO is killed."

I hopped off the bunk, took a quick bird bath, brushed my teeth and bounced. The unit looked like the gutter. I was almost ashamed to be walking with Crip as he hobbled along, pathetically dragging his legs on crutches.

By the time we reached the chow hall, Crip was breathing hard and drenched in sweat. Guards stood like sentries out front. The warden and Captain Turner had positioned themselves in front of the chow hall door. They looked up as I passed. They spoke with the cons, but their eyes stayed on me. The captain folded his arms over his chest.

I had never seen so many people in one confined space. It was filled with mostly Spanish and white cons. A few black faces were scattered throughout. The convicts sat in segregated sections and there wasn't a guard in sight. The noise was so loud I could barely hear Crip talking to me.

"They gonna kill you. A shot to yo dome," I heard someone say.

I turned around to see who had said it, but all I saw was a thick chick with a fat ass, small waist and pretty face. Her large breasts held me captive. She had smooth olive skin; her beige Prada sweat pants matched her complexion. She sashayed by, smelling like something sweet enough to eat. She waved at me. We exchanged amorous glances.

Crip nudged my ribs. "Aye young'in. Aye!"

"Yeah," I answered, watching the chick.

"That's Anthony Fields. We call him Fe Fe."

"Who?" I asked.

Crip nodded toward the thick chick I was eyeballing.

"That's a dude?" I asked, disgusted.

"Yep, she is a *he* and a cold-blooded killer. He killed his lover and everybody else in the house. He also took a razor and sliced his shit clean off. Damn-near bled to death."

"Dayum!" I cringed, grabbing my nuts.

Four big-ass white guys with lots of tattoos and shaved heads walked up. One of them had a Mohawk with a crazy Helter = Skelter look in his eyes. I remembered seeing him standing out in the hall talking to the warden. He intentionally bumped into me. It was four against one. Out the corner of my eye, I noticed Crip ease away from me. I reached into my pants and cuffed my shank. They walked off. I exhaled a deep sigh.

"Come on," Crip said with a nervous smile, "they just a bunch of wannabe ABs." He added, "There they go over there. That's where Chicago and BGs sit."

I got my food and glanced over at the table. They were at least three tables deep, and a lot of them were dressed in BG traditional blue. Their faces were masked with deadly intent.

"The big dude standing at the head of the table, his name is Lobo," Crip informed me. "He's head of security, the enforcer for the BGs."

We neared the table, "Wuz up, Crip?" Lobo said, halting our movement. Four tables of dudes stopped what they were doing and looked at us. Dudes at other tables watched us like vultures, including Gee and his crew.

"This here is IC. He *say* he's from Chicago and his brother is a BG shot-caller." Crip spoke as if I could have been an imposter.

Then he hobbled off.

There were at least forty pairs of eyes watching me.

"Who yo peoples?" Chill asked.

"TC, he a 47$^{th}$ Street Black Gangsta shot-caller all the way to the wild hundreds on the south side." Instantly everyone at the table knew who my brother was; some even stood and gave me dap.

"Now I remember yo young ass. You de kid they used to bet on in those high school games. I heard 'bout 'cha. You the little homie fo-reel."

Chill offered me a place to sit down and someone passed me a plate filled with fried fish and macaroni and cheese. I threw down. Talking with my mouth full, I told them about how I had been framed, convicted, and sentenced to death. I explained how I had killed a white dude in the shower. They all looked at me, eager to hear my story. I told them about how the warden seemed to have a personal vendetta against me. To my surprise, they all laughed at my naivety.

"Cracka probably mad 'cause you killed one of his flunky AB snitches. We heard the big rat had got killed, but, damn, you did it?" Chill said in a booming voice as he pointed at me.

Everyone erupted in laughter.

I held my head proud. If they only knew, that white man had tried to rape me in the shower and I had killed him accidentally, out of fear.

Milkman, the only white boy at the table, changed the subject. His corn silk, blond hair and blue eyes made him almost look like a college student, except for the two tear drops tattoos under his right eye and the brawny muscles bulging under his shirt.

"I lived at 48$^{th}$ and Calumet and went to Englewood High School," he told me.

I thought for a second, remembering a white family that had lived in the last building on the block. One of the children was a pretty mulatto girl, and the rest were white.

"You got a little sister named Marie?"

Milkman smiled. "Yep."

"Man, I remember you!" I blurted out as it suddenly dawned on me who he was. They never had no electricity or running water in the big abandoned building they lived in. I had once helped his little sister and his crack addict mother tote water into the old building that was they lived in. I continued to eat and talk, but something told me to take a casual glance behind me.

Lobo knocked over a table and pulled out a shank as long as a sword.

"Oh shit!" I jumped up.

At least a hundred white cons ran up on us. Milkman shoved me to the side and everyone in the section stood. Tables and chairs scattered across the floor. The white clique made a path. Suspense lulled and the rest of the convicts looked on.

"Hold the fuck up right there!" Lobo shouted, aiming his shank and taking a step forward.

There wasn't a guard in sight.

I looked over at the other tables.

The Crips, Bloods, DC Crew, M-13, and Latin Kings were all watching.

The AB's leader was Lugar. He had a tattoo of the Grim Reaper on the back of his head. He wore a green army coat, combat boots, and tiny rimmed spectacles that made him look sinister. He stood with his hands clasped together. On his index finger was a large silver skull and bone ring. "666" was tattooed on his knuckles with a clover on his hand–the insignia of the Aryan Brotherhood. Standing next to him was someone I recognized Bruce Sinclair. He whispered something in Lugar's ear.

"Yo! Chill! We need to talk!" Lugar's voice boomed brusquely.

"Why de fuck you bring the whole fuckin' clan wit you just to talk?" Lobo asked.

Chill stepped into the chaos. Out of respect, he held his shank at his side and silenced Lobo with a wave of his hand, leaving little doubt he was the driver of the Black Gangstas. "You bring all them muthafuckas with you to talk?" Chill inquired with fury.

"Better to talk now instead of dying later," Lugar responded. As he spoke, more and more white convicts walked over to join him. I just stood there trying to understand what the fuck Bruce was doing.

"I need to talk to you about *him*." Lugar pointed at me.

"Me?" I retorted.

Lugar ignored me.

"First off, as you personally know, I'm always ready for dying or killing. Second, if you got something to say, say it now!" Chill said acidly.

"In private, me and you," Lugar said. "All y'all move de fuck back!" He waved the shank making a path for himself and Chill.

The two of them walked off.

The chow hall had taken on an eerie quietness. I glanced over at Gee and his DC homies. They were clocking our every move. I looked at Bruce. He gave me an evil scowl. I glanced back over in Chill and Lugar's direction. For some reason, Chill was doing most of the listening.

Milkman whispered to me, "If Chill strikes dude and shit pop off, it's gonna get ugly in here fast."

I knew what he meant.

Moments later, Chill returned and the tables turned.

# Chapter Thirty-Seven

We sat back down and huddled around the tables waiting for Chill to speak. He took a deep breath and exhaled. He looked at me and then spoke. His words came hard like a slap across my face. "Nigga, you didn't tell me you was convicted of raping and murdering a little white girl."

"I told you they set me up!" I raised my voice in defense.

"Yeah, but you pled guilty." "They tricked me into that shit, man!" I shot back.

Chill shook his head dismissively and continued. "Lugar says you crept Mark Hudson in the shower when he had his back turned. He said that's how you were able to kill him."

"Man, that's a lie!" I said honestly, searching the faces of everyone at the table in hopes they'd believe me.

Chill leaned forward in his chair. "Lugar said the only reason you killed Mark in the shower is because he had threatened to expose you to everyone. He said that you are a snitch working for Captain Turner and the only reason they let you off death row into the compound is to infiltrate us."

"Whaat!? Snitch? Infiltrate?" I noticed a few of them slide their chairs away from me like I was contaminated.

Chill gave me a blank stare. "Nah man, you got a bad bone on you. Even though your brother, TC, is a high ranking BG in the organization on the streets, a nigga respects dat to de fullest but dis de chain gang and I can't risk going to war over you."

"Chill, I think we should vote on this," Milkman cut in.

"Vote on what? This nigga pled guilty to raping and murdering a child and now he's suspected of being a snitch? I can't take a chance on harboring a fuckin' rat!"

I stood with lightning quickness, knocking over a chair. "Nigga, you got me fucked up!"

"Nah, but I can have you fucked up, bitch-ass nigga. Keep runnin' yo muthafuckin mouth!"

"Chill out!" Milkman hissed.

Lobo was all up in my grill, his chest bumping mine. "Nigga, you betta sit yo ass down!"

I didn't budge or move.

Lobo shoved me toward the door. My first instinct was to swing on him.

"Nigga, just chill out," Lobo whispered, sensing my distress. He continued shoving me toward the door.

Chill and I exchanged hateful stares.

Chill yelled loud enough for everyone to hear. "Hot-ass nigga! You need to check in 'cause Black Gangstas ain't protecting yo child-rapin' ass."

I flinched and stopped in my tracks. I turned and started to go back until I saw Gee and his homies watching me. I had been thrown to the wolves.

# Chapter Thirty-Eight

I walked outside the chow hall with a heavy heart and a shank in my pants pocket. I looked up to see a platoon of guards headed straight for me. I walked toward them, head-on. I welcomed the encounter, hoping they would lock me up.

They passed by, but gave me the evil eye and barely enough space to walk by.

I slowly walked to my unit taking special notice of all the grimy white cons that loitered around my cell. Back in my cell Crip sat at the desk in front of a skinny window. A beacon of sunlight shone across his withered face; a syringe was plunged into his arm, which was tied off with a belt.

He gazed up at me. His right leg twitched uncontrollably and he spoke in a slurred voice. "Slim, you gon' hav'ta find you another cell. You too much trouble. They gon' come get you." Crip went into a perpetual nod.

"I ain't goin' no fuckin' where!"

Crip's eyes popped open and a smile tugged at his mouth. He spoke lethargic words and spit them at me. "All you got left, young'in, is your fuckin' balls and your manhood. You fight for what you believe in or die tryin'! No compromise. Never! You hear me boy?"

I nodded my head somberly, staring at the spike in his arm.

Scarlet blood stained the floor. Crip looked down at his arm. Realizing his blunder, he turned away from me.

"Damn, I'm high as a muhfuh ..." he drawled. Removing the syringe and the belt from his arm, Crip began to rub his aging bicep.

There was a sharp rap on the door.

I looked up to see Gee with his two hoodlum homies. They entered the cell. True to his word, Gee had returned.

"Wuz up?" I said courageously with all the bravado I could muster. I eased my hand into my pocket for my shank.

Crip slid his chair away from me.

"Nigga, you know what's up. Dem niggas ain't fuckin' wit 'cha and now we know why." Gee crept closer and eased the shank out of his sleeve. "Nigga, didn't I tell you I was gonna come back and holla at yo ass?"

I took a step back, bracing myself. I needed to get the shank out of my pocket and stab him first. He had me cornered against the wall. I had to do something fast.

Just then the door opened wide. Gee turned his head for a fleeting moment. I was about to stab him when a muscular build intimidatingly filled the doorway. It was Lobo.

He spoke in a deep baritone. "What's up lil' homie? Y'all 'bout to have a party without me? What's up Gee, Meatball, J-Rock, where's the party?" He bumped into Gee and his flunkies as he made his way into the cell.

Milkman was behind him. He stepped onto the toilet seat to get a better view. An older dude, who looked just as intimidating, followed. Crip sat back in the chair with heavy eyes. He was determined not to nod off. With a raised brow Lobo asked, "It take all y'all niggas to step to dude?"

"I just came to get something straightened out," Gee answered.

"Well, did you get what you came here for?" I retorted, taking the shank out of my pocket. I was suddenly feeling emboldened by the hometeam presence.

Gee shrugged his shoulders. "Let me get the fuck outta here!" he snorted angrily.

Lobo stood, still blocking their path.

Gee took one last look at me. He placed his shank in his sleeve and brushed by Lobo. The other two followed.

"I'ma holla at you later, slim." He tossed words over his

shoulders.

"Holla at me now, nigga!" I challenged.

He was gone and the cell door slammed after his departure. Lobo turned and faced me. "Yo, Pop, give us a second to holla at dude," Lobo said to Crip.

Crip gimped out the door.

Milkman hopped off the toilet, causing metal to cling. He must have been strapped with several weapons under his hoodie. I was still trying to figure out where they got all their gear. I never knew cats in prison dressed like cats on the streets. The door opened again and a dude with a patch over his right eye and a deep cut chiseled into his forehead dipped his head inside the door. "Lobo, you want us to stay or go?"

"Go," Lobo commanded with a wave of his hand. At least a half dozen BGs had been posted up outside my cell door.

"Lucky for you I peeped the move with Gee and them grimy DC niggas. They planned on punishing yo ass."

I ran my fingers through my hair in frustration. The shank was still in my right hand. "This shit is crazy man! This nigga, Chill, put me on blast, calling me hot. Now everybody thinks I'm a rat. He gon' believe that fuckin' cracka over me?"

"Yep," Lobo answered matter-of-factly. He continued. "Chill don't have much choice, either that or go to war with the ABs. Lately the warden has been shippin' all the blacks out, moving in hardcore white dudes from other maximum security penitentiaries. That's why they outnumber us three to one. With you killin' that bad ass, to save face, they sayin' you crept him in the shower. We all know Mark was the warden's personal henchman."

"Well, if y'all know that, why won't y'all help me?"

Lobo rolled his shoulders. "If you were Chill calling shots for the entire BGs on the compound, would you go to war over a dude that was a convicted child rapist and was sentenced to die, when every day your crew is shrinking and the enemy is growing?"

Lobo had a point. I looked over at Milkman and the dude standing next to him. I searched their eyes for a solution.

Milkman spoke in a soft, polite tone. "Your brother, TC, that's my nigga for life. He saved my life one time when some Cobra Stones had me cornered. I had got shot up pretty bad. They caught me slippin', coming out a chick's crib. Your brother drove up, shot up the spot. He damn-near got kilt tryna save my ass. He took me to the hospital. I still almost bled to death. He saved my life, and dude was only fifteen. Now you here and y'all look identical. You da homie and I got yo back."

"It's the warden and the captain that are after me—"

"It ain't just you," Lobo interjected.

"Oh, yeah, this here is the homie, James," Milkman said, introducing the older dude that had been standing idly by.

James stepped forward. He was slim with long, wiry arms and he was about my height. His short wavy hair was sprinkled with gray. He smiled pleasantly at me, then shook my hand. "I know your entire family, Big Mama, TC, Uncle Dough," he said, giving me a light hug.

Lobo commented, "James used to be Black Gangsta. He retired at forty. He ain't on count no mo, but he still respected as Black Gangsta."

This was the dude Half Dead had said to holla at once I hit the compound.

"Oh, shit!" Lobo exclaimed, looking out the cell window.

We all turned to look. The warden, Lieutenant Vice, and several guards were heading straight for my cell.

"Out! Everybody out! Now!" Lieutenant Vice yelled.

We were all lined up on the wall. The warden walked over and stood behind me.

"You make friends fast, Inmate Miller," he said sarcastically. Then he looked at the guard. "Search 'em."

The guard searched Milkman and pulled not one, but three shanks from his pants leg. The guard blew his whistle. Next, they searched Lobo. He had a shank on him longer than Milkman's. They found a shank in James's sock and one in my pocket. They handcuffed us all.

The warden called out, "Remove the handcuffs from Inmate Miller."

Both Lobo and Milkman cut their eyes at me suspiciously.

The guard shoved Lobo, "Walk, boy."

Lobo resisted. He turned around and glared at me. "I try 'ta help you and you set me up!"

I was dumfounded. I stood there embarrassed and ashamed.

The mumbling of angry voices rose like a tidal wave in my ears. I looked to the next tier and saw Chill talking to Gee and his crew. My heart slammed against my rib cage. I walked back into the cell and turned the light off. "God, pleeze help me." I muttered a prayer out loud to a God that had long ago abandoned me.

# Chapter Thirty-Nine

Crip walked in the cell and snapped on the light.

"Turn it off," I said.

He hit the switch.

"You need to find you another cellmate, young'in," Crip said timidly.

"Nah, I need a knife."

"Young'in, you shouldn't have let the warden play you like that. By letting you go and taking Lobo n' 'em to the hole, it makes you look like a snitch. That ain't a good look."

"What the fuck was I suppose ta do?" my voice screeched.

"Bitch-slap him. Kick him in his ass. Something! In the chain gang all a man got left is his reputation and his muthafuckin' balls. Once they take that you ain't got shit left to live for young'in'."

I turned away from Crip, agitated and frustrated. I ran my fingers through my nappy hair. I peeped out the cell door window again. Lugar and several of his AB buddies congregated around a water fountain. They were talking to Gee.

"Crip, pah-leez, man. I need a knife!"

"A shank is the last thing you need. What you think, I'm stupid? You gon' get me locked up to, so you can have the cell and lower bunk."

"Look!" I pointed.

He looked out the window. "Oh, shit!" he grumbled moving away from the door.

Gee walked up, shielding his hand against the light. He peeked inside the cell and walked in with his goons. With a flick of a switch the light flooded the cell. "I thought we told ya ta get this 'bama outta yo cell," Gee said brusquely.

"I tried! I tried, but he won't go," Crip whined.

Gee stepped closer.

I looked around for something to pick up and swing.

Meatball said, "Crip, nigga, just because you the homie don't mean you can't get it too!" He walked up on the old man and punched him in the face.

Crip fell to the floor and blood spewed from his nose.

"Slim, your war daddy locked up. You was rappin' real slick shit the last time I was here. Waz up wit dat?"

"I ain't looking for no problems," my voice squeaked. I was scared.

Crip began to moan pitifully.

Gee pulled out a 12-inch shank. "Nigga, I know you the warden's boy. I know you got punk in your blood and you new in de system," he hissed. He stepped closer to me. "I know you need a war daddy, somebody to give you a second chance." He pressed the tip of his shank against my throat. "Ain't that right?" he whispered.

I swallowed the tight lump in my throat. "What do you want from me?" I brazenly asked through fear.

"What do I want from you?" Gee said in a sing-song voice. "I'll tell you." He looked at me, "Nigga you gon' suck all our dicks and give us a shot of ass or I'ma stick yo bitch ass so many times it's gonna take a shovel to clean yo ass up off the floor. You hear me?" Gee pressed the blade harder against my throat.

I felt something warm trickle down my neck.

Gee unfastened his pants. Taking his dick out, he began to stroke himself. "Niggas, what you waiting on? Take them pants off!" he shouted at Meatball and J-Rock. Gee removed the knife from my throat and reached down to pull my pants off.

After Gee touched me, I swung so hard that Gee fell backward. Then I followed up with a wild right hook with my eyes closed. The contact was so hard that I heard the bones in his face shatter. Gee dropped his shank and it slid across the floor. Gee's knees buckled. I shoved him off me.

Meatball lunged at me with his shank in his hand. He reached over and stabbed me twice savagely hacking into my flesh and bone.

I felt stabs of pain explode in my chest and shoulder. With all the strength I had, I shoved Gee into Meatball.

They stumbled out the door.

I looked down at my shirt. I was leaking blood. I picked Gee's shank up off the floor and rushed through the door. Niggas gave me distance. "I ain't no muthafuckin' snitch! I ain't nobody's rat! These crackas gave me a death sentence. I'll die first before I let one of you fuck-ass-niggas or crackas try me. You gotta bring some ass to get some ass and I ain't got shit to lose!"

The entire unit looked at me in disbelief.

An old dude named Big Red walked up within five feet of me. "Why you hollering, slim? What, you tryin to do, make a check in move? If you tryin' ta make it happen, just walk yo ass over there and step inside the TV room and give my dude Gee a headup fight."

"Nigga, it didn't start in the TV room when them fuck niggas came in my cell wit dat bullshit!" Lugar and Bruce stood at a safe distance.

On the far side of the unit Gee's homies had him propped up against the wall. There was blood everywhere.

Lugar turned away and whispered to Bruce.

A wave of nausea consumed me. I saw blood oozing from the hole in my shirt. I stumbled inside the cell.

Crip tried to help support me but he wasn't strong enough.

I pulled away.

Meatball came to the cell door.

I waved his homeboy's shank. "Come in, fuckboy!" I challeged.

He laughed.

I glanced over at Crip. His nose was severely broken. Blood formed around his nostrils and top lip. I looked down at my chest and could see bone and blood. I began to pant. My body felt like it was on fire.

"Shit, man! Shit, man!" Crip lamented. "We gotta get you to a hospital. You can't die in here!"

"I'ma be alright," I croaked dryly.

"Listen, slim," he whispered, "I'm goin' to find the CO and tell 'em you cut up bad. You can't die in here."

"Fuck that! Didn't you say all a man got in prison is his balls?"

The cell door opened and in walked Gee and Meatball. Gee had a long metal pipe in his hand. "Pussy nigga, you right. You ain't gotta go to the TV room. Let's handle it right here!" Gee said loud enough for everyone to hear.

Crip gimped to the other side of the cell.

I struggled to hold the shank. I was faint, fatigued, and seeing stars.

Gee lowered his voice, "Gimme back my joint and check in, bama. Don't be no fool!" His jaw was disfigured. He inched closer and swung the pipe. It whistled toward my head. I ducked in the nick of time causing the pipe to collide with my hand. Pain exploded through my body. I jabbed at him with the shank and missed. The shank fell to the floor.

Gee reached back to swing and Meatball lunged forward simultaneously. They bumped into each other.

I made a futile attempt to kick.

We heard someone shout outside the cell, "CO comin', pull up!"

"I'll be back nigga," Gee yelled.

I reached down and picked up the shank off the floor. "And I'll be waiting on you when you come back." I retorted.

The cell door closed. I leaned against the wall. My hand was throbbing and my chest was hurting.

Crip was whimpering.

With a quickness, the door opened. Someone threw something at me.

I ducked.

The liquid doused Crip's body. The scent was familiar.

"Gasoline!"

In the backdrop I saw Bruce and Lugar. One of them tossed in a match.

Flames roared throughout the cell.

Crip screamed in agony. His entire body was aflame.

I had to do something, and quick. Reacting on survival mode and instincts I kicked Crip in his ass pushing him out the door. Crip ran.

Weary and depleted I stumbled back into the cell, fell against the wall and slid to the floor.

I was delirious. My eyes opened and closed. I began to loose consciousness. I opened my eyes one more time and the most beautiful, angelic face I'd ever seen stood before me.

It was Tamara. She was my guardian angel.

# Chapter Forty

I pushed my body alarm and radioed for help.

Staff arrived in herds. A fire extinguisher had been used to stop the old man from burning but it was too late. His lifeless body laid in the middle of the unit, still smoldering. Guards and medics frantically worked on the convict. I directed the medics to Innocent's cell.

The warden, captain, and Lieutenant Vice arrived with more staff. They all looked around at the bleeding bodies covering the floor.

They all stormed toward me.

"What the hell happened here?" the warden asked, outraged.

I took a timid step forward, cleared my throat and spoke in my most professional tone. "While I was making my rounds I observed an inmate run past me on fire. Upon further inspection, I noticed another inmate." I pointed. "I was bleeding badly. That's when I looked into the cell and saw this inmate on the floor in a puddle of blood. I immediately pushed my body alarm, called for help, and secured the inmates back into their cells."

The warden turned and looked at the bodies. Innocent was escorted out of the cell. He was bloody as hell, languid, and weary; but he was still alive. The prison medics placed him on a steel stretcher.

The warden turned to me. "You saw him stab one inmate and set another on fire?"

"I didn't see anything," I replied.

"Yes, you did. I want a report on my desk by the end of your shift. Lieutenant Vice will be by to talk with you. Is that understood?"

"Okay."

The warden and Lieutenant Vice stalked off.

Captain Turner lingered behind. He stared at me. "That inmate, IC Miller, is a fuckin' beast. Sho gon' make my job interesting. Nowadays, I can't wait to come to work. It's too bad though cause in a month or two, they gon' kill his ass." He chuckled and meandered off.

The warden yelled at the medics. "Take him off that stretcher. Put his ass in chains. He can walk to the prison hospital."

The guards shackled and chained him.

I turned and walked away. At the time I didn't realize it but my eyes were filled with tears. At the station I tried to write the report for the warden, but I couldn't tell the lie he wanted me to tell.

In walked Lieutenant Vice with a lit cigarette dangling from his thin lips. He snarled. "You are to write a shot on Inmate Miller charging him with arson, two counts of assault with a deadly weapon, murder and possession of a weapon."

"But I didn't see anything," I said vehemently, placing my pen down.

"It doesn't matter what you saw. This is how we do things around here. This inmate is a child rapist and murderer sentenced to death. When the appeals court hears his case the warden wants this on his record to make sure they execute him. Understood?"

My jawbone clinched tightly as I spoke. "No, I don't understand and I am not going to lie on him for you. Understood?" I shot back at him with my lips bunched up and pushed to the side of my face: ghetto malevolence.

Vice's bushy eyebrows gnarled. He took a step forward and placed his hands on the desk. I could see dirt caked under his fingernails.

"Listen here, Ms. Jenkins, your conduct will not be tolerated. Let me remind you, you are still on probation and just as I hired you I can easily fire you. Either you write the fuckin' shot or you're fired."

I hopped up from the desk, but before I could speak, Vice continued. "You are to immediately write the shot and go hand-deliver it to the SHU where Inmate Miller is being housed. If anyone asks you, tell them these are my orders. I sent you!"

I looked at him with contempt.

"Write the fuckin' shot and go!" Vice shouted like a lunatic.

I nodded and sat back down to write.

The SHU building housed the maximum solitary confinement, the PC, or Protective Custody, as well as the psychiatric ward. I approached the SHU and I looked inside the booth.

A pudgy, black man with thick bifocals, sagging chins, and a mane of ridiculously unruly red hair with a rather large bald spot on the top, barked at me. "What do you want?"

"Uhm, I'm here to investigate a discipline report on IC Miller. I need him placed in the interrogation cell so that Lieutenant Vice and I can question him." I waved a blank discipline report like I was all business.

"Where is the Lieutenant? Why is he not here with you?" he asked annoyingly.

My heart pounded in my chest. "He, he told me if anyone asked to tell them these are his orders."

"Okay, hold up a second and let me give him a call." He picked up the phone and began to dial.

"Fuck!" I scuffed.

"What did you say?" Pudgy asked, stopping mid dial.

"Nuttin', nuttin'," I muttered, panic-stricken. My mind switched gears into overdrive as I strutted up and looked into the booth.

He stopped. He held the phone up to his ear and looked at me.

"Hey, can you help me? As you can see, I'm kinda new 'round here."

He continued to look at me. I unbuttoned two buttons on my uniform shirt and reached inside like I was having trouble adjusting my bra strap. His thick glasses began to fog up. I continued to tease him with my brown breasts.

"Ooph, damn," he moaned.

One of my supple breasts almost slipped out of the bra cup. I smiled flirtatiously. Finally, I got the strap adjusted and looked at him in mock embarrassment.

He put the phone back on the cradle and opened the door.

"Make it quick," he said.

I smiled and sashayed through the door. "Thank you." I adjusted myself and walked down the tier. A stench assaulted my nostrils making me cover my mouth fighting the urge to vomit.

"I want to talk to you when you come back," the guard called after me.

"Okay, boo," I teased.

I headed toward the Interrogation Cells. Convicts began hooting and hollering at me. I pretended I did not hear them.

An electric snap gave way to a buzz. "Go in," Pudgy announced.

I walked inside the cell. It smelled like old disinfectant and dried semen. There were two dilapidated chairs, a desk with a gray typewriter, and several law books strewn about. I took a seat and waited for Innocent to be brought in. My nerves were on edge. After all, this was the man who had walked out on me and his unborn child when I was only fifteen years old. I didn't know whether to be pissed or happy to see him.

A few minutes later, Innocent was escorted in by two white guards. He looked horrible.

"Do you want us to stay?" one of the guards asked.

"No," I replied. "I'll be fine."

The guards chained Innocent to a steel rod on the wall.

"Radio me when you're finished." They left.

We sat stewing in stifling silence. My heart pounded in my chest.

Innocent looked over at me and spoke first. "At first I thought you were an illusion. I thought I was dreaming or that I had died and went to heaven. What are you doing here? You're a prison guard?"

I looked at him. "You look horrible." I had to get that off my chest. "I should be asking you that question. You were charged with rape and murder—*of a white girl*? What, black pussy wasn't good enough for you when you ran off and left me pregnant with your child?" I said acidly.

"Tamara, I swear ta God, I ain't do that shit! They set me up." His voice was quivering. He coughed violently, and his body shook.

"What happened? Tell me everything." I walked over to him and stood inches from his face. "A real nigga handles his business, but you got me pregnant, gave me a disease, and ran off. You left me with a child that didn't ask to be here. Now you want me to help you? Shit!" I hissed through clinched teeth. My fists were balled tight at my sides.

"Tam, I don't know why. I don't know why I left you and our child. I guess I wanted a better life. I wanted to go to college. I wanted to make something of my life. I had to get out the ghetto. Tam, I'm sorry." He reached out with the arm that wasn't chained to the steel rod and grabbed my wrist. "Baby, I need for you to get my court transcripts and the DNA test. The nurse from Douglasville, Georgia's name is Desiree Harvey. She'll testify that they tortured a confession out of me. My brother is coming to Atlanta to get me a lawyer. I'ma tell him to find you. Tamara, baby, we gonna beat this case. We gonna be together again, you, me and the baby."

"No. No," I said shaking my head. "I can't forgive you. I can't forget!" I said.

He looked up at me.

"Now you fucked up and you expect me to risk my job to help you? What about me and my son? You never helped us. You have no idea what I had to do just to survive. We needed you!" I said.

"Baby, I'm sorry," he groaned, pulling me closer. He placed his forehead on my stomach.

I felt his heat and inhaled his pungent scent.

"Tam, sweetheart, you said I had a son. What's his name?" Innocent asked.

"*My* son's name is Tyres, and as far as I am concerned his father is dead." I moved away from him.

Innocent frowned.

I continued. "Inmate IC Miller you are to address me at all times as Officer Jenkins. Is that understood?"

He looked stunned.

"Now, I am not going to submit the discipline write-up. Innocent, we make choices in life. You made a choice that you didn't want to have nothing to do with me or your child, so the choice you made, you're going to have to live with, or die with it. I promise you, nigga, you'll never see your child!" I turned my back on him.

"Tamara, I ain't kill nobody. But they intend to kill me, execute me for a crime I didn't commit." Innocent began to pant as he struggled to talk.

It took everything in my power not to turn around and hold

him in my arms.

"Any day now they're going to hand down a ruling on my case. Please, get the court transcripts and get in contact with Nurse Harvey and my brother. You two have always been cool."

I glanced over my shoulder. Innocent was bent over and fresh blood dripped off his elbow. "The warden and the captain been out to get me, making bets against me. It's because of them that I killed a man in the shower." Innocent began to cough. He spat blood on the floor.

My hands trembled. "Interrogation cell to confinement duty officer, Inmate Miller is ready to be taken back to his cell."

"Ten-four, I'm on my way," a baritone voice responded.

I turned around. I didn't want to face Innocent.

The cell door opened with an electric snap and the guards walked in.

"Take the inmate to the infirmary. He needs immediate medical attention."

One of the guards looked at me with a raised brow.

"These are Lieutenant Vice's orders," I lied convincingly. I watched them take Innocent away.

"I ain't kill nobody, but they gonna kill me if you let 'em," Innocent yelled as they shoved him out of the cell. He looked back at me.

On my way out I gave Pudgy a fake phone number and pouted like I would be really disappointed if he didn't call me. After blowing his ugly ass a big kiss I bounced to the records department. "Can I get IC Miller's file. Also I need his court transcripts."

# Chapter Forty-One

At three o'clock I left work an emotional wreck. My hands trembled so badly I could hardly get my key into the ignition. Guards continued to picket with their signs and a news van was parked in front of the prison.

Innocent's pleas for help rang in my ears. I drove through traffic clutching the steering wheel so tightly that my knuckles turned white. I pulled into the driveway and parked next to Kanisha's Ferrari. I had Innocent's transcripts and prison file tucked in my bag. I ran to the front door, but couldn't find my keys so I had to ring the doorbell.

Ebonyze pulled the door open. Her smile died when she recognized me.

I stalked past her.

She slammed the door shut behind me.

"I'ma take a shower. I'll be back in 'bout an hour," I said to Kanisha, who had come into the room from the kitchen.

She glanced at her watch and folded her arms over her breasts impatiently.

I walked up the stairs, tired from a bad day at work. After my bath I dabbed on a touch of perfume and put on my sexy nightie. I rolled up a blunt and puffed on it while I did my hair and makeup in the mirror. I looked in the mirror and Innocent's face appeared. He was the boy I used to love. "Fuck 'im!" I cursed and closed my eyes to erase the bittersweet memories. I got up with the smoldering blunt burning between my fingers and stared at Innocent's court transcript on the bed. I began to pace the room back and forth. "Think. Think. Think," I said out loud. "Nurse Harvey! Innocent told me to get in contact with some chick named Desiree Harvey."

I picked up the phone and dialed information for Douglasville, Georgia. The operator gave me three families listed under D. Harvey. I dialed the first two numbers and was rudely informed that I had the wrong number. On the third call I was starting to feel like I was on a wild goose chase. The phone rang with no answer. "Fuck it!" I scoffed. I was about to hang up when someone answered.

"Hello?"

"Uh, may I speak to Ms. Desiree Harvey?"

"This is she," an amicable reply came.

"Uhm, I'm calling in regard to IC Miller. I'm his baby's mama. Uh, I mean he's my baby's daddy," I said stumbling over my words.

"Thank God! Thank God!"

I felt the hairs on the back of my neck stand up and a chill raced through my body.

"That boy ain't kill nobody. They set him up. I saw it with my own eyes and tried to help him. I even took the witness stand for that boy. They retaliated by killing my son and they burnt down my home."

I sat on the edge of the bed with my heart thumping against my ribcage. The transcript fell on the floor scattering everywhere. "Ma'am, what are you talkin' about?" I asked softly while cupping my forehead in my hand squeezing my temples hard.

"I'm talking about the boy from the hospital. Thank God you called. I've been praying so hard for him. He ain't kill nobody! You hear me?"

I nodded my head.

Nurse Harvey continued. "God don't like ugly! Just recently there was a big scandal here with that ole crooked judge, the courthouse, and the jail."

"Scandal? Courthouse?" I interrupted.

"Yes, Lawd and it's something awful."

"What?"

"Bubba Ray, the police officer that IC paralyzed—"

"Paralyzed! Innocent paralyzed a cop?"

"Innocent? Who is that?"

"IC is Innocent," I told her.

"Oh. No, no, it was by accident. The cop had been harassing him. Even Dr. Ferguson testified witnessing that," Ms. Harvey sighed. "One day he had enough of the cop's harassment. They struggled over the gun, it discharged, and the cop was shot in the neck. But the child is innocent. I tell you that boy is innocent."

# Chapter Forty-Two

After I got off the phone, my mind twirled with the daunting possibilities. What could I do to help?

I heard the doorbell ring and decided to go downstairs to make some money. I took two more deep tokes off the blunt, one last look in the mirror, then left my room. I strutted like I was a supermodel, but as soon as I took my first step down the stairs, my heel turned and I tripped. Sliding all the way down the staircase, I was certain that I had broken something. I heard the Korean chick laugh out loud, and someone else giggle. I tried to play it off by getting up like nothing had happened, but it hurt like hell.

Kanisha sucked her teeth as she walked up on me. "What the fuck was that?" She suppressed a laugh.

I ignored her and watched Ebonyze stroll to the door. That bitch got there before me. I bumped into Kim and cut my eyes at her. "Biiitch!" I muttered under my breath.

Her brow gathered with alarm and she took a hesitant step away from me.

Ebonyze opened the door, "Oh, my God!" she clamored in a fitful frenzy.

I craned my neck to look past the girls, toward the door.

"Oh, shit!" I got excited, too. Dude was a serious rapper with lots of cheddar.

He strolled in and looked around. I could feel my heart pounding in my chest as he strolled in examining each girl. Kanisha welcomed him. "Welcome to the Meat Market." She smiled.

He walked in front of us girls and stalled in front of Carmen. They exchanged sex faces. She moaned when he pulled her royal blue sarong to the side exposing her breasts. He finally moved on to the next girl, Amanda. She sucked in rows of fat. Her chubby cheeks were flushed red. He moved along to Kim. At first look, dude's eyebrows shot up. Then he stepped closer and she opened her robe to show him her curvy body. He stifled a groan and caressed himself wantonly.

Kanisha continued talking, "Our models are available for your video shoots."

Dude ignored her babbling and reached out to Kim's nipples. He rolled each one between his forefinger and thumb.

She purred for him.

He was attracted to the Korean beauty. "Yeah, I'm gonna use one of these chicks for my lead model in my next video," dude confirmed.

I knew I had to do something and fast. I bumped into Kim and nudged her out the way. I let my nightie glide to the floor. I held him captive like a snake charmer. I peeled off my bra and tossed it in his face.

Kanisha gasped in horror. "Oh, my God."

Standing nude, I hit him with a sexy pose. I put my hands on my wide hips and turned around. I bent over and jiggled my ass. I made it bounce and clap. I wasn't going to let this nigga get away.

Kanisha had her fingernails in her mouth.

I saw the rapper smile. He grabbed my hand. "Damn, ma! You got skills and you killing 'em with the green eyes and the ill-ass body. If these chicks is dimes, you gotta be a quarter!" he exclaimed excitedly with a heavy New York accent.

I blushed and smiled from ear to ear. "You like?"

"Will that be cash or credit?" Kanisha asked anxiously.

"Come on, you know a nigga go hard. I'm paying with a Black Card. I'm gonna save all the Benjamins for the tip drill, na' mean." He pulled out a wad of cash with a rubber band wrapped around it. He slapped me hard on my ass. Dude tugged my hand toward the stairs.

I made a pit stop at the bubblegum machine and pointed meekly.

He pulled out his bankroll. "That's what you want?" He dropped two bills in the machine.

I wiggled my ass with a handful of pills. "Ta, ta hoes. Don't hate, appreciate." I strutted up the stairs with one of the hottest rap niggas in the industry.

Dude wanted to fuck me in my ass and I let him for a large fee. It hurt like hell, too. We had sex on top of the dresser and then I straddled him in the chair. We fucked like wild rabbits and went through three condoms in less than three hours. While he slept I dipped off in dude's pockets, popped his rubber band, and relieved him of eight bills.

I was that bitch, pah-leez believe!

# Chapter Forty-Three

My eighteenth birthday came and went. I continued to work at M&Ms and started to build my own clientele. My main focus was to get my own place for me and my child. I also continued to work at the prison.

After work, when I wasn't dog tired, I'd go over Innocent's transcripts. I hadn't seen him since that dreadful day I snuck into the SHU. I didn't want to take a risk going back there again.

Saturday morning, I woke up with a splitting headache. I was tired from another week binging on pills, alcohol, and a buckwild lifestyle. After showering and getting dressed, I sparked a blunt and padded down the stairs through the foyer. The morning sunshine stabbed at my eyes.

Kanisha was arguing with one of the night security people over a pay dispute. "I don't give a fuck!" she hollered. Directly behind the security guard were several other disgruntled employees.

I decided to let her be. I went into the TV room and plopped down on the couch next to Kim. She had the nerve to cut her eyes at me with an icy stare. I balled up my fist and thought about hitting that ho in the face. Instead I picked up her can of soda, popped the top, and guzzled it down. Leaning forward, I belched loud in her face. She frowned and scooted away.

I could still hear Kanisha arguing. I flipped the channels and came across the news. It was a special news broadcast about the Atlanta drug wars. A camera showed where four bodies were found beheaded, butchered, and hacked to death with a machete. Other victims had also suffered multiple gunshot wounds.

"Dayum!" I droned thinking back to the night I was caught up in all that drama. After the news broadcast went off, I needed something to get into. Some of the commotion in the room started to die down as soon as Kanisha walked out of the door. I scanned the room; Ebonyze was perched cozily on the loveseat looking stunningly sexy. She was sitting with her legs curled underneath her, reading a magazine, or at least looking at the pictures. I glanced over at Amanda, then at Carmen. They were talking loud, all animated 'n shit, arguing about who was the cutest between Chris Brown and J. Holiday. Then I looked back over at Ebonyze. She put the magazine down and reached her hand into the cushion of the loveseat, retrieving a raggedy brown baby doll dressed in shabby old clothes. She began to play with it. I did a double-take. This grown-ass woman was playing with a doll.

"Hey, psst, psst, hey!" I gestured to get Amanda's attention. She and Carmen cast a wary glance my way and went back to debating. "Look!" I hissed again.

Amanda turned around and looked at me. A tight line had formed across her forehead. The whole time, Kim continued to howl, singing Soulja Boy's "Crank Dat", screaming, *"Youuu!"* while doing that stupid-ass Superman dance.

"Never mind." I turned my attention back to Ebonyze. "Ebonyze, how old are you?"

She pretended not to hear me.

"I know you heard me."

She looked at me the way a young girl does when she's irritated, "I turn thirteen in May," she answered in a heavy African accent. "Amanda is seventeen, Carmen is fourteen, and Kim is fifteen," Ebonyze continued, talking absentmindedly as she played with the doll.

Disgusted, I sat there, numb. I looked around the room. The girls were dressed in fake maturity. They were all underaged girls. "Scandalous-ass bitch!" I said out loud. I was fuming!

Kanisha had an elite clientele of rich customers. She was the proprietor of M&M's, an exotic whorehouse, and she was making a killing. No wonder she didn't want the girls working the night shift with the other professional prostitutes. It was too risky. The underage girls would be detected.

"Scandalous bitch! Just like her mama," I said again.

Kanisha walked in, "What's all the noise?"

With a panicked expression on their faces, the girls frantically moved to hide. I jumped up from my seat and rushed over to Kanisha.

"Bitch, what de fuck kinda shit you tryin' here? Got me in here with them young-ass girls." I bumped into her, ready to fight.

She tossed her weave back and glanced between me and the door fearfully as if she expected it to come flying open.

"Not now," her voice quivered. "I promise, I'll explain everything to you. This is a lot bigger than you think."

I stood back, folded my arms over my breasts and snaked my neck. "I got time bitch; start explainin'."

The door bell chimed and Kanisha flinched.

I kicked into gear and everyone went scrambling, frantically bumping into each other. Kanisha had trained us all well.

Ebonyze made it to the door first. She opened it, and Kanisha muttered dreadfully, "We in big trouble."

A cacophony of voices filled the parlor. The front yard and entire parking lot was full of Haitians.

"Oh, shit!" I scoffed.

Bleu Baptiste and his big henchman, Boss, walked through the door.

"Beech whur mi muddafuckin' moni at? Yu steal from mi, mi finna kill all yu beeches!" he hollered.

Boss, with a machete in his hand, walked straight toward me.

# Chapter Forty-Four

Bleu quickly moved to Kanisha. He slapped her so hard that her neck snapped back.

"I'ma get your money, Bleu. You don't have to—"

He slapped her again before she could finish. "Hush up!" he shouted, lassoing his hand around her long hair.

She squirmed, fearful of the next slap. "Bleu, please—"

He held his hand up to silence her. Then he looked over to me. Paralyzed by fear, my whole life flashed before my eyes. God only knew what Kanisha had done to these crazy-ass Haitians to get them all rowdy. And now, she had gotten me caught up in some teenage prostitution shit. I began to pray like hell.

"Yu, dat hur! Dat hur!" Boss babbled unintelligibly and reached out, grabbing me around my throat with so much force he lifted me off my feet. Boss reached back to swing the machete.

This time it was Kanisha that screamed a piercing shrill. "No!"

Bleu rushed over and grabbed Boss's arm. Boss, I know dats err, but you can't hurt err. Let err go!" Bleu commanded in an undeniable tone of authority.

Boss released me. My feet plummeted to the floor. I clutched my throat. It felt like he had damn-near crushed my windpipe.

"Luv, mi nevah mint tu hurt choo," Bleu said in a soft voice. He took my hand.

"Why in the hell y'all come in here scarin' us and shit?" I spat.

"Kanisha owe mi moni—"

"I'ma pay you—"

Bleu interrupted her. "Hush up wumon or mi tell Boss tu chop off yu head." Bleu walked closer.

I could smell his cologne. "You smell good," I cooed.

"Luv, yu dun't have tu work here. Mi nevah stop tinkin' about yu since de last time mi see yu. Mi had tu take a trip back tu mi countree, Haiti. Mi recently come back."

I had almost forgotten that this crazy nigga was sprung off the poonanny. Kanisha's scandalous ass picked up on it instantly. She gestured, waving at me to work my charm on dude. I was going to, but it wasn't for her conniving ass; it was for me. I wasn't trying to get my ass killed. I needed a quick exit out of M&M's—especially when I looked around and saw all the scared girls. Hell, I was scared too.

"Tell Boss and the rest of your boys to chill out! Y'all scarin' us!" I pouted somberly. "Bleu, you and him are scaring us." I pointed at Boss.

Bleu yelled at his cousin, "Boss, go stand outside. Tell 'em tu be quiet."

Boss scratched his head, dumbfounded, and walked out the door.

"Dat feel bettah luv?" Bleu asked.

I nodded.

"Mi wanna spend de week wit yu. Mi make it worth yu while."

"A week?"

He squeezed my hand. I felt an electric jolt.

"Bleu, uh, I don't know, that's a long time." I didn't want to hurt his ego and end up getting us all killed, but I didn't know what exactly to do or say.

"Luv, mi pay yu triple! Take yu on a shoppin' spree, give yu de finner tings in life," Bleu persuaded.

Kanisha gestured for me to accept.

"Okay." I hesitantly accepted Bleu's offer.

During my week with Bleu we went on several shopping sprees and he bought me a brand new Mercedes truck. But I didn't stop thinking about Innocent and those underage girls working at M&Ms.

I continued to stack my paper. I worked at the prison and at M&Ms. Things were going okay until a riot ensued in the SHU one day when I wasn't at work. One prison guard, two ABs and an inmate had been murdered. I called the prison, but I couldn't get any information. The institution was on lockdown and an investigation was pending due to the killings. Government officials were demanding Warden Scott's immediate resignation.

I was in a tizzy, and to top it all off, I had not heard from Nurse Harvey concerning the corruption in Douglasville. That information could free Innocent—that is, if he was still alive.

October 22 was a fabulous night at M&M's. The mansion was banging full of ballers, professional athletes, and other rich clientele. I was high off "Cush" and "X", and drunk as hell. I found out that night how scandalous Kanisha's ass really was.

# Chapter Forty-Five

Morning came too fast. I was awakened by the sound of keys jingling. My breakfast was placed in the food slot in the cell door.

Benny, my new cellmate, hopped off the top bunk with a thud and stomped across the floor. He was bare foot. He retrieved both breakfast trays.

The guards barked. "If you goin' to the rec have the bunks made and be ready when I come back."

"We ain't goin' to rec," Benny said. He cut his eyes at me.

"Yo, CO, I'm goin'." I spoke loud enough for the guard to hear.

"Be ready in five minutes!" he called back.

The slot slammed shut.

Benny turned to me and frowned. "You going out there? Lobo and them think you a snitch. They gon' kill you." He raised his voice and tried to pass me a tray.

I waved him off and eased off the bunk. I walked to the toilet to take a leak. With my back to Benny I spoke with more confidence than I actually had. "I ain't nobody's snitch. I ain't runnin' from them niggas because that would make me look guilty as hell. I don't have a choice."

"Betta to look guilty then to be dead. You do have a choice,"

Benny said, walking over trying to glance down at my joint.

I turned my back. "Get the fuck away from me."

"You can check in with me."

"What? Check in with you?"

"Yeah, it ain't so bad back here. Hell, they was raping me taking my booty so much I had to get stitches and wear a tampon to stop the bleeding. I couldn't even hold my mud—"

"Hold up man! Hold the fuck up!" I said, shaking my joint depositing it back into my pants.

Benny looked up at me startled.

"All that personal shit, I ain't tryna hear it!"

The guard banged the keys against the door. "Ready for rec?" he shouted.

I placed a little razor shank in my draws.

"Lets go!" the guard shouted.

"Don't go!" Benny whined in a feminine twang.

I ignored dude and walked to the door. As I looked out the cell I saw three big rednecks with crew cuts, leather gloves, and shiny boots. The guards were to search each inmate before being led to the rec yard.

I stood with my legs apart as they patted me down. "What 'cha shakin' for?" the guard asked.

"I ain't shaking."

His hand passed over the shank in my pants. "Put your hands out."

I was cuffed and then led out the cell.

At rec there were fenced cages everywhere. The first cage was filled with Spanish cons. The shank was easing down my pants.

Someone called my name. "IC Miller."

I looked up to see Milkman, Lobo and James. "Yo, CO put him in here! Put him in here!" they all yelled in cunning persuasion.

The guards stopped.

"Come on nigga! Bring yo ass in here!" Lobo shouted, waving a meaty fist at me.

"I'ma go in there with them?" I asked. The shank continued to ease down my pants.

The Spanish clique in the next cage kept me on their optic radar. The guards shuffled me to the cage and removed my cuffs and leg irons. I walked inside. Lobo and the rest of them rushed me as the guards walked off.

"Man, on everything I love I ain't no snitch!" I said, reaching in my pants for the shank. The razor hit the pavement. I quickly bent down to pick it up.

They stopped and looked at each other then Lobo pointed toward it. "What you gon' do with that, scratch us to death?"

Everyone laughed.

"I thought y'all was gonna jump me," I confessed.

Lobo stepped up. "Nigga, you the homie. We was just testing where your heart wuz at." He gave me a firm pat on the back.

I winced in pain.

"We know you didn't snitch. We convicts, not inmates. We just played along to fool the warden and the rest of them fools so they wouldn't fuck wit you since they thought we was going to come after you."

"Well, it didn't work. After they took y'all to the hole, them niggas from DC came at me. I got stabbed twice." I opened my jump suit to show them my bloody gauze. "The Dirty White Boys threw gasoline on Crip."

"Nigga, we heard you put some work in on them DC niggas and the Dirty White Boys, though," Lobo said with his top lip snarled.

Directly behind him, James and a couple of cons stood idly watching us.

"Man, I don't know what's going on with all this bullshit. I got a death sentence hangin' over my head and now all this shit with the warden, the ABs, and DC niggas trying to kill me," I vented.

"Look man, I don't know what the fuck is going on but I do know you gotta be strong. This prison shit will break the average nigga. You got to be strong—especially after all the shit you've been through," Lobo said.

Milkman nodded his head in agreement. "Like it or not, you a death row con with a body count. Muthafuckas in prison gon' respect you for that," Milkman spoke.

James nodded his head in agreement.

"Yo, if they don't move your bad ass back to the row I'm moving you into the cell with me. Chill and the rest of 'em gon' to have to accept you," Lobo said, placing his hand on my shoulder.

Milkman continued, "Since you already got a death sentence all they probably gonna do is place you under investigation, drag yo ass in the hole for a minute, then take you to kangaroo court here."

"Oh, shit!" James shrieked and he walked to the other side of the cage. "Goon squad! They are the warden's personal henchmen. Something 'bout to pop off."

The recreation yard suddenly got silent. The guards headed straight for our cage.

"Get rid of that razor and go stand at the back of the cage with your back against the wall," Lobo whispered.

"For what?" I asked, flustered.

"Just do it!" Lobo screeched, never taking his eyes off the approaching guards.

"I—"

Lobo shoved me before I could get the words out.

I walked over toward James. They quickly distanced themselves from me like I had the plague.

"Which one of you is Inmate Miller?" a tall muscular guard with a crew cut asked.

"I'm Miller," Lobo answered before I could speak up.

We had the same last name.

Lobo shot me a silent warning with his eyes as he stepped to the gate.

"You got a separation so we have to move you to a separate cage."

"Damn Joe, it take all y'all to move a nigga?" Lobo said sarcastically as he flexed his brawny muscles.

"Unless you wanna find out, walk your ass over here," the guard challenged.

"I don't want no problems." Lobo threw up his hands in mock intimidation.

As they cuffed him, the other guards stood around sharp-eyed. They looked like they were expecting trouble.

"We're placing you in the next cage—warden's orders. Seems like you's a bad man," the guard told him.

His cohorts snickered. They moved Lobo to the next cage across from us.

"Man, why you do that?" I asked.

"I thought they was coming to tap that ass," Lobo responded from across the yard.

"Yeah, a few more fights and yo skinny ass gonna run outta places to get stitches," Milkman laughed.

"We got yo back lil' homie," James told me.

"Thanks," I smiled. "Aye, you knew my uncle, David?"

"Yeah, we called him Dough. Muthafucka was crazy as hell. We had some good times, though. Back then we ran everything, the streets, the hoes. You name it, we did it.

"What you in here for?" I asked

"I'm serving life for murder," he told me.

"You ain't heard nuttin'on your appeal?" Lobo called over to me as he shadow- boxed.

"Nah, I ain't heard nothing."

Lobo walked over to the fence eyeing movement in the yard. "If they put them ABs in the cage with y'all, there's going to be trouble."

We looked at each other. Four ABs were headed right for us.

# Chapter Forty-Six

The guards stopped in front of our cage. The ABs had shaved heads and tattoos over most of their bodies.

"Miller, you got company!" the guard bellowed.

"Oh, fuck, they gon' kill'em," Milkman muttered.

Lobo continued to stand his ground as each AB was uncuffed and placed into the cage with him.

He strategically positioned himself in the cage so that he could watch the clique of white cons. They didn't waste any time getting loud and rowdy.

Lugar approached Lobo. "You got a problem or something?" he spat. "Why you keep cutting your eyes at me?"

They were standing real close to each other. Lobo didn't move. Then he rolled his shoulders and cracked his knuckles.

"Look like he got a joint!" I hollered.

Four cons walked up on Lobo.

"Fuck y'all doin', Silverstein?" Milkman yelled, shaking the fence with both hands.

"Nigger lover, what, you his bitch or something?"

Lobo stole on Lugar hitting him in the jaw. The other ABs rushed Lobo, but somehow he managed to keep them at bay by swinging his arms with his back against the fence.

The Spanish convicts in the next cage began to cheer. "Beat his ass, ese!"

Lobo swung a wild overhand right, knocking one of the cons down. He delivered a barrage of blows to the next one's face and torso. Lobo continued to swing, throwing punches all over the place. Then one of the cons jumped on his back and caused Lobo to stagger. Silverstein caught him with a solid overhand right and then another. The two other ABs regrouped and pummeled Lobo with smashing blows to his face. Lugar got up off the ground and even though he seemed dazed, he reached into his coat sleeve and pulled out a crude ten-inch shank.

"Lobo, look out!" Milkman yelled.

Lobo looked up, but it was too late.

# Chapter Forty Seven

The shank tore into Lobo's thigh muscle. He screamed in agony and fell to one knee. He still managed to throw blows; but by then, it was pointless. He was getting punished.

The Spanish clique banged their fists on the gates, cheering and laughing with excitement as all four of the ABs beat Lobo unmercifully.

All of Lobo's strength had been depleted. He continued to fight back even though he was nothing more than a human punching bag.

Milkman shouted, "Lobo, man, get up!"

Blood spewed from his nose and mouth and there was a deep gash above Lobo's left eye. Silverstein kicked Lobo in the face and more blood spattered.

Seeming to get a burst of energy Lobo hit one of his attackers in the throat severing his jugular vein. Blood squirted everywhere. The man dropped to the ground. His body laid there motionless.

Lobo then flipped the AB off his back and stabbed another with a shot to his gut with the shank. "Take that mutharfucka'!"

Silverstein and another con quickly moved out of his way.

"Yea! Yea! Yea!" we all chanted jumping up and down with joy.

The Spanish cons in the next cage stood silent.

Lobo staggered with the bloody shank in his hand. He was tired and out of breath. He stepped over the dead body, making his way back to the fence. He held his arms up over his head and smiled. Blood ran down his face. "Fuck, yea!" he shouted.

One of the white cons called up to the gun tower, "Help us!"

A piercing shot fired from the gun tower.

"Lobo, get down!" I shouted. It was like in a dream

The shot resonated and echoed between the buildings. The inmates scattered, trying to protect themselves from any stray bullets. When the dust cleared we all checked to make sure those around us were unharmed.

Milkman called across the yard, "Hey, Lobo, you alright?"

Lobo was lying on his back. The shank was still in his hand. When we looked closer we saw that the entire right side of Lobo's head was missing.

"Nooo! Nooo! Nooo, man! Lobo, get up! Get up, Lobo!" Milkman yelled. "Lobo, get up! Get up, man!" Milkman looked up at the gun tower. "Y'all didn't have to kill him! You fuckin' bastards!"

A voice called from the tower, "Lie on the ground with your arms and legs spread!"

The gun was now aimed at Milkman's head. All the other cons on the rec yard were already face down on the ground.

"Fuck you, pig! You didn't have to kill him!" Milkman called out.

The warden and captain came storming into the yard. The warden walked up to me. "Inmate Miller, you have more lives than a three-legged cat," he quipped.

With the sun high in the sky, bright as an orange ball of fire, we were forced to lie on our bellies on the hot pavement. Captain Turner and the warden frantically rushed about giving senseless orders with futile results. Afterward, like human cattle, we were shackled and led back to our cells in a single file line.

Back in my cell Benny greeted me like I was a long lost soldier returning home from war. The cell was cleaned up. He had on pink boxer shorts, a handmade wife beater, and he wore a ton of cheap perfume, so strong it made me sneeze.

"They killed Lobo," I managed to say.

"Good!" Benny spat while placing his hands on his bony hips.

"Fuck you! What do you mean, 'good'!?" I scoffed, trying to control my temper.

"He was gonna kill you," Benny stuttered.

"I'm so happy you're safe," he beamed coyly.

"Yeah, me too."

"Can I get you anything?" Benny pursed his lips femininely.

"Yeah let me have a cigarette."

His smile brightened as he reached into his bunk and retrieved a cartoon. "You know ain't nothing wrong with a man getting oral sex from a queen." Benny finagled.

"Is that so?" I said.

"Lemme suck yo dick and I'll give you five cigarettes."

"Five?"

"Yep," Benny intoned and nodded his head with excited vigor. He looked at my crotch lustfully.

"Okay."

Benny looked at me and then he looked down at my crotch. Timidly, he walked toward me. "I been wanting to do this for a while," he purred. Benny reached down to fondle my dick.

I slapped the shit out of him. "Get the fuck away from me."

"What you hit me fo?" he whimpered.

I snatched the carton out of his hands. "Get the fuck on and tell'em you want a cell change."

"Why?" he asked.

I raised my hand to slap his ass again.

"CO, CO, CO!" he screamed like a bitch. Benny beat on the cell door.

I sneezed.

"Why you doin' this to me?" he cried.

"You gotta go! If you want your smokes back tell that nigga Fields to holla at me!"

"Who, Fe Fe?" Benny asked, perplexed.

I nodded my head menacingly.

"What's going on here?" the guard asked once he reached the cell door.

"I want a cell change, ASAP," Benny cried.

The guard laughed at Benny's request. "I want, I want, I want," he taunted. "To be in this shit hole, y'all sure make a lot of demands."

"Please, if you don't—"

"The institution is on lockdown," the guard told Benny cutting him off. "Even if I wanted to, it can't be done." He looked at me and then back at Benny. "Have fun."

I stormed toward the door.

"My name is IC Miller. I'm a death row convict. Check my file. Go tell the captain or the warden, I'ma kill this fuck nigga in five minutes if y'all don't move him."

"Ohh noo, please help me!" Benny pounded on the door, crying louder than before.

With a disgusted look on his face the guard left only to return within minutes flanked by a platoon of guards.

"Inmate Benny Scott, cuff up! We're moving you to another cell."

"Good!" Benny mumbled under his breath while he packed his gear and stood by the door.

"Tell Fields to get at me!" I hollered.

Once again I was alone with my thoughts.

# Chapter Forty-Eight

The entire prison was on lockdown. By the fifth day I was going crazy. The doctor came and took out my stitches. I didn't even bother to look down at my chest.

As soon as the doctor left, I walked over to the window and looked outside at freedom. A glorious bright sun sat up in the celestial sky, causing me to daydream. An intrusive knock at the cell door broke my thoughts. The warden pushed his way in.

He had a serious expression in his opaque blue eyes that was hard to read. His lips were thin and his weary face was aged with folds of wrinkles. His shirt tie was askew. Behind him, convicts called his name, but he ignored them.

"Miller, since you've arrived here you have been involved in a lot of shit and it's becoming a problem."

"Problem!?" I shrieked. "It's you that's the problem! You set me up and tried to have me killed. I ain't never did shit to you. I don't even know you, man! Now Lobo's dead 'cause of you!"

The warden leaned forward and whispered, "I might have made a mistake. Look, let's start over with a clean slate." He rubbed his hand across his mouth and continued talking in a low tone. "How about if after the investigation is over with and the Regional Director leaves, I place you back on the compound with no more hassles?"

I stepped away. "You 'bout eight bodies too late to talk about some peace treaty shit, man. What the fuck you got against me?"

He spoke in a whisper. "Tomorrow, Federal Agents are going to come ask you about a few suspicious deaths. One of the deaths occurred when Mark Hudson slipped and fell in the shower. The others are about what happened last week on the rec yard."

"What about when you tried to have me killed in the unit?" I asked.

"Like I said, that was all a big mistake. That was the past and this is the present. -I'm being investigated." His voice was stern.

"So you want me to lie for you after all the foul shit you did to me? You killed my homie and tried to make me look like a rat," I said bitterly.

"You need to understand, once the Regional Director and investigators leave, you will be here with me and I promise you I'll succeed where I failed before. I can make your life a living hell or I can make your stay here as comfortable as possible.

"Just do like the real cons do when the investigators question you. You haven't seen nothing and you don't know nothing." The warden smiled and took a step away from the door. He adjusted his tie and looked over his shoulder suspiciously. Then he turned back toward me, waiting for my response.

I nodded my head and croaked a dry reply. "Okay, warden."

"Good, as soon as the investigation and lockdown are over I'm going to have you placed back in population not on the row. Would you like that?"

I didn't answer him.

The warden looked at me closely then sang, "I'll have one of my officers bring you the phone."

I nodded my head. In the joint a telephone was like a lifeline.

The warden walked off to the sounds of convicts shouting his name.

The next day, Federal investigators came to pay me a visit after lunch time. They asked me a lot of questions but I kept my mouth shut like the warden and I had discussed.

That night in my cell I thought about Lobo. I thought about a lot of shit. Faces and thoughts ran through my mind nonstop. I rushed the cell door, kicking and yelling. "CO! CO!"

Finally a guard, an old redneck, came wearing a dirty wrinkled gray uniform.

"I need to use the phone!" I shouted.

"The prison is on lockdown. No phone."

"I'ma flood this bitch and start throwing piss and shit. The warden said I could use the phone."

He looked at the name tag on my door. "Let me go check."

I paced the cell. I needed to call Big Mama to ask her a question. There was something about James. I needed to find out who he was.

The door opened and a phone appeared. "Hurry it up!" He spat, sitting the phone down hard. He walked off.

"Fuck you, cracka!" I shouted behind him. I dialed Big Mama's number with a trembling hand.

Big Mama picked up on the first ring.

"Big Mama, it's me, IC."

"Haaay, baby!" Big Mama exclaimed. "Are you okay? We tryna get the money up to get you an appeal lawyer. I'm selling plates of food. Your brother in Atlanta right now. That boy gotta bunch of money. He don't think I know he hiding it in de house."

"Gramma?" I called, interrupting her. "Gramma, I met James."

Silence.

"Gramma, is he—"

"Innocent. IC, baby, please, you gotta read your Bible and leave it in God's hands."

"Who is he?" I screamed. "Is he the man who killed my mother?"

"Innocent baby—"

Gramma didn't deny it.

"Nah Gramma, he killed my mama. It's now in my hands."

"IC, you ain't got no choice. You gotta leave him alone."

"Nah Gramma, he didn't leave my mama alone. So I'm not gonna leave him alone. I'm already on death row and he won't be the first man I killed. It's because of him I'm in here and I'm a killer."

"IC, I don't ever want to hear you talk like that again! You hear me?" she spat. "You're not a killer. Your father will pay for what he did. Please just let that man be."

Her words stunned me.

"Father?"

"Yes, IC," she said solemly, realizing what she had just told. "James is your father."

"My father?" I repeated. "Gramma, why didn't you just tell us?" I asked, hearing my voice crack with emotion. Tears welled in my eyes.

"Because, you and your brother were both traumatized. It was years later through a blood test that it showed he was your father. You adored what you remembered about your father, so I just couldn't tell you. It would have broken your heart. IC, promise me you'll leave it in de Lord's hands?"

"I can't promise that, Gramma. You have no idea what this place has made me. These people have made me into a killer. Even your Jesus, who you brag about, has forsaken me!"

She gasped.

I continued, "I should have been in college making something out my life." A tear rolled down my cheek.

The phone beeped, "Ten seconds," the operator reminded.

"I'ma send you some Bible verses, IC. You gotta start trusting in the Lord and let Him fight yo battles," she told me.

"And if I did that I'd probably be dead already."

"Child don't say th—"

The line went dead. I hung up the phone and climbed into my bunk. I thought about how I was going to kill James, my father. That was, if this judicial system or the convicts didn't kill me first.

Two weeks later I received a letter. Someone slid it under the cell door. The envelope was written in neat handwriting, and there was no return address:

*I don't want you to think I forgive you for what you did to me and my child. I think you would have to be a woman to truly understand or better yet, a real man just to understand how much it hurts when a man abandons his child for another woman. So, if you were rotting in hell I would happily provide you with gasoline and a match to make your stay as miserable as I felt when you left me.*

*On a brighter note, I did manage to get in contact with Nurse Harvey. There is a big scandal going on in Douglasville. It has something to do with the cop who shot you. There is a chance it may involve your case. I don't know, I'm just a messenger. I'm not even a friend, more like a concerned citizen or better yet, just a bitch you dogged and abandoned with a child. Don't expect me to do anything else for you.*

*Sincerely yours,*

*A bitch you once claimed to love*

*Innocent*

251

# *Chapter Forty-Nine*

## IC MILLER
## ONE MONTH LATER

On September 3, breakfast came early. I stumbled in the dark to get my food tray. The institution was no longer on lockdown. I sat on my bunk and watched the first hint of the morning sun. After eating, I decided it was time to take care of business.

"Hey James! Hey James!" I yelled.

No answer.

"Lil homie, IC, is that you?" I heard a voice call out moments later. It sounded like Milkman.

"Yea!" I yelled. "Tell James I need to talk to him about some legal advice."

"Bet that up, homie. They at my cell now, but as soon as I hit the pound I got'cha."

I still had pain in my shoulder, but physically I was fine. I was strong enough to do what I needed to do: Kill my flesh and blood, my father. I stepped outside the shower to the sound of a sharp rap at the cell door. I hoped it was Tamara. I wanted to talk to her about that letter she had written me. I walked over to the door wrapped in a towel and wiped the steam off the cell window.

"Oh, shit!" I said.

It was Fe Fe. He had on a small uniform shirt that showed off lots of cleavage. Dude's hair was wavy, and with just a touch of eyeliner and lip gloss, he looked just like a bitch.

"What?" I asked brusquely.

"Um, Benny told me you tried to take his booty and when he wouldn't give you none, you beat him up. He said he had to get the CO to put him in another cell before you raped him, *and* you took his cigarettes. He said you talkin' 'bout you wanna get wit me!" He snaked his neck and shoulders with homosexual sassiness, emphasizing his last four words. "For yo information, I already got a man! Touche!" He snapped his fingers.

"First off, dude, Benny lying."

"Hold up! What you call me?" He rolled his eyes. "My damn name ain't no fuckin' *dude*! Do I look like a *dude* to you? Call me 'Fe Fe' or don't call me nothing at all."

I heard the guard call him, "Yo, Fields!"

He threw up a bent wrist in disgust.

I walked over to my bunk, retrieved the carton of cigarettes, and passed them to him under the door.

The guard called his name again.

"Listen man, oh, I mean Fields. I ain't try to rape Benny. I don't get down like that. If it don't bleed once a month I ain't hittin' it."

Fe Fe cuffed the cigarettes. He smiled as he stared down at the bulge in my towel.

"A while back you told me not to go on the rec yard because I would get shot in the dome. How did you know?"

His facial expression froze and he looked flustered and nervous. He glanced over his shoulder.

"Come on man, I mean, Fe Fe."

He gave me that same look with no answer.

"I'm goin' back to death row for a fucked up crime I ain't commit," I told him bitterly.

He walked up closer. "I know."

"How you know?"

He shrugged his shoulders. "I was in the warden's office fixing his sink. I heard him on the phone talking to someone in Douglasville. He said your name, IC Miller, then he mentioned something about a test result and whoever he was talking to, he said not to worry. He said that you would get shot in the head or beat to death, whichever came first."

My mouth dropped open in shock. The guard's keys jingled loud. The CO was walking toward us.

"Gotta go!" Fe Fe sashayed away.

I sat back on the bunk and thought back to Tamara's letter. She mentioned a cover up in Douglasville and something about the cop. Now Fields said he had heard the warden say something about Douglasville and a test result. I started putting on my clothes.

Someone called my name from the other side of the cell door. "IC Miller."

I looked up to see Captain Turner.

"Yeah, wuz up?" I responded coldly.

"The investigation is just about over. You did good not to run your mouth."

"I did good? Why? Just because I didn't tell them crackas y'all playin' with nigga's lives, like this is a game?"

The captain laughed, "A game? I never thought of it like that. Yeah, I like that, Miller." He smiled at me. "Anyway, you're being released back on the ground pound until the court makes a ruling on your case. Think you can go out there without being involved in anymore killings?"

I sneered at him. "Think you can stop setting a nigga up to be killed like you did my homie, Lobo? That bullet was meant for me, not him, but you already knew that, didn't you?"

"No, that bullet served its purpose. That inmate assaulted and killed two inmates with a weapon. We check you before goin' to rec. He was a crafty son of a bitch. The officer that shot him was only doing his job. He was a threat and we gotta keep y'all safe. Because the officer was protecting you all, I personally put him in for a bonus."

"Bonus? That's bullshit and you know it, man."

"Look, I got a job to do and I'm doing it. I can't help it if y'all make my job easier by killing each other." He smiled.

I looked away from him and felt my heart pounding in my chest.

"Oh, and just so y'all know, I'm releasing Silverstein back into the pound along with your homie Milkman. Now, *that's* gonna be entertaining." He smirked.

I hated him with every fiber in my body.

"You can have a firsthand seat right up front to watch the

whole thing, boy. So, can you be a good lil' nigger until it's time for your execution?"

"You know what man, you fucked up! All y'all fucked up! This place and this prison fucked up!" I yelled.

He laughed. "It's all a game, Miller. It's all a game."

# Chapter Fifty

The day I got out of the hole, the sun was sitting high in the majestic blue sky. Birds soared above me, free; and for the first time in my life, my biggest concern was survival. Nothing else mattered. Nothing else existed. I was an inhabitant of a microcosm of a kill or be killed world. It was now my choice to become predator or prey. Survive or die. It wasn't even an ultimatum. It was a solution.

I needed a knife.

I walked into D-Unit and there they were: the ABs, the Dirty White Boys, and their wannabe affiliates. They were at least a hundred deep, and they all stared as I approached.

I knew I was in trouble.

Bruce stepped up and blocked my path. He had gotten bigger. "If it ain't ole Oreo Blizzard man himself, he queried.

I wasn't even scared. The worse they could do was kill me. With my hand in my pants, I bumped Bruce hard.

"Watch where you're going, nigger!" he spat.

I continued walking. On the fifth floor I saw a lot of familiar faces.

"IC! IC Miller!" Milkman rushed up on me and gave me a hug.

A few other homies came over. We exchanged daps.

"What cell you in?" Milkman asked.

"526," I responded.

One of the homies carried my gear.

"Nah, you moving in with me," Milkman told me.

I didn't say anything. I just shrugged and gave a wary smile. I walked into the cell and noticed that it was clean. It smelled of Simplegreen and prayer oil. Nude pictures of Coco, Ice-T's wife, decorated the walls. J Holiday's "Suffocate" played on the radio from a speaker box underneath the bunk.

"I need a joint bad!"

"Nah, you gonna need two of them, dawg. I'm surprised they let you back on the compound. How you pull that shit off?"

I didn't say anything.

Just then, homies came in with a pizza, a brown paper bag with wine, and a thin joint of weed rolled in toilet papers. Because I had held it down to the fullest, niggas was showing me mad love. I was respected as a gangsta.

"I ran into Lugar and a dude named Bruce Sinclair downstairs. They was drunk. Crackas tried to shine on me—spook a nigga, too," I said apprehensively. "Something was wrong; shit looked different. I dunno." I shook my head and hunched my shoulders. "Maybe it's me."

"Nah, it ain't you. While we were in the hole the warden had over half the blacks and almost all the DCs transferred. We like sitting ducks now."

"What?" I screeched in disbelief.

Milkman gave me a subtle nod. "I'ma kill Silverstein and Lugar and make them transfer me." He threw his head back, pushing some blond hair from his face.

"A'ight, cool. I'm gonna help you kill Silverstein and Lugar, too, but first I need to find the old dude, James."

"Ok, that's no problem," Milkman said.

"And when I find him, I'm gonna kill him."

"Damn, man!" Milkman shot to his feet. "Fuck you talkin' bout? Ain't but a few of us left. He the homie! What he do?"

"Dude, you know he in here for murder."

"Shit, who ain't?"

"He knew my mother."

"Okay." Milkman shrugged his shoulders.

"He knew her well enough to kill her."

"What? You serious, man?" Milkman quizzed.

"Yeah, man. I figured it out while I was in the hole. Then I called my grandmother and she verified it."

Milkman plopped back down on his bunk.

"You know what's even more fucked up?" I added.

"What?"

"The nigga is my ole man."

Milkman looked at me like he couldn't believe what I had just told him. He got up and placed something over the cell door window so nobody could see in. Then he took the cover off the air vents, removed two shanks, and handed them to me.

I held them in my hand and felt a surge of power. I thought of how it would feel to kill James. Murder was no longer a thought; it was my instinctive action. Now, it was my nature. It was my world and I intended to claim it.

"James lives on the third floor in A-Unit. I don't know what cell he's in. You want me to go with you?" Milkman asked.

"Nah, I'm good."

"You know Chill and the rest of the homies gon' be fucked up with you."

"Man, fuck Chill. Them bitch-ass niggas watched me get stabbed the fuck up by some white boys and them DC niggas and didn't come to at least try and break it up. I'ma kill dat bitch-nigga too, if he get outta line." I fumed. A grin spread across my face. "You shoulda seen the look on them crackas' faces when I walked in the unit."

Milkman smiled. "One thing about prison or any other place for that matter, if you kill up a bunch of muthafuckas you gon' earn some respect," he said assuringly.

I nodded my head.

Milkman continued. "You got cats leery of you—especially the ABs. They should have killed you as soon as you stepped into the unit today."

"But they didn't."

"A lot of bodies done dropped since you hit the compound. If you go kill your own father, man, that shit crazy. Can't you give him a pass?"

"Would you give him a pass if he beat your mama to death like she was a fuckin' man?" I scoffed. "That shit happened in front of my eyes, man. I won't ever forget what I saw." consistent

"What about your appeal?"

I looked at him through squinted eyes. "What about it? I'ma die right here in this prison. Do you think after all I've been through I have any faith in this white man's legal system? I'd have a betta chance of escaping."

"Man don't be saying no shit like that." Milkman's blue eyes filled with sympathy.

I closed my eyes. "You know we got a homegirl who work here."

"Who?"

"Officer Jenkins."

Milkman thought for a second and suddenly snapped his fingers. "Yeah, I think I know what chick you talkin' about. The one with the big ass, lil' waist, and she's cute in the face."

"Yeah, that's her."

"She cool as fuck, man. She won't write nobody up."

"You know who that is, right?"

"Naw, who?"

"That's crackhead Alicia's daughter."

He frowned at me.

"Older redbone chick. She used to turn tricks across from your building."

"Oh, shit! Now I know who you're talkin' 'bout! She had that nappy head, bad-ass girl named Tomica."

"Tamara," I corrected him.

"Damn, that is her? Shit, she turned into a fuckin' brick house!"

"Yeah, she did."

"You know she working on this floor right now."

His words struck me like a bolt of lightning, causing me to stand straight up. "You sure she working right now?"

"Yeah, you didn't see her when you walked by the office?"

"Hell naw."

"She cool as shit. She don't fuck with nobody, though. Dudes be gunnin' her down and some mo shit."

I frowned.

"Fuck wrong with you man?"

"Man, that's my baby's mama." I walked over to the sink and splashed cold water on my face.

"Get the fuck outta here!"

"Yup, but now she can't stand a nigga."

"Man, you need to go holla at her. Hell, she might even bring in some work."

"Yeah, I'm finna holla at her now." I placed the shank in my pants. "But first I want you to walk downstairs with me. The cracka Bruce said something slick out his mouth and it irked the shit out of me. I'ma straighten him out.

"What he say?"

"He called me a *nigger*."

"Aw man, you can't let it go? Them ABs crazy as fuck! Didn't you see how many of them it was?"

"They crazy and I am too." I walked out the door.

Milkman scrambled to grab his shank and coat and he followed me.

# Chapter Fifty-One

As soon as I walked out of the cell I noticed Chill.
He approached me.

I stopped abruptly and placed my hand in my pants.

"Yo, it was a misunderstanding. I didn't think shit was gonna pop off like that-na'mean? Plus Lugar sprayed you, saying you was a rat and a child rapist." He extended his fist for me to give him dap. I left him hanging.

"Yeah, and you believed him," I said with a scowl on my face.

Milkman walked up.

Chill shrugged his shoulders and continued. "The DC niggas wanna squash the beef. Ain't that many blacks left in the compound and they wanna come together. Niggas see you gangsta. They recognize you as a thorough young nigga." He extended his hand again.

Again, I left him hanging. "Get the fuck outta my face, fake-ass nigga! I'm suppose ta be dead nine lives ago with you runnin' yo mouth, calling me hot!" I was loud enough for the entire unit to hear.

I heard Milkman grumble, "Calm down, man."

"I ain't got no beef wit'cha," Chill shot back defensively.

"I can't muthafuckin' tell, nigga," I gritted.

Milkman stepped in between us.

I walked off and headed toward the exit where Gee, Meatball, and a couple of other DC niggas was loitering. "Nigga, wuz up?" I grilled them.

"Slim, you a pain freak or sumpin," Gee said. He took a step toward me.

Behind him, Meatball reached for his joint.

"Let it go, 'bama. Shit gonna be twice as nice next time. We'll blast that ass," Gee said.

Milkman shoved me from behind. "Yo Gee that shit over with."

"You betta talk to that crazy-ass nigga!" Gee threatened.

I walked off toward the office. I walked down the stairs at a brisk pace with Milkman on my heels. Once at the office, I could barely see Tamara's head. She was sitting behind a desk at the computer, typing. I kept walking.

"Man, you on some suicide shit. This is like walking into the lions' den. You gon' get us both killed."

"Just watch my back."

"How the hell I'm suppose to do that with over a hundred bloodthirsty ABs on my back?"

I ignored him and continued walking. I didn't stop until I reached the lions' den.

There they all stood just as I had left them. When Milkman and I approached, their laughter stopped.

Silverstein, Lugar, and Bruce stood next to each other. At least four dozen other white convicts stood behind them.

Lugar said, "Miller, you got a lotta fuckin' balls. I'ma tell you that much. What do you and that nigger-lover want?"

"Nah it ain't balls, it's more like a guaranteed insurance policy, a policy that ensures I'ma die. But the thing is from here on out when I die, I'm taking more muthafuckers with me. You tryna go?"

Milkman reached under his coat and pulled out two shanks. A couple of ABs walked off. Silverstein wrinkled his brow.

"A hundred against two of you? What you tryna do, use us to dodge death row and the lethal injection?" Lugar sneered.

"Nah, you lied sayin' I was a rat and your fat fuckboy Bruce over there," I pointed, "you called me a nigger a couple hours ago. I'm tryna see either one of you in the TV room. We can go heads up or y'all can line up. It don't matter who go first."

"Nigger, I'll beat your skinny ass!" Bruce yelled. He attempted to rush me.

His people grabbed him and there was a tussle as he struggled to get loose.

I pulled out my joint and so did every AB and Dirty White Boy in the unit.

Lugar's face was beet red. He pulled out a butcher's knife from his coat. "How 'bout all my men just commence to stickin' yo black ass."

"How 'bout you give a dude a headup fight like he asked for?" a guttural voice said from behind me.

I turned around. Gee and the entire DC crew was behind me. The BGs and Chill was with them.

Silverstein rubbed his hands together. "I'm more than certain that Bruce or my humble Aryan Brother, Lugar, would be more than happy to accommodate you in the TV room."

I took off my sweatshirt.

Milkman whispered, "Don't do it."

"Let me at him! Let me at him! I'm gonna beat you so bad, your own granny won't know you!" Bruce yelled.

His crew was still holding him back, but with great difficulty.

"Okay, you first, fat boy. You and I in the TV room, one on one."

"Let's go asshole!" Bruce raged. He slung one of the ABs to the ground.

"Bruce, you got yo knife, I got my knife, let's go." I turned and looked at Lugar. "You next?"

Bruce suddenly stopped struggling to get loose. Lugar's eyes bulged wide.

"You heard him. What's the fuckin' holdup?" Gee interjected. He and Meatball came and stood beside me.

Bruce's cheeks were flushed red. He walked within five feet of me, flanked by at least ten ABs, including Lugar and Silverstein.

"Boy, you fucking crazy. I ain't going in no TV room with us having knives. Bet you won't go in there without the weapons." He arched his brow.

Someone said, "Take his ass into the TV room!"

"I knew you was a bitch," I said.

"Fuck you!"

"Okay Lugar, you can take his place," I challenged.

"What I look like? A crash dummy? You got a death sentence? You want a motherfucker to kill you? It ain't happening, buddy!" he spat.

"Just like I figured, all you AB muthafuckas wanna be warlords except when it comes to dying. Me, I ain't got shit to lose."

"Kick rocks motherfucker, beat it! Find somebody else to take you out yo misery 'cause it ain't happenin' here!" Silverstein assured.

I chuckled and turned around to walk away.

Silverstein bellowed, "Milkman you gonna turn against your own people, your own superior race? You realize you're gonna have to be dealt with."

Milkman whirled around.

I grabbed his arm and pulled him toward the stairs.

"Y'all racist bastards ain't gon' fuck with me!"

"We'll see, traitor! We'll see just how long you'll last around here!"

That day, I became friends with Gee and the DC crew. Unity became a necessity.

We walked back to the third floor. Milkman and I lingered behind intentionally.

With Milkman posted out front, I veered to the right inside the officer's station. Tamara looked up. She looked startled to see me. My shirt was off and my pants were sagging low.

She gasped and placed her hand over her mouth. "Inmate Miller, what you doing here?" she asked in a corrosive voice.

She caught me looking at her.

"I, I need to talk to you."

She bolted from her seat. Her large breasts strained against her uniform. "Innocent, I mean, Inmate Miller, I'm not going to tell you again, you are to address me at all times as Officer Jenkins. Now boy, what do you want?" She huffed and stole a glance at my chest. She cringed again.

"Cut the bullshit, Tamara! I asked you for help. I got your letter. What scandal is going on in Douglasville? You said something about some results. What results?" I took a step toward her. Then I took another. I basked in the sweet scent of her perfume and the fragrance of her hair. "These people intend to kill me. I don't know what's going on. The warden is out to get me and the captain, too." My voice quivered. "I'ma die right here in this prison if you don't help me."

Tamara shrugged her shoulders and began to shake her head adamantly. She sighed and rolled her eyes. "You just don't understand how bad you hurt me do you?" she pouted.

"I know I hurt you, Tamara. I'm sorry. But did I hurt you so bad that you'd let me die?" I had the overwhelming urge to touch her, to hold her in my arms. I glanced over my shoulder at Milkman standing outside the door and with one quick motion, I grabbed Tamara and pushed her in the office behind us.

"Boy, stop!" she screeched, pounding my chest with the palms of her open hands. "Let me go! Let me go!" she hollered.

I held onto her tightly until she stopped resisting. It felt good as hell to have her in my arms.

"You gon' get me fired," she said weakly.

"You gon' get me killed," I whispered in her ear.

"Innocent, I swear. I hate you."

"I know, Tam, you hate that you still love me. I'm yo baby daddy."

We cuddled and she nestled against my chest. It was just the way it had been when I would steal sweet kisses off her lips as a kid.

"Tell me what the nurse said?" I asked in a lusty voice. I eased my hand inside her shirt.

"Hmm ..." she moaned, "Ohh, there was a big scandal going, on, umm, Innocent don't do that ... hmm." She smiled. "Why you unfasten my bra? We gon' get caught."

"What else she say?" I asked while kneading both of Tamara's firm breasts.

"She said there was a big scandal going on in Douglasville and that the cop that shot you got caught up in something."

"In your letter you mentioned something about test results. What results?" I asked, taking off her uniform shirt. I continued to caress her breasts.

"She said, uh, she said something about missing, or DNA test results that had been tampere with." Tamara paused as I fumbled with the zipper on her pants.

"Why didn't you tell me that in the letter?" I asked, helping her out of her pants.

"Because I was mad at you. I know once you get out, if it's true what she said, you would go and fuck with some other bitches."

I kissed her hungrily while squeezing her ass. I slid her panties down around her ankles. "Listen Tam, you gotta believe me, if I beat this case I wanna marry you. I still love you. I want my son to have a father."

"You're lying. I know you're gon' hurt me again. Innocent, I've been hurt enough. You was my first and only love." She broke down crying.

I held her nude body in my arms. "It's okay," I cooed. "I'm here now."

"You don't know what I've been through," Tamara said through tears.

"Tell me."

"What I'm going through now is a bunch of shit and if you knew you wouldn't even want me."

"I doubt that. I got you now. I'm not letting you go." I inhaled Tamara's scent, wanting to keep it with me forever. "Tell me what's up."

Tamara took a deep breath.

"You remember Kanisha?"

"Yeah, what about her?"

"I've been working for her." She sobbed harder.

"Working where?" I asked as I kissed her neck and made my way to her chest.

She hesitated, "M&M's."

I stopped, stunned by her answer.

Kanisha was the bitch that had burnt me with an STD. When she had found out I had a big dick she'd seduced me, knowing damn-well her best friend, Tamara, was my girl. She was no good and I could just imagine what she had Tamara wrapped up in.

"Tam, you gotta get out of that situation."

"I know," she sniffled. "I know."

"Where is my son?" I asked, continuing to her kiss on her.

"With my mom."

I looked at her.

"She ain't smokin' no more," she confirmed. Tamara pulled my pants down. "We gotta hurry up. What you want me to do to you?" The words slipped out of her mouth. She was so used to talking to tricks.

"Tamara, I'm not a client. I'm a nigga that loves you."

She blushed.

"I wanna make love to you like my days are limited on this earth, like you are the only woman on this planet. Tam, I just wanna make love to you passionately and slowly, okay?" I kissed the tears from her face.

"I love you, too," she whispered as she caressed my rigid, stiff manhood. "Damn, you got a big dick," she droned. She turned around and bent over the desk.

"No, not like that." I looked around and grabbed her coat and spread it on the floor. She laid on the floor and spread her legs for me. I eased between her thighs and slid gently inside. Her stifled whimpers turned into lustful cries as I road the ebb and flow of a lover's tide. I came within thirty seconds, but I wasn't about to stop. Tamara grabbed her heels spreading her love wide open. I plummeted deeper as we made love on the prison floor like we would never make love no more.

Almost an hour later, she laid in the crook of my arm raking her fingernails over the rigid scars on my chest. The sensitive feeling made my toes curl uncontrollably.

"They're not going to kill you, Innocent. I'm going to do my best to help you get out of this place."

"Even if I have to escape?"

"Yep."

"My brother is in town. He will find you and help get me a lawyer or help me escape."

Tamara didn't reply. She stood up and started to get dressed. Just that fast, her mind was in that sphere, a place where a woman's mind goes when regret and daunting fear reaches the surface. I couldn't help wondering if it was me. Finally, she spoke.

"I'm dating a dude. His name is Bleu Baptiste."

"What you tellin' me for? You my baby mama. I'ma always have you."

"He's a big-time drug dealer."

"So."

"Stop being so hard headed, Innocent. I'm just saying I can bring you anything you want."

I looked down at the shank next to my pants. "Hey, can you do something for me? I need you to tell me what cell a dude named James King stays in."

"He's in Unit A-3, five thirteen," she said in a clipped tone. "Don't you go get in anymore trouble. I'm gonna call Ms. Harvey. Oh, I gotta get you a cell phone. What else you need?"

I didn't hear her. I was thinking about slamming my knife into my father's chest.

"Innocent!" she called.

"Officer Jenkins! Officer Jenkins!" a deep baritone voice called out.

"Oh, fuck! It's the captain and lieutenant with the warden." She slid out the door and closed it behind her. I could still hear the muffled conversation from my position on the floor. I recognized the voice of Lieutenant Vice. "Where have you been, Jenkins? We've been calling for you on the radio."

"I've been here," Tamara replied. "I was looking at some schedules on the computer."

"Warden Scott wants you to secure Inmate Miller's cell. Immediately! The Governor has just signed his death warrant. Before the four o'clock count I want Inmate Miller placed back on C-Unit death row with a lockup order signed and delivered to my secretary."

I heard Tamara gasp loudly.

"Vice! Let's go!" Captain Turner called out.

When they left, Tamara walked back into the office. Tears filled her eyes as she rushed over to me and held me in her arms.

She cried hysterically. "They was lookin' for you."

"Shhh, don't cry. We gonna be a'ight." I tried to wrestle her arms from around my neck. She wouldn't let go.

There was a knock at the door. Tamara inched in open and peered through the tiny crack.

"Tell IC it's time to go," I heard Milkman say to her.

I rushed out the room without saying goodbye to Tamara. "Where the fuck you been?"

"My bad dawg, I had to put my ticket in."

That day we caught James King sitting on the toilet. He was taking a shit with his pants down around his ankles.

He never saw us coming.

# Chapter Fifty-Two

## DEAD MAN WALKING
### TAMARA

I packed Innocent's property.

The incessant interruption of the prison's PA system was loud in my ears. "IC Miller, report to Lieutenant Vice's office."

They were trying to find him to take him back to C-Unit—death row.

In his property, I found the letter I had written to him. Just holding it in my hands choked me up. In the month that I had been working at the prison, I learned that convicts are sentimental, too. They cherish the most trivial of things, like a visit from a loved one, pictures, and letters. These are all mementoes that they treasure like frozen moments in time that can never be replaced.

I received a communication over my radio to stop by the warden's office before I left for the day. Halfheartedly, I walked to the office. My nerves were on edge. Was I about to be fired? Would I ever see Innocent alive again?

I knocked on the warden's door. My knees shook and my heartbeat quickened.

"Come in."

I walked inside and saw the warden's secretary sitting behind a desk humming to classical music. Normally, Ms. Glandy was talkative, but was unusually reserved. She couldn't even look me in the eye. "They're waiting for you in there," she nodded toward the door.

"Thank you," I muttered.

The warden puffed on a large cigar. Lieutenant Vice and Captain Turner sat across from his desk.

"Sir, you called for me?" I asked.

Lieutenant Vice looked up at me and blew smoke in my direction.

"Yes, there's about to be some major changes around here and you're one of them."

"Me?" I asked.

"Yes. Today when we confronted you about Inmate IC Miller, you appeared to be somewhat unsettled."

My heart began to race. I couldn't get fired now. Who would watch out for Innocent? He needed me.

"No. No, I had a long day that's all and—"

"Also, I went over your prison conduct along with your past employment background and qualifications entitlements. Other than your conduct today you have shown exemplary work standards."

I nodded my head.

He continued. "You have an exemplary educational background. And I try to observe equality in my hiring practices. So, Jenkins, there is a position open for a lieutenant. If you like, the position is yours. You'll be the first black female lieutenant the prison has ever had."

Lieutenant Vice cringed in his chair. Captain Turner continued to stare at me.

I was shocked. My hand went to my mouth.

"I, I don't know what to say."

"Say you'll accept the position and it's all yours." The warden grinned at me.

"I'd be honored to Warden Scott, sir."

The warden stood and shook my hand. Lieutenant Vice continued to squirm in his chair.

"I look forward to working with you as an authoritative member of my staff." He shook my hand hard.

I left the warden's office and a body alarm went off. I thought nothing of it and hurried my ass out of the building. I was officially off work. I was mentally and physically exhausted.

When I got home, all the girls were lounging around. They were all there except Ebonyze. She was upstairs with a customer. Since I had found out about the girls, I had grown attached to them—especially Ebonyze.

"We got a big client in the house. You're not going to believe who it is," Kanisha bragged. "It's on and poppin' tonight so wear something sexy."

The first thing I did when I got to my room was call Nurse Harvey.

She picked up on the first ring. "Hello?"

"Nurse Harvey?"

"Yes, who—"

"Nurse Harvey, the Governor signed Innocent's death warrant today and I'm so scared. I don't know what to do or who to turn to." I broke down crying on the phone. "Baby, everything's gonna be okay. Matter of fact, people from advocacy groups are headed for Atlanta and I'm coming with them," she told me.

I nodded my head as warm tears streaked my cheeks.—

"I'ma be damned if I let these crackas kill another child if I can help it. I personally saw with my own eyes what they did to IC. They shot him. They beat him. They tortured him. They put a gun to his head and forced him to confess. A person that won't stand up for somethin' will fall for anything. So we coming down there to fight for that boy's life. I have not lost my son in vain! They are not going to kill IC. Do you hear me, child?"

"Yes ma'am." I wiped at my tears.

"You better hear me cause we coming down there to raise hell."

"What about the DNA results?" I asked.

"I'm still working on that. In fact, I have a friend that will let me know as soon as anything pops up in the database. The thing is, there's several hundred thousand vials of DNA that were contaminated, discarded, destroyed, or misplaced."

"Damn," I muttered.

"What about Bubba Ray?"

"Bubba Ray is dead. He jumped out of a fifth floor window at three o'clock this morning at the Veterans Administration Hospital."

"He jumped? I thought you said he was paralyzed."

"He was."

"How could he jump out a five story building? Somebody had to kill him, tryna' cover up what he knew."

"Yeah, maybe. I thought about that, too. Maybe he knew too much."

"I dunno."

"Have they set a definite date? Who are his lawyers?" Nurse Harvey asked.

"I'm not sure, but I'll find out," I responded.

"You do that. But in the meantime, we're coming there and I also have some helpful information."

"What's that?"

"The prosecutor's star witness is Wanda Clark. She gave a sworn deposition that she saw IC running from the scene of the crime with a gun. After speaking with her, she has recanted her statement and said she lied because the prosecutor said they would let her out of jail for violation of probation and possession of drugs."

"Dayum," I droned, kicking off my shoes.

"So, all of us are comin' down there, including the media. You goin' to church with us when I get there?"

"Church?"

"Yes, Lord, people need to see you and that baby in church grieving for IC to come home. A camera can tell a million stories."

"Yes ma'am. I look forward to going to church with you," I reluctantly told her.

We said goodbye and then hung up. I undressed and turned on the radio. Mario's song, "Crying Out For Me" was just going off. Then the radio's top of the hour newscast cut in:

*"Today Governor George Banks signed the death warrant for convicted killer and child rapist, IC Miller; however activists and anti-death penalty groups are picketing outside the Governor's mansion at the moment. The United States Federal Penitentiary in Atlanta, where Miller is housed, is the most violent prison in the nation, and is back on lockdown after the recent onslaught of murders. We have just received word that Miller is suspected in a recent killing at the prison. The inmate James King, Miller's alleged father, was found dead this afternoon. King was serving a life sentence for killing Miller's mother. In other news, today on Wallstreet, stocks reached an all time low."*

I turned off the radio. I was in a state of shock. Innocent had killed his own father, and I had helped him by telling him what cell he was in. My God!

I took a hot bubble bath and a nap to get prepared for that night's special guest. I needed to make all the money I could.

*Innocent*

# Chapter Fifty-Three

I awoke from my nap and started getting ready. I puckered my lips and applied strawberry gloss. I dressed provocatively in sheer thong panties and a matching low-cut strapless bra. I topped off my ensemble with a see-through silk wraparound dress. I slipped into my brown suede stilettos with four-inch python heels. And just for them hoes that wanted to hate, I put on damn-near every piece of jewelry that Bleu had bought me.

The full moon shown high in a fuschia colored sky. Down below, the parking lot was nearly packed to capacity with luxury cars. I heard music coming from downstairs along with the delicious aroma of food. I sparked a partial blunt and sucked on it till my lungs were on fire. I almost burned my lips.

I strolled down the stairs shaking my hips, being careful not to fall and bust my ass. Rocko's joint, "Umma Do Me" was jamming through the speakers. Every night Kanisha hired a DJ to work the mansion. That night, it was the Dirty Boys from station Hot 107.9. The place was crunk. It was filled with more professional prostitutes than dudes. My competition was fierce. One bitch walked around nude. She was ugly as hell, though. I saw one of my clients trying to holla at her. I was more than pissed.

Exotic lights flashed along to the beat of the music.

"Haaay!" I sang along, snapping my fingers. I caught a whiff of some good- smelling weed. I looked over at the bubble gum machine. It was half full. All I needed was a trick to buy me a few.

I turned around and an older dude dressed in khakis, a navy sports jacket, dark sunglasses, and a big-ass wide-brimmed hat touched my arm. "Ms. Lady, may I have a moment of your time?"

I rolled my eyes. He was old and tired and he spat corny-ass lines. His English was so perfect, it sounded rehearsed. I leaned back on my heels to check him out. It looked like he had on a disguise. I could see a ring of gray hair that shadowed his temples underneath the hat with folds of wrinkled skin around his cheeks and chin. He had to be in his late fifties or older.

"Yeah, wuz up?" I said, annoyed. My intention that night was to stack as much paper as I could and then bounce.

The old dude walked up closer. He was invading my personal space.

I was about to tell him to leave me alone, but he reached into his pants and pulled out a stack of hundred dollar bills.

I pushed up on his ass fast. "Hey boo, my services are for hire. What' cha gon' do wit all that money?" I asked. I slid my tongue in his mouth.

"Good lawd! Jesus Christ, have mercy!" he exclaimed as he pulled up his glasses.

"How much for an hour of your time?" the old dude inquired.

I caught him looking at my breasts. "Oh, it just depends on what you want me to do." I smiled coyly. I reached out and took some of his money. I pressed up against him, allowing my succulent breasts to collide with his chest.

He gulped air like a fish out of water.

"Go over there and get me a couple of those candies out the machine and we'll talk about my services when you come back." I commanded. I gave him a gentle shove.

"Hurry, I'm in heat," I mouthed seductively.

Old dude did as he was told. Within minutes, he returned and passed me three pills. He leaned forward and whispered in my ear, "I'm celibate. I want to perform anilingus and cunnilingus on you."

"Nah, you crazy if you think I'ma let you anna cunna on me!"

I snapped, taking a step back. "Listen partna, I ain't into that freaky shit where you gonna beat and strangle the hell out of me to get a nut. You need to find you a white chick for that shit, 'cause I don't get down like that!"

"No! No! No!" he placated, throwing up both his hands.

I balled my fists and took a step back.

Behind me, I heard Kanisha's big-ass mouth.

"Haaay, Reverend Ronald Dollar! Good to see you again!"

"Reverend?" I retorted derisively.

The reverend cringed. He pulled the wide-brimmed hat further down over his head, looking around suspiciously.

"Didn't I tell you not to call me that? You are to address me as RD." He bristled with anger.

Kanisha gestured with an exaggerated wink. Then she smiled and gave him the thumbs-up sign. "S'cus us," she said, pulling me to the side.

"All his ole ass wants you to do is sit on his face so he can lick your asshole raw while he masturbates. He likes to use them big-ass words. Tamara, calm down girl." Kanisha quipped gleefully. "Cunninglingus means to eat pussy."

"Oh girl, I thought he was tripping. Thought his old ass wanted to choke me or some shit like that." I was embarrassed.

The reverend gestured for me to come back.

Kanisha pulled my arm, walking fast with her mouth moving even faster. We strolled through the congested room as several customers tried to get our attention. A huge, muscular security guard stood in front of the Boom Boom Room. Kanisha yelled over the music, "I got someone who is dying to meet you. He says he has a crush on you."

"I can't! The old reverend wants to trick with me," I yelled back, showing her the money.

"I got a better proposition for you."

"What's that?"

"How about that fine-ass football player? He just asked for you, specifically."

"Whaat? You lyin', gurl!" I swatted her arm with delight.

"Him and his boys are in the Boom Boom Room waiting for you. They want a private dance and he might want to sex you. I got three G's and I'ma split it with you. I could have picked one of them bimbo broads, but he asked for you!" she exclaimed.

I was flattered. I looked at Kanisha. "Let's go!" I said, tossing my long hair over my shoulders.

My eyes had trouble adjusting to the psychedelic lighting in the Boom Boom Room. Everybody in the room was nude. On a long velvet couch I saw a guy getting his dick sucked by two gorgeous chicks. While he leaned back, another chick had her legs up in his face while he licked her cunt. Next to him, two chicks lie on top of each other, passionately kissing and caressing. All around me people were performing orgies.

I followed Kanisha over to a group of nude men and she whispered, "Take off your clothes and do what I say."

Instantly, I recognized the handsome football player and his buddies. The entire offensive line was there, naked and hairy.

"Here she is, right here!" Kanisha said excitedly.

I smiled and looked into his sexy brown eyes. Then I glanced at his dick. The nigga was hung like a horse.

He spoke to Kanisha, "Okay, this bitch will do, but I asked for a redbone." He looked at me and continued. "You ever been fucked by eleven dudes before?" He was dead-serious.

"Who the fuck you callin' a *bitch*?" I knotted my brow tight.

He was taken aback by my response. "Chill, ma. No offense."

"And what you mean *redbone*? Kanisha said you asked for me specifically and that you gave her three G's." I cut my eyes at her.

"Three grand? What the fuck you think we are? We gave her twenty-one thousand, ma." He had confusion in his eyes. He looked over at Kanisha.

I turned to face her, too. I reached out, pulling her shirt so hard that the thin material tore and caused her breasts to pop out.

"She'll do it," I said to dude and his boys. "Won't you, Kanisha? You're a *redbone* just like they requested."

"I, I ..." she stuttered.

"Either do it or give them back their money," I gritted. "It's that simple."

Kanisha smiled nervously. The bitch had tried to play me. I was interested in seeing how the fuck she would get her cunning ass out of this mess this time.

"My bad," she said as she shrugged her shoulders. Kanisha slowly began to undress.

Eleven football players huddled around us, ready to get their money's worth.

She continued to undress and asked timidly, "How do y'all like it? What y'all want me to do?" Her hourglass figure and large breasts swayed from side to side as she stepped out of her G-string. Nude, in high heels, her butterscotch complexion looked incandescent in the dim light.

I took a step back and watched.

"You hit that shit from the front," the first ball player told a guy to his left. "You hit that shit from the back," he told a guy to his right. "And you," he commanded to a hefty guy, "lay down. I wanna see this bitch ride."

"Assume the position, ma."

Kanisha did as she was told and mounted the dude.

The other football players cheered them on.

It took both of Kanisha's hands to guide his dick inside her. She smiled *and* grimaced. The next dude came up from behind her and spread her ass cheeks. Someone else slapped her on her butt hard. She squealed in pain.

They all hooted and hollered in boisterous laughter as they wilded out. The guy holding her ass cheeks shoved a stack of ecstacy pills in her anus and then spit on his hands lubricating his ten- inch dick. It was as thick as a pop bottle.

If Kanisha could handle all of that, girlfriend deserved a medal. She deserved a trophy, a Bozo sticker, or some kind of award for taking all that dick up her ass. From the painful scowl on her face, with both dudes pounding away inside of her, she looked more like a rape victim than her Pimpstress persona.

The dude hitting it from the back rammed her hard.

Kanisha hollered out. It could have been ecstasy or pain.

When she opened her mouth the leader poured champagne all over her head then shoved his dick in her mouth.

Kanisha attempted to suck on his dick. She extended her hands in a futile attempt to jerk off two others at the same time. True to M&M's motto, "The Meat Market aims to please."-

They all changed positions. Another football player opened her legs wide, and they poured more champagne all over her head. Then one of the guys shoved his fist in her pussy.

Kanisha let out a painful scream.

I knew right then that it was time to leave. Not only leave the Boom Boom Room, but leave the Meat Market. I knew that I needed to grab the money I had stashed and leave this house and never look back.

I stumbled out of the room feeling sweaty and slimy.

The security guard raised his brow. "Where's Kanisha?"

"In there getting what she deserves."

I walked away. My damn feet hurt and my head was spinning. Someone grabbed my arm. I whirled around to give them a piece of my mind. It was Bleu.

I smiled at him.

"Where yu been luv?" "I just came out the Boom Boom Room," I shouted above the music.

He frowned at me.

"No, no, no! I wasn't in there doing anything. Kanisha's nasty ass tried to set me up in some shit. Now, she payin' the price. That ho in there fucking an entire football team."

"Good! She betta get mi monee," Bleu snorted and then smiled. "I com ta spen sum time wit' cha."

"Hmph, that's my song!" I said, trying to change the subject.

Bleu reached out and pulled me in his arms. "Luv, mi haf a question fo yu. Mi wunt yu ta be mi wumon?"

I cringed. My body went rigid in his arms. *Why did he have to ruin the fuckin' moment?* I had just decided to leave. We could never be together.

Bleu reached into his pocket and pulled out the biggest diamond ring I had ever seen.

It took my breath away. "You shouldn't have," I said, dramatically placing my hand over my heart. "Bleu, I can't accept this."

He ignored me. He reached for my hand and placed the ring on my finger.

"I love it!" I looked up to give him a big kiss. "Oh shit!" I shouted as I saw someone I knew coming up behind Bleu. Boss appeared from out of nowhere, grabbed the man, and put him in a full nelson. Bleu instinctively spun around pulling out his burner.

# Chapter Fifty-Four

I grabbed Bleu's arm.

"No! No! Don't shoot him! That's my friend; don't shoot."

"Yu whut?"

"That's my friend," I repeated, still holding onto Bleu's arm.

"Boss! Let 'im go! Put 'im down befo yu eurt 'em." Bleu had to repeat his words three times before Boss released his captive.

"TC, what are you doing here?" I screeched as I wrapped my arms around him.

"I oughta bust a cap in yo big giant ass;!" TC muttered, pointing at Boss.

Boss frowned at both TC and me.

I introduced Bleu to TC and surprisingly, the two gangstas had heard of each other's infamous reputations. TC was terrorizing the city of Chicago, getting money and lots of media attention with an onslaught of gang wars and dead bodies just as Bleu was doing in Atlanta with the drug wars over turf and product distribution. Bleu emphatically apologized three times to TC. He assured him Boss's actions had been the result a big misunderstanding. Afterwards, the two of them immediately started politicking. I had never seen Bleu show any dude that much respect. The two of them must have talked for damn-near an hour.

Finally, Bleu turned to me. "Mi look forward ta doin' business wit yu friend. I got tu go," he said, nodding his head toward a group of people standing by the fireplace. "When you finish talkin' wit yu friend, go ta yu room. Mi wunt an answer." He kissed me passionately.

"Damn girl, look at you!" TC said with beads of sweat rolling off his forehead. As usual, like his twin brother, he was dressed nice in a Rocawear outfit, a large dooky chain, and diamond earrings. Even though he and his brother were identical twins, I could always tell the difference. It was in the slants of his mischievous eyes. Unlike his amicable brother, IC, TC was corrupt. He didn't have a friend in the world. He killed them all as soon as they got too close to him. He ran the organization with an iron fist and a body count.

"How did you find me?" I asked.

"How did I find *you*?" he repeated.

"I been here since this morning. Done tricked with every bitch that works for Kanisha except a big ole fat white chick named Amanda."

"Do you know how old these girls are?" I blurted out.

He shrugged. "If they old enough to bleed once a month, suck a dick like a pro, and can keep a secret, I won't tell if they don't." TC snickered giddily.

I took a step back from him, folded my arms over my chest and rolled my eyes. But that was TC for you—cold and callous. I changed the subject to something that was dear to both of us: his brother, Innocent.

"You know the Governor signed your brother's death warrant today."

He nodded his head.

"I work at the prison. I was promoted to lieutenant today. Allegedly, Innocent stabbed an inmate in retaliation for what he did to your mother."

TC grinned holding his chin high. "Better him than me. That muthafucka, James would have been gone a long time ago if it was up to me. Ain't no way in hell a nigga gon' live somewhere, a prison out of all places, with a muthafucka that killed his mother." His voice was cold. "Don't worry about my brother. We gon' get him out, even if we have to break his ass out or I have to die taking his place. But right now, I'm finna put my hustle down and get my brother the finest lawyers money can buy." TC looked around. "I can't believe you got with Kanisha and this operation. She killin' 'em. Did you see that safe in the office?"

"Yes, she doin' alright," I agreed with him, "but you know that bitch ain't shit, though?"

A chick with big breasts, wearing a gold sequined dress walked up. Out of nowhere, she flicked her cigarette lighter.

"Bitch, can't you see I'm talkin' to him!" I snapped.

She rolled her neck at me and frowned.

"Hold up, ma, I'ma be with you in a minute." TC took the lighter and gave her a slight peck on the cheek. He looked back at me. "Them crackas railroaded my brotha, the only thing I love." TC grabbed my arm and pulled me within ear shot. "Don't trust that bitch, Kanisha. Tomorrow I want you to leave! Hear me?"

I nodded my head. I had already decided it was time to go. I needed to get my child. I needed to help Innocent.

"Take my cell number." I put my number in his cell phone and saved it.

TC gave me a sweaty hug. "Leave tomorrow!" he whispered in my ear again.

I walked off to go and pack my bags so that I could leave. I thought about what I would tell Bleu when he showed up in my room. I glanced at the diamond ring on my finger and decided I would tell him nothing. I would just go.

I weaved through throngs of horny people. I ignored the customers that wanted my services. I just wanted to get to my room to take off my high heels, hop into the Jacuzzi and gather my cash and clothes so I could leave.

I neared the stairs and saw the reverend still waiting on me.

"Reverend?" I said.

"Are your services still available?" he asked, taking a quick glance at his watch.

"I have a splitting headache," I yelled above the music.

"What about the money I gave you?" he asked.

I had forgotten all about it. "Come back tomorrow. Your credit is good here, sweatheart."

He opened his mouth to complain.

I cut him off. "Or I can send the money to that mega church you have as a donation from the Meat Market; and by the way... did I ever tell you I'm only fourteen?"

"I, I'll see you tomorrow." He fidgeted with his hat before he pulled in on, low enough to conceal his eyes, and walked off.

I laughed and walked up the stairs with a bottle of Patron in one hand and a fist full of tokens in the other. I was high as hell. I stopped outside the girls' room to gather my thoughts. I thought about rescuing them from Kanisha, but then I realized I couldn't because I had to rescue myself first. I walked inside of the room and surprised each girl by giving her a sisterly hug. I noticed the bars on the window. I thought about taking Ebonyze with me, but instead, I left the bottle of Patron with them. "Good night, girls."

I removed my shoes and padded to my room barefoot. On the way, I wondered if I should tell Bleu I was leaving. I had to give that Haitian nigga mad props when it came to spoiling a chick. Plus that nigga wasn't too proud to beg. When I entered the room, I felt a cold draft hit my legs. I walked over to the dresser and checked my reflection in the mirror. I sat the tokens on the dresser. One of them rolled onto the carpeting. I took off my jewelry. The diamond ring on my finger sparkled. Unfortunately, the ring felt like it was cutting through my skin and causing my finger to turn purplish-blue. I spit on my finger and wrestled the ring off my hand. I placed it next to the tokens on the dresser. I ran a hot bath and lit scented oils and candles. Then I eased into the tub. I closed my eyes. I saw Innocent in his cell on death row. "Shit!" I splashed and sat up straight. I needed to start packing.

After my bath, I dabbed on some perfume, put on a silk G-string and hurried to the closet to pack. I rummaged through the closet past expensive designer clothes and purses. I pulled out the shoebox full of cash that I had stashed away. It was almost one hundred grand in all. I felt the cool draft again. This time it was accompanied by the familiar smell of a cigar.

I heard the familiar sound of a gun being cocked and I froze like a mannequin.

"Goin' somewhere in a hurry, shawty?"

Hesitantly, I glanced over my shoulder. My heart damn-near stopped. "Oh, my God. I thought you were—"

# Chapter Fifty-Five

"You thought I was dead?" Pharaoh Greene said with his eyes narrowed into tiny slants. His gun aimed at my head. "Take the shoebox and go sit on the bed," he ordered.

I complied.

"The only thing that saved my life that night was that me and my niggas was all dressed in black. Niggas in black all look the same when shit start poppin' off. Yeah, I took six slugs and dove to the ground playing dead. I managed to get away, but when the rumor spread the next day that I was dead, I decided to go along with the program to seek revenge."

"Revenge?" I chirped.

"Yep. Revenge on Bleu and yo girl, Kanisha."

"You might be making a big mistake. Bleu is on his way up here any minute."

"Good, that's what I want. I want to kill three niggas wit one stone."

"Three?"

"Yep. Bleu, Kanisha and *you*."

"*Me*? What I do?" I groaned. I sat the box of money on the bed next to me.

"Bitch, don't play dumb. You stole my chain and then yo ass

got out of line. You should have checked yoself." He played with a strand of my hair. "You don't have a clue what you done got into, do you?"

"I ain't steal your chain. You left it in my hotel room the day yo baby's mama came lookin' for you." I was pissed.

"Shut the fuck up and listen, bitch!" He gestured with the gun in my face. "The day I walked into the hotel lounge when we first met, it wasn't by coincidence. It was by design." He smiled.

"Kanisha set it all up," he continued. "It all started when we were at the airport waiting to get a thirteen-year-old Japanese girl. Kanisha is heavy into child prostitution and pornography. It's a multi-billion dollar a year business. The girl never showed up, but you did."

"Lucky me," I quipped.

"Kanisha desperately needed an underage girl. The Japanese girl cost plenty of money to purchase and when she didn't show, she had to do something. Kanisha is in big debt. So from day-one her plan was to recruit you without you even knowing it by using me as bait. She said you was young, dumb, and foolish enough to go for the okie doke, because you was a gold digger. When I first met you I thought you'd recognize game, 'cause game recognize game. But you went for me hook, line, and sinker. The only problem was, Kanisha is smart. She's much smarter than you and I will ever give her credit for. That day, with the help of the waitress, they tried to set me up. Yeah, them bitches tried to set me up. They called my baby's mama and then planted two ounces of crack in my whip. Lucky for me the cop that searched my ride was on the take. I paid him off. If not for that, a nigga would have had a free ticket to hotel Fed."

I shook my head in disbelief.

"Oh, it gets better, or should I say worse in your case. Once the waitress called the police station and found out I was only charged with simple assault and had bonded out, Kanisha called me saying that Bleu and the BHM boys was at the club and it would be a good time to kill him. I jumped on the opportunity because she knew me and dude was at war and, I'd either kill him or he'd kill me. You see, Kanisha borrowed six-hundred grand from me and nine hundred from Bleu. So if one of us or both of us got killed or went to jail, she straight, na'mean?"

As PG told me everything, my mind flashed back to the night at the club. That's why Kanisha was trying to rush out and she was pissed at me for trying to holla at Bleu. "Kanisha's ole girl was a boss-bitch before she died and left her a small business, but she parlayed that into M&Ms. That's how she also got in debt to the mob."

"Mob?"

"Hell yeah! That's who controls child pornography and the prostitution ring in Atlanta."

"Well, can't I just pack my shit and leave?"

PG took a step closer and laughed. "It ain't that easy, shawty. You know too much now. You in too deep."

"No I ain't," I grumbled pensively. "I don't know shit. I don't know you, Bleu, or Kanisha. Hell, I don't even know myself anymore."

"You're a smart girl," Pharoah told me, "but you in too deep with me unless you help me set this nigga up."

"I can't do that. He would kill me!"

"Bitch, I'ma kill you!" he said with a terrorizing scowl. Then he slapped me. "You gon' do what the fuck I say, understand?"

I whimpered and nodded my head in agreement. I rubbed the side of my jaw. My ears rang and eyes watered.

"Dat nigga make millions of dollars a year by smugglin' drugs and money in bodies and caskets they make inside that big-ass mansion. His granny into some Haitian Black Magic voodoo bullshit. Remember that night I shot at him at point blank range in the club? I missed!"

"Please, I need some time to think about it. Can't you give me about a week?"

Pharoah's eyes flashed angrily.

"All you muthafuckas come down here to the dirty south thinkin' we country as hell and slow. So I'ma tell you what, if this nigga come through dat door I'ma murk both y'all asses. Now pass me that box of money." He gestured with the gun.

"Nah, pah-leez don't take my money!" I pleaded.

"Bitch, you can quit all the begging." Pharoah grabbed a handful of my hair and pushed me down toward his zipper.

I noticed that his dick was hard.

"Suck my dick!"

"I told you Bleu is on his way up. Plus you gon' take my money and kill me?" I wailed.

"I might not. If you top that shit you did last time. I *might* let you go," he sneered.

I glanced at the door and back at him, then at the box of money on the bed.

*God, please don't let Bleu walk through the door while I'm givin' this nigga head*, I prayed as I scooted to the end of the bed and struggled to unzip his pants. He pulled his dick out and placed a hand atop my head.

I gobbled his ass up with a frantic, jackhammer, suction cup motion. Quick, fast, and in a hurry, all the while I was crying and slobbering all over the dick. I knew a nigga of his caliber got off on dominating. Sure as shit, he grabbed the back of my head and shoved his dick down my throat, causing me to gag. But I never lost my rhythm. I spied the door while I rubbed his balls. I needed for him to hurry up and cum.

I cried harder and sucked faster.

Finally, he grunted and his body jerked. Pharoah let out a deep moan. "Yeahhh, yeahh, suck the dick, swallow it, bitch." His body jerked as he came.

I choked and cum spewed out of my nose.

"I said swallow it, bitch!"

I did as I was told. I needed to get his ass out of my room.

He pulled his dick out my mouth, still spewing cum. He pushed me back on the bed and placed his gun to my head. "Let a nigga get some of that pussy."

"I told you Bleu was on his way up!" I said. I began to cry again.

"Shawty, life ain't no fun without a nigga takin' a risk to cum," he intoned wittily as he shoved my panties to the side and ran up in me dry and raw.

"Ouch! You hurtin' me, I crooned. "At least use a rubber." I cried out.

"Hell nah, and ruin all dis good pussy, shawty?" He deep-stroked me painfully with his gun still pressed against my head.

At that moment I knew I had to do something. At any minute, Bleu was going to come walking through the door. I remembered the gun I had stashed in the nightstand. The pills started whispering to my brain for me to do some outlandishly bold shit. I was gonna have to lullaby this nigga.

"Oooh, yesss, baby, that feels good," I moaned loud, spreading my legs wider and throwing it back at him. "Don't cum in me yet," I begged. "Let me get on top and ride it, big daddy."

"Hell yeah. Now that's what I'm talkin' 'bout." PG rolled

over with me on top.

I worked my tight vagina muscles, riding his dick like a stallion. When I leaned forward, he started biting on my damn nipples so hard it took everything in my power not to scream. I positioned my hand inches from the nightstand. Nervously, I chewed on my lip as my fingers crawled closer to the nightstand.

Pharoah closed his eyes, grabbed my hips frantically, and began thrusting inside of me. "That's it, bitch. Fuck a nigga like you mean it."

I finally got close enough to the gun to I ease it out of the drawer.

The contorted expression on Pharoah's face told me that he was cumming.

I felt his warm liquid shoot inside of me. He thrust upward and grabbed my hips, allowing his cum to shoot deeper inside me. "Damn it!" he shouted.

I placed the barrel of the gun at his temple.

Pharoah opened his eyes.

I pulled the trigger.

*Innocent*

291

# Chapter Fifty-Six

*Click! Click! Click!* The gun was empty.

"Oh shit!" I shouted.

Pharoah backhanded me in my eye. I flew off the bed.

"Trick-bitch!" he shouted, showing me the gun's cartridge.

There was a knock on the door.

Pharoah pulled up his pants, then picked up the shoebox filled with my money. Frantically, his eyes searched for a place to hide. He dashed toward the closet. "Remember, kill three niggas with one stone unless you agree to help me set this nigga up." He pulled the door closed.

My bedroom door opened.

I stumbled toward it trying to maintain my compsure.

"Luv, why dun't yu answer de door?"

"Uhm, I was asleep," I said.

"Whut happin' tu yu eye?" Bleu asked. I could tell he was drunk.

"I didn't wash my makeup off when I laid down," I lied and turned away from him.

He walked up and held me in his arms. "Why yu shakin'?"

"I don't feel too well," I muttered, spying the closet door. I saw Pharoah with the gun aimed at the back of Bleu's head. I panicked and nudged Bleu toward the bedroom door.

"Luv, yu nevah answer mi question."

"I'm sorry. What question?" My mind was all over the place.

"Yu know, be mi wumon."

"I told you I wasn't feeling well," I yelled. I saw a light gleam off the barrel of the gun as Pharoah took aim to shoot.

Bleu looked at my breasts then down at my torn G-string. My pussy was wet. "Luv, let mi taste yu."

Pharoah aimed at Bleu, but Bleu shoved me on the bed. I stumbled and he fell on top of me. The closet door swung open wide. I could see the silhouette of Pharoah's body emerge from the darkness along with the eminent threat of certain death as Pharoah took aim.

Bleu wrestled with me, pulling my G-string down. He buried his head between my legs.

"Hmm, yu tast like mi grandmudda's molasses," he hummed, lapping up Pharoah'scum.

Pharoah stepped closer and leveled the gun at the back of Bleu's head.

I screamed. "Yesss! Yesss! I'll do it! I'll do it!"

Drunkenly, Bleu babbled, "Yu like dis, huh."

Pharoah stood behind Bleu menancingly. A gloating grin plastered on his face. Pharoah nodded his head in agreement of our coup against his adversary, Bleu Baptiste. He pulled my bedroom door open and exited quietly.

Then PG did something strange. He did something I could never explain. It would come back to haunt me miserably. He looked onto the mirror, touched something, then he took all of my jewelry including the diamond ring Bleu had just given me. He also took the shoebox full of money. With the gun aimed at Bleu, PG pulled his hoodie over his head and put on dark shades. Then he eased out the door. All the while, Bleu continued to gluttonously munch on my coochie.

Exhausted, I passed out while Bleu continued to eat my pussy. When I woke up, it was morning. I had a splitting headache.

Bleu was sitting at the foot of my bed. "Wuk up, luv!"

I groaned and pulled the pillow over my head. "What time is it?"

"One o'clock," Bleu told me, kissing me on the lips.

My eyes were sore. Last night's nightmare returned to me.

Sitting up in the bed, I stared at the dresser. Fuck! My jewelry was gone. Slowly, I scrolled my eyes over to the closet. The door was wide open. "Shit!" My money was gone, too. I wanted to break down and cry. Pharaoh, the unwanted guest from the night before, had taken everything.

Bleu kissed me again and squeezed my titty.

"Not right now," I moaned again, holding my head. Sex was the last thing I wanted.

"Luv yu nevah answer mi—"

"Bleu, for God's sake, Jesus Christ, not now. Can a bitch breathe?" I snapped.

"Get dressed! Yu cummin' wit mi." I just wanted to lie in bed and be left alone.

"Cum!" he snatched the covers off me.

I padded to the bathroom, took a shower and got dressed. I put on a denim outfit and my brown, four-inch, Jimmy Choo stiletto heels, with the lace-up leather straps. I felt wack without my jewelry. At least I still had my gold crucifix chain around my neck.

Bleu took one look at me and smiled with satisfaction. He asked, "Where's your ring, luv?"

"I put it up for special occasions," I said with a half smile.

Bleu liked that.

Downstairs, Kanisha sat on the couch. She had an ice bag on her head.

My blood boiled at seeing her.

I turned to Bleu. "Lemme speak to Kanisha for a sec. I'll be right out." I told him sweetly.

He glanced at his watch. "Hurry up!" Then he walked outside.

I rushed over to Kanisha. "Bitch!" I slapped the shit out of her.

The ice bag flew off her head. "What you hit me for?"

I balled my fist up.

Kanisha shied away from me. "I got stitches in my ass and they had to pump my stomach!" Tears welled in her eyes.

"Bitch pah-leez, I know what you did."

"No, it was a misunderstanding. I, I thought *he* was talking about you."

"That ain't what da fuck I'm talking bout! You set me up. I just happened to be at the wrong place at the right time—at the airport. You followed me to my hotel. You put that nigga Pharoah on me."

Kanisha's mouth flew open. She was in shock.

"Not only that," I added, "but, you borrowed money from Pharoah and Bleu, knowing damn well they were at war with each other. So, when your little trick failed at the hotel, you, or someone else, tipped off Pharoah that Bleu was at the club that night we went out. That's the reason why you were so anxious for us to leave. I was in the way of your plans to kill him."

Befuddled, Kanisha asked, "How do you know that?"

"Because Pharoah Greene is *still* alive! He ain't dead. Last night he raped me, took all my fuckin' money and my jewelry."

Kanisha shook her head. She was in denial. "He can't be," she grumbled.

"He is and shit finna get crazy 'round here."

Kanisha looked around the room as if searching for a solution. The girls looked on, perplexed and scared. Suddenly, an image flashed in my mind of the day I had seen Kanisha having a heated argument with a white man when she pulled over to the side of the road. I had a feeling he was a member of the mob. Pharoah had said she borrowed money from them, too.

"What am I going to do?"

"First off bitch, you might start by not being so fuckin' scandalous, and if dat don't work, dig a hole."

"Dig a hole?"

"Yep, 'cause all the bullshit you done did, yo ass is good as dead. Digging a hole would make it much easier to bury yo ass cause Pharoah is gonna kill you," I spat. Then I turned on my high heels and strutted out the door.

I rode next to Bleu in his black convertible Bentley. It was one of those lazy Saturday afternoons. The wind played in my hair. Bleu's hand was inching up my thigh. I realized something that I couldn't deny; I was catching feelings for Bleu Baptiste. I found it hard to imagine another chick sitting pretty in my position.

We pulled into Bleu's gated community and a car pulled up beside us. The window slowly descended and a billow of smoke curled out. Once the smoke cleared, there sat TC.

"What you doin' here?" TC and I asked in unison.

I laughed.

TC didn't.

"Folloh mi car," Bleu said. He sped off, burning rubber.

TC followed.

"What he doin' here?" I asked Bleu.

"We gonna do sum bisness. Mi sell 'im product."

I had to smile to myself. TC was dead-serious about getting his twin brother the best appeal lawyer. We parked a few feet from an imposing statue spewing water. Up ahead in a ten-car carport there were four black hearses. A convoy of luxury cars parked beside us. TC's whip stood out by a mile. I had to give him his props—that nigga was flossing hard. Haitians got out their cars, rambunctious and rowdy as usual. Bleu and TC greeted each other by exchanging dap.

"Did yu bring de money?" Bleu asked, squinting his eyes from the sun's brightness.

"Right here, dawg!" TC responded, holding up the Louis Vuitton duffel bag.

Bleu smiled in return. "Mi decide tu give yu tree extra bricks since yu ole friends wit mi wumon." He patted TC on the back.

We all walked through the front door and were hit with a delicious aroma. My stomach churned.

Bleu's grandmother, Delia, met us in the spacious living room. Her gray locs hung down her shoulders. She had on an A-line silk, black dress with an assortment of colorful beads around her neck. Eeerily, she looked to be a Voodoo Priestess. She gave me the creeps.

Bleu planted an affectionate kiss on her ebony cheek. The two spoke in Creole.

TC mimicked Bleu's accent nearly perfectly. "Boy, mi hearr yu grandmudda cook a wicked curry goat beans n' rice, lemme teast?"

Everyone in the room cracked up in giddy laughter. Delia was laughing the hardest. Everyone knew she took exceptional pride in her cooking. After Delia recovered from her laughter, she rushed off to make TC a plate of food.

TC cut straight to the chase. He placed the big duffel bag on the glass table in front of Bleu. "Bingo! One million cash for one-hundred three bricks of pure Columbian flake cocaine."

"Someone count de moni," Bleu ordered.

"Dat's what I'm talking 'bout. I likes to do business with a nigga who know de business," TC said while rubbing his hands together.

Bleu picked up the phone and threw up one finger. He spoke in Creole. After the phone conversation he said. "Pro-duct soon cum."

TC smiled with satisfaction.

A money counting machine sat on a table a few feet away. Lil' Phazzy put the money in and turned it on.

"How long hav yu tu known each otta?" Bleu asked.

I crossed my legs and said, "I've known TC almost all my life, since I was a little girl. His grandmother used to be the candy lady. I had a big crush on his brother." I glanced over at TC, but he didn't look back at me.

A dark-skinned Haitian walked in. He was carrying two duffel bags. His taut, wiry muscles coiled and flexed, showing off an eight pack of abdominal muscles. His Knickerbocker shorts were sagging. He was snaggletoothed; his two front teeth were missing. His hair was matted and nappy. He smiled at Bleu. The two began to speak in Creole. Lil' Phazzy stood with the money as Delia walked in with a plate of food in her hands.

Bleu asked, "How ja know bout mi gradmudda cookin'?"

"Oh, Tamara told me," TC lied. He wiped at the sweat on his forehead.

The smile on my face died. I sat straight up in my seat.

Lil Phazzy stuck his hand into the duffel bag and grimaced.

TC went into action. He pulled an automatic gun out from underneath his shirt. He rushed over to Delia and grabbed the old woman by her hair. "Everybody freeze or granny here is dead!"

# Acknowledgement

First I would like to thank God Almighty for blessing me with the ability to write and helping me on my literary journey. Leo Jr. and Christie, my son and daughter whom I love dearly. In order for us to move forward you all are going to have to forgive me for being gone out of your lives. Let go of the past by embracing the future. Imagine us all together with love in our hearts, a family!

To my angels; Desire, Lamaya, and Jasmine, my babies. I promise y'all won't hurt for nothing!

Neil Muneil, the preliminary editor of Innocent 2 you're a beast! The check is in the mail. You with me?!" To my step-dad Samuel and my step-sister Sharon and brother Tracy, I can't wait to see you all again.

Dr. Mutulu Shakur, Tupac's father, you instilled in me, the true sense of our struggle as an oppressed people. It was you that breathed this revolutionary fire into my mind. It was an honor to have you as a mentor and best friend for over a decade. It pains me now to no avail that them devils places you in supermax 23/7, hours- no human contact in Florence, Colorado. Just because you dared to teach us our real history. Free Mutulu!

Ms. Vickie M. Stringer, my boss. For a moment I can't lie, I got tired of wrestling with you over that big ass Triple Crown purse you be toting around. I wanted some of that, "Obama "Recession-Proof" Money. And just when things were starting to look more discouraging, after three failed contract negotiations and seven months later, you finally opened that purse and broke bread, giving a brotha some steaks. Thank you so much! Now if I can just get you to go in your bra and get that other stash for the sequel... that would be lovely!

To Danielle Ferneau, the new editor- in- chief. I know I drive you crazy at time with my demands. I humbly appreciate your civility and kindness in a business where patience is a burden, disguised as a virtue. Thank you and the rest of the Triple Crown Family.

Cynthia Parker, the editor of this project. We've shared differences in the past. I felt slighted and so did you. I had no idea you would be assigned to this project and I'm happy you were. Who knows my work better then you? Hopefully you'll be a part of *Innocent 2*.

Kanish Winebush! Thank you for all your helpful knowledge of Hotlanta's crazy underground clubs and prostitution houses and dope activities around the city. Girl, your ass is a trip! I'm going to put a bean on my tongue with you and party in the Boom Boom Room (smile).

P. Stone, even though we crushed the car on that lick (actually I crushed the car). From day one you have kept it 100% on some ride or die shit and to top it off you have brains and beauty. I loved your novel, *Institutionalized*. Check her out at www. pebblestone.com.

Auntie Antoniate Sullivan, the matriarch of the family. You really tried to hold us up together.

My cousins Alicia and Ariah Sullivan, that day is coming soon! So get ready!

To Taya R. Baker, I am truly blessed to have a strong black sista in my life as a best friend, a confidante. None of this would be possible without you! Your relentless dedication and staunch devotion to me and my writing career is invaluable. You often tell me what I don't want to hear. Critiquing me and pissing me off! But in essence, you keep me grounded. You keep me focused protecting me from myself. I love you Taya B. And I'm coming to your wedding first.

To the following people, I would like to thank them, no they are not forgotten: Jimmy Smith down there in Sarasota, see you soon. Marvin Johnson and his beautiful wife Kay and their new baby. Kiss! Kiss! Leon Blue, what happened? I heard you finally got back with your girl Terri Woods. If so, I got your publishing co. surrounded! To my number one biggest fan and personal friend Stephanie Grip and her beautiful daughter Amber. Love Yall! And I can't forget my sista Tajuana Hardinson, and her girls Teresa Woods, Sharon Milton, Michelle Woods, and Tracy Jarman and their book club "Just Us Girls," in Greensboro, NC. My dude Hollywood Joseph L. Holmes, dirty they say it gets greater later! Keep your head up. Valentine boy we did it! The check is in the mail. Thank you for your typing skills on this project's early stages.

Important people that reached out in a major way: My dude Brice Wilson, former member of the Grammy Award-winning, over 20 million albums sold, popular group "Groove Theory". Brice is also a movie producer, director, and actor. Thank you for inviting me to be a part of your HBO special and just the opportunity to work with you. You're constantly reaching out to me; we'll be a good team.

To my other phenomenal dude Snake down with Grand Hustle Music. The rapper T.I's personal assistant. Every time I call and need a favor you bend over backwards for me, whether it is tickets to a show, a personal favor to impress a chick or loved one. Then you'll get upset whenever I don't call my dude, I'ma take you up on that offer to pop bottles and visit The Strip Clubs ATL style as soon as I bounce.

Ms. Kashamba Williams: author and publishing company owner of Preciousty and Entertainment. I know I bug you to death when I always seek out your advice. And as a man I am not ashamed to say I consider you, a black woman that has been in the game longer than me, as a mentor and friend. I can't wait until we work on a project.

Jamie Ramsey, girl now you know I'm a novelist. I hope this comes as a surprise to you, after keeping my identity a secret for over a year. Someone told me I should write a book about us. All those times I told you I worked odd assignments out of this country, now you know the truth. Still care?

Halema Simonsi intellectual, artistic, beautiful, brilliant. There are not enough words to describe you in the English language, so I'ma keep it real and call you my souljah. Thank you for everything boo.

Renita Walker, I wish you much success on your new publishing company and the release of your new book *Night and Day*. I can honestly say, never have I met a chick in the business that has more drive and tenacity, you grind hard. I respect your hustle, and you always try to look out for a brotha. When you need me.

Role call to my peeps on look down!: Tony Walker, and Marcus Sanders, in Colemon Pen. Tom Colemon. Rock from Alabama. In Atlanta Pen: aka the gas-man. The big homie James Isum, Rosevelt Smiley. Joe Lee Burt. The C.O. Smitty down there in Edgefield. S.C. C.O. McQueen. Chu and his beautiful wife Deborah. I owe ya'll a kit. Darryl Hawk. Jamie Fuller down there at Henderson, N.C. Jerry I haven't written back yet. Keisha Caldwell, wuz up boo! Gina Phillips in Jessup, MD. To sexy Chocolate Paris Higgs, ma, you really got it going on! To my dude Jame Mitchell representing dpt. BK, keep your head up. I got your kit, we good. To my girl Aracelis Dorticos: Dare to struggle. Stay determined and believe in yourself. I believe in you ma! Natalya Williams, use the time wisely by educating your mind: READ! READ! READ! Then write some more. Nicholas Martinez, if we turn prisons into think tanks: (intelligentsias) they'd free us all! To my dude Graylin Kelly, AKA 'Gee' you had trail on the street! I aint forgot about you and Sasha. Where is zoo at? Hmmm....

Triple Crown Authors on lockdown: My sista Tanika Lynch and her book 'Whore,' is still crushing shit, stay strong love. Yafeese Johnson (AKA Feme Fate) in Bruceton on Fed. I'm making you a TCP author. I aint forgot you boo. Victor Martin, I wish you much success. I enjoyed chopping it up with you on the 'horn. That was gangsta. I heard you had a new book out. Darrell Debrew, a seasoned veteran in the game with a new book about to drop as well. I can't wait!!!

To my fans, I love you all! I try to respond to every last one of the thousands of letters I receive, because it doesn't take much to make a brotha or sista smile. To show them they are appreciated, especially if they are locked up. Feel me?

At this critical junction in my career, the market is oversaturated, inundated with urban books. My competition is fierce! In order to countermine that, I am giving my fans a double does of myself with *Innocent* and the sequel *Innocent 2*, so don't look at this as the end of the book. Look at it as the intermission to a good movie and go out and buy some popcorn and the sequel. Get cozy because you're not going to believe what scandalous ass Kanisha, T.C., Lil-half Dead, and the rest of the characters are up to while Tamara continues to frantically race against time to save Innocent from being executed. www.leolsullivan.com.

You can write him at:
Mr. Leo Sullivan 10024-017
FCI Yazoo City Medium
P O Box 5888
Yazoo City, MS 39194

# ♛ Triple Crown Publications

## Order Form

P.O. Box 247378   Columbus, OH 43224

| Name | |
|------|--|
| Address | |
| City | |
| State | Zipcode |

| QTY | TITLES | PRICE |
|-----|--------|-------|
| | A Down Chick | $15.00 |
| | A Hood Legend | $15.00 |
| | A Hustler's Son | $15.00 |
| | A Hustler's Wife | $15.00 |
| | A Project Chick | $15.00 |
| | Amongst Thieves | $15.00 |
| | Baby Girl Pt. 1 | $15.00 |
| | Baby Girl Pt. 2 | $15.00 |
| | Betrayed | $15.00 |
| | Bitch | $15.00 |
| | Bitch Reloaded | $15.00 |
| | Black | $15.00 |
| | Black and Ugly | $15.00 |
| | Blinded | $15.00 |
| | Cash Money | $15.00 |
| | Chances | $15.00 |

**Shipping & Handling**

1 - 3 Books          $5.00
4 - 9 Books          $9.00
$1.95 for each add'l book

Total $_____

Forms of accepted payment: Postage Stamps, Personal or Institutional Checks & Money Orders. All mail in orders take 5-7 business days to be delivered.

# ♛ Triple Crown Publications

## Order Form
P.O. Box 247378  Columbus, OH 43224

| Name | |
|------|--|
| Address | |
| City | |
| State | Zipcode |

| QTY | TITLES | PRICE |
|-----|--------|-------|
| | Chyna Black | $15.00 |
| | Contagious | $15.00 |
| | Crack Head | $15.00 |
| | Cream | $15.00 |
| | Cut Throat | $15.00 |
| | Dangerous | $15.00 |
| | Dime Piece | $15.00 |
| | Dirty Red | $15.00 |
| | Dirty South | $15.00 |
| | Diva | $15.00 |
| | Dollar Bill | $15.00 |
| | Ecstasy | $15.00 |
| | Flip Side of the Game | $15.00 |
| | For the Strength of You | $15.00 |
| | Game Over | $15.00 |
| | Gangsta | $15.00 |

**Shipping & Handling**
1 - 3 Books          $5.00
4 - 9 Books          $9.00
$1.95 for each add'l book

Total $_____

Forms of accepted payment: Postage Stamps, Personal or Institutional Checks &
Money Orders. All mail in orders take 5-7 business days to be delivered.

# Triple Crown Publications

## Order Form

P.O. Box 247378   Columbus, OH 43224

| Name | |
|---|---|
| Address | |
| City | |
| State | Zipcode |

| QTY | TITLES | PRICE |
|---|---|---|
| | Grimey | $15.00 |
| | Hold U Down | $15.00 |
| | Hood Rats | $15.00 |
| | Hoodwinked | $15.00 |
| | How to Succeed in the Publishing Game | $15.00 |
| | Imagine This | $15.00 |
| | In Cahootz | $15.00 |
| | Innocent | $15.00 |
| | Keisha | $15.00 |
| | Larceny | $15.00 |
| | Last Bitch | $15.00 |
| | Let That Be the Reason | $15.00 |
| | Life | $15.00 |
| | Love & Loyalty | $15.00 |
| | Me & My Boyfriend | $15.00 |
| | Menage's Way | $15.00 |

**Shipping & Handling**
1 - 3 Books      $5.00
4 - 9 Books      $9.00
$1.95 for each add'l book

Total $_____

Forms of accepted payment: Postage Stamps, Personal or Institutional Checks &
Money Orders.  All mail in orders take 5-7 business days to be delivered.

# ♔ Triple Crown Publications

## Order Form

P.O. Box 247378   Columbus, OH 43224

| Name | |
|---|---|
| Address | |
| City | |
| State | Zipcode |

| QTY | TITLES | PRICE |
|---|---|---|
| | Mina's Joint | $15.00 |
| | Mistress of the Game | $15.00 |
| | Queen | $15.00 |
| | Queen Bitch | $15.00 |
| | Rage Times Fury | $15.00 |
| | Road Dawgz | $15.00 |
| | Sheisty | $15.00 |
| | Stacy | $15.00 |
| | Stained Cotton | $15.00 |
| | Still Dirty | $15.00 |
| | Still Sheisty | $15.00 |
| | Street Love | $15.00 |
| | Sunshine & Rain | $15.00 |
| | The Bitch is Back | $15.00 |
| | The Game | $15.00 |
| | The Pink Palace | $15.00 |

**Shipping & Handling**
1 - 3 Books        $5.00
4 - 9 Books        $9.00
$1.95 for each add'l book

Total $_____

Forms of accepted payment: Postage Stamps, Personal or Institutional Checks &
Money Orders. All mail in orders take 5-7 business days to be delivered.

# ♛ Triple Crown Publications

## Order Form

P.O. Box 247378   Columbus, OH 43224

| Name | |
|---|---|
| Address | |
| City | |
| State | Zipcode |

| QTY | TITLES | PRICE |
|---|---|---|
| | The Set Up | $15.00 |
| | The Reason Why | $15.00 |
| | Torn | $15.00 |
| | Vixen Icon | $15.00 |
| | Whore | $15.00 |
| | | |
| | | |
| | | |
| | | |
| | | |
| | | |
| | | |
| | | |
| | | |
| | | |
| | | |
| | | |

**Shipping & Handling**
1 - 3 Books          $5.00
4 - 9 Books          $9.00
$1.95 for each add'l book

Total $_____

Forms of accepted payment: Postage Stamps, Personal or Institutional Checks &
Money Orders.  All mail in orders take 5-7 business days to be delivered.

CPSIA information can be obtained at www.ICGtesting.com
Printed in the USA
LVOW061520250413

330968LV00002B/243/P